Stella Scura: Dark Star Rising

Volume Three

Book Five: Now I am become Death

Book Six: A Child Once More

A Novel by

J. Matthew Neal

Stella Scura: Dark Star Rising

Volume Three

Book Five: Now I am become Death

Book Six: A Child Once More

Astronomical photos courtesy NASA/Jet Propulsion Laboratory/Space Science Institute.

Printed in the United States of America
Dunn Avenue Press
Muncie, Indiana 47304

ISBN 978-1-7349372-2-0

Book Five:

Now I Am become Death

"Now I am become Death, the destroyer of worlds."

—J. Robert Oppenheimer

Chapter Fifty-One

After returning to Earth, *Stella Scura* flew from Aurora City in the direction of Polaris, the North Star, towards central Alaska. She had been that way in the old armor, obviously, but not without it. Nick had given her a GPS device inside the helmet to get where she needed to go. She had disabled her NDB (non-directional beacon), which broadcast her call sign; this was against FAA rules, but Nick knew that she needed some privacy at times.

It was strange to go back after all this time. Six weeks was a lot of time, at least, at her age. She didn't want to call after what happened; she just hoped things were okay. Yet, she knew that things would never be the same again, as she had changed forever.

She flew over North Pole towards the west part of town and went out another ten miles to a seemingly familiar place, although she had rarely actually seen it. There he was, out in the yard, as usual, this time of evening: about nine PM.

Jack Marshall was bringing in firewood as he saw the fallen leaves on the ground blowing. For some reason, he turned around to see the helmeted female figure in a form-fitting dark blue costume floating twenty feet above him in midair, faintly illuminated by the *aurora borealis.* He gasped and dropped his load of firewood.

"You—is that really you, Paige?" She approached within ten feet of him, now hovering eight feet off the ground.

"What? Who else could it possibly be? Santa Claus? I do not see colors very well, but I am pretty sure my outfit contains no red. While I have eaten well as of late, I have not gained any weight."

"How long have you been up there?"

"About ten minutes. You cut firewood as poorly as you always did, Jim who has long been off the grid."

"*Jim?* What do you mean by that?"

"I think you know; we will discuss it later, pater."

"But how can you see at all? Electronics?"

She shook her head. "No. There are advanced avionics and communications devices in this fancy helmet, but they do not help me see. It is a long story, one I will not go into just yet."

"It's only that you startled me. How did you get here?"

"Strange questions for which the answer is obvious. How do you think?" She landed and walked towards him and removed the helmet as they walked back towards the house.

"Your hair is black, just like on television."

"So it is." She shook her head as her hair reverted to its native Titian color. "Is this better?"

"How did you do that?"

"Magic." She changed it back to black.

"No, really."

"Phase-change carbon nanoparticles. As with many other new developments, I will explain later, to the extent I am able."

"Where have you been?"

"Aurora City and Washington, with a couple of stops in New York and Armstrong City. Where else would I have been?"

"Armstrong City? How did you get there?"

"The shuttle, of course. I do not think I can reach escape velocity by myself. I have only been a little over a hundred thousand feet on my own, although that was easy, and I did not push it."

"Do your powers work there?"

She nodded. "Yes, it is seemingly no different. While I can counteract gravity on Earth, I discovered I can actually create it in space. I made several lunar orbits on my own, with a protective suit, of course. The radiation would not be kind to my skin."

"What was that like?" he asked.

"A bit boring after the first orbit. Very dark on the far side."

"Of course—but you flew here like that?"

"Yes, it is only a short journey. The suit is gone; you must surely know that. And you have certainly seen this getup on the news."

"Yeah, but we've been very worried about you, Paige." She watched as Petra came out, who stared at her as if she had seen a ghost.

"Why? I called you a few weeks ago."

"Well, that sure didn't give us reassurance that you were okay or let us know where you were."

"You know that was not possible, for reasons I cannot go into." She stared back at her mother who was staring from the back porch step. "Did you not know I was coming out for a night on the town, o Nobel physicist of great renown?"

"What did you say?"

"Never mind, but I imagine you heard me."

"I figured you would show up eventually. I just was not certain what to say to you when you came back. Or even if you *were* coming back."

"I see you have the Russian accent back. How convenient."

"Humph. Is that all you have to say after all this time?"

She snickered. "Oh, no, just wait. I have plenty more in store, and I will definitely not be a bore."

"At least *that* has not changed about you."

She put her hands on her curvy hips. "Yeah? Actually, there is a *hell* of a lot that has changed about me; this you will soon see."

Jack gave her a hug. "I'm proud of you for what you've done. You saved Air Force One and the thousands of people in Aurora City who would've been killed by the crash."

She looked around in paranoid fashion. "Maybe we had better go inside. You never know who is watching these days, even with it being overcast."

"I guess you're right." They went inside through the back door into the kitchen and sat down as Jack removed some milk from the refrigerator as she took a bite of oatmeal raisin cookie from a plate on the table. Thankfully, he had clearly made them and not Mom.

"So, tell us about things," Jack said.

"Things, huh? Well, where do I start? Saving that plane was challenging, but I had some help from the *Science Squad*. Without them, none of this would have been possible."

"Those dumb old guys? Are you kidding?" Jack asked.

"No. They are quite an impressive lot for a group intended to entertain a tot."

"How many of them?"

"All, except Wendy and Mom, of course."

Petra looked at her and touched the visor. "I have seen the pictures on the news feeds. What is this simple device that allows you to see? It cannot possibly function by the same technology as the armor. Rather, it doesn't look complex at all." She walked around her and tapped on it. "Curious."

"Well, look at it for a moment and figure it out. You are a smart lady, from what I hear."

Petra stared at it for two minutes. "Okay, but how is this possible? It seems to be sapphire, by its unique texture and reflective properties, but what can that do?"

"Yeah, that is what it is, a synthetic version; you are brilliant. It is doped with several rare-earth elements to increase its opacity."

"Humph. Yes, I can see that, but I don't see how that can—"

"Apparently, I am not truly blind, it is just that my eyes became so sensitive after the *Darkkday* blast that my brain now 'shuts off' when my retinas are exposed to even a tiny amount of normal light. A protective mechanism that kicked in after the atomic explosion in 2016. Bella finally figured it out after Dr. Royce G. Bivereaux III did a thorough examination of my retinas and found no damage. None of the others could solve the problem. It is made of dark blue synthetic sapphire, as you mentioned. I seem to be able to see in the near-infrared range, but I do not see much color."

"Is your visual acuity normal?" Petra asked.

"It is definitely above average, about 20/5, although we do not have the color thing sorted out yet, if that is even possible. I seem to see well into the near-infrared range, of whatever use that is."

"20/5, wow. Not quite as good as mine."

"Aww, so sorry to disappoint you. You have to be better than everyone at everything, yes?"

"Isabel solved this perplexing dilemma when even I couldn't?" Petra felt the smooth sapphire. "Sensory overload triggered by the original blast threw your brain into a protective mode where even small amounts of light are now interpreted as overloading? That never would have occurred to me."

"The others thought it was ridiculous, but there it was."

"It was my belief that nothing could harm you," Petra said. "Why hasn't your vision returned to normal, then?"

"I have no idea. But Bella is apparently pretty good at figuring things out that have stumped others."

Jack scratched his head. "I'll be damned."

She shrugged. "But, about that—it appears that my touching

another living being confers my invulnerability to that person, but it dilutes mine to a proportion equivalent to the mass of the other person. That is how you got your hearing back—the blast combined with that somehow transferred abilities to you and explains the partial recovery of many individuals in the D.C. area after the blast who were within a certain radius."

"So, why have you come back now?" he asked.

"Why? You are my mother and father. How can you ask? Did you think I deserted you or something? My cybernetic armor was damaged beyond repair, and I did not want to leave here. I had every intention of coming back. How was I to return until now?"

"You were a damned fool, going out in that armor by yourself. What did you think you were going to accomplish?"

"Perhaps, Dad, but who is the bigger fool—me, or the person who showed me the armor in the first place? You all started it."

"Paige is right for once in her life," Petra said. "I am a damned fool, for sure."

"Stop it." He shrugged. "We all had a role to play, and we can't go back. However, if you've encountered the grand trio of Bella, Nick, and Wendy, then you must know it all."

"Yes, I do. It was hard to believe at first, but I have come to terms with it. I did not believe Bella until she told me of the birthmark on my right buttock."

"What we did, hiding you from them all—was done for your own good until you could stand on your own feet. You must surely understand that," Petra replied harshly.

She tried not to get angry, but it was hard. "*For my own good?* You could not have told me of my heritage? That my father's sister is the President of the United States, for God's sake? That my mother is scientific royalty, now living like an eccentric hermit in an Alaskan hick town? No, I do not understand it at all, Mom."

Petra pointed at her. "You had best watch your harsh tone with me, daughter. While you are mighty, I pack a wallop myself."

She laughed. "I would not advise it, Mom. I am capable of things I did not think were possible, so do not make things worse by starting a fight. You never could take me on with words."

"You're the one who came back here, Paige, so some sage advice to you as well: don't ever start something you can't finish. I am capable of a few things myself of which you are surely unaware, so underestimating *me* is a colossal mistake. There are many graves filled with those who did."

She laughed. "Yeah. Ming, the Tosian dictator, for one."

"What?" Mom stared at her for fifteen seconds.

"You heard me. The funeral home sure earned its money that day, sewing his head back on and all for the service."

"I . . . won't ask how you know about that, but, yes, it's true. He was a horrible being who deserved to die horribly."

"You are God, is that it? You get to decide who lives and dies? You ripped the dude's head off!"

Petra nodded. "I did, and I'm glad. I'm not the one who shot off that nuclear missile and killed our family, so do not ever judge me. While my existence is simple and beyond your limited comprehension, it serves a purpose."

"We were both just trying to help," Jack said. "Learning to fly, for example. We live out in the middle of nowhere. Would we have been able to do that in Washington, San Diego, Aurora City, etc.? I don't think so."

"Maybe that is correct, but do you know how hard that was to swallow? It is not like my aunt is a desperate criminal or someone to be ashamed of."

"No, not a criminal, but far worse than one."

"Look who's talking. You assassinated someone, so who's the real criminal here?"

"I did what had to be done." Petra threw a glass into a wall and shattered it. "Maybe you are not ashamed of her, but do not ever speak for me—"

"Sputtering your trademark hyperbole, as usual."

Mom shook her head. "No, for once, I am not. There are things you don't know about your wonderful aunt. She is not always the beneficial being you believe her to be."

"And you are such a great person? All the lies?"

Petra crossed her arms angrily. "I don't answer to you. I also never said I was perfection personified."

"Neither did she, and Wendy would be the first to admit that."

"Shut up, both of you." Jack frowned and turned back to her. "How would knowing any of that stuff earlier *possibly* have helped you with anything? We did what we thought was right. Wendy is no better than any other person; however, she can help protect you and your identity. You would rather have her as friend than foe. She has been your friend long before you ever met."

"We live out here, while we would truly be wealthy were we to live back in the Midwest or Washington. Think of the things we could have if we had taken advantage of them—"

"*Wealthy?* Is that all you can think about now?" Petra shook her head. "I'm sorry the material things are all you see today, Paige, or Aurora, or *Stella,* or whatever you call yourself these days. That's too bad, but predictable."

"Hey, wait a minute. Do not talk down to me."

Jack poked her in the chest. "No, *you* wait a minute. If you flew up here to tell us off, I have a few things to say to you, too, since I can see your preexisting bad attitude has been kicked up a few notches."

She puffed out her size 42D chest, far superior to that of her equally muscular but small-breasted mother. "Yeah? So what else is new? I like my new attitude, dude, do not be such a prude."

"I'm sure you do. I also observe that being around your few remaining other relatives like Bella has had the negative effect I had long anticipated." He shook his head. "I don't blame you, as you're still just a child. Fitting, as those people act like entitled children sometimes. Look at Jay; he's basically a sixty-year-old with the maturity of a teenager. Will is probably more mature than he is."

"Really?" She sneered and pointed at Jack. "Well, regarding Wendy, Bella, Jay, and Will, at least *they* are my blood relatives, something you will *never* be—"

Her poorly chosen adolescent words were interrupted as her mother slapped her hard in the face with her right hand. Mom had never struck her before.

She looked at her mother with astonishment as she realized something else new that she had never experienced.

A stinging, quite unpleasant feeling across my face.

What the hell?

Is this what pain feels like?

The sensation only lasted a few seconds, but the emotional impact was even more stinging as she touched her cheek and stared at her as tears poured from her eyes, now leaking from the visor.

"Now, you have a snappy retort to that, Aurora?" Petra said, arms crossed.

"My God."

"You have something to say, invincible hero?"

"Mom, that—*hurt.*"

Petra nodded. "Yes, I know, that was the point, duh!"

"You—know?"

She nodded. "I do. Aurora Darkkin, how *dare* you say such a terrible thing to your father, you insolent spoiled brat! Superpowers or not, this is still *our* house, and we are still your parents. I shall not tolerate it."

"Petra—it's all right," Jack said. "Let it go. She's just a kid. Kids say and do dumb things."

"But it's not all right, do you not see? She has crossed the line of responsibility where acting like a child is no longer permitted. You of all people, Aurora, named after the goddess of dawn, should see the truth." Mom stood up and stared down slightly at her. "Jim gave up everything to make a life for us both after *Darkkday*. Maybe it wasn't a perfect one, but theirs isn't either, in case you think it is. He gave up the love of his life to help us."

"Bonnie, don't say any more—"

"No, I will say what I please to my selfish daughter. Response?"

"You did that, Dad? Who was it?"

"Nobody. I'm sure she's forgotten about me."

"I bet not. Aurora, you have surely met this person."

"How? Who is it?"

"Your aunt's Secret Service detail chief, that's who."

"*Jackie?* Dad, you were with Jackie?"

He nodded. "It was a long time ago. I don't want to talk about it now, as things have changed forever."

"I am sorry, Dad. I did not know."

"I just wanted *you* to know others gave up things to help you, Aurora. Money doesn't solve all problems. I know; I grew up with it. Wendy did, too—do you think her life was happy as a teenager? No way, she lived in Dysfunction Junction. I took on the job of being a high school math teacher for you—I sure didn't get anything out of it, except maybe some inner peace. But if you want to live with your fancy new relatives, then you are free to leave, obviously, because you are an adult now, as you are so fond of declaring."

Mom had actually stopped ranting and had a sense of clarity she hadn't seen often. "Mom, I think I understand, but—"

"No 'buts,' Aurora. You think you understand much, but you comprehend little about the world." Mom spread her arms wide. "This house—which may not seem like much to you after visiting the palatial Stannous estate or the White House—is always open to you, but on one condition—our home, our rules. That's not negotiable. If not—you don't need a plane ticket to leave, obviously. As much as I love you, *that* I shall never endure, not even from you. It's so hard tolerating being among you people of inferior intellect, with no one besides my synesthetic construct to talk to. I may not have been a very good mother, but I did the best I could with the hand that was dealt us. The only thing we ask is some respect and some forgiveness for the flawed human beings we are."

She crossed her arms and frowned. "You cannot have it both ways, Mom: arrogant and dismissive of the 'mere humans' one minute, and a member of the 'flawed ones' the next. Decide which you want to be."

"Hey, don't you start in with your junior-attorney arbitration gibberish. I am trying as hard as I can."

"Really? You think I am not? All this is so much to become accustomed to. However, let us not forget the fact you lied to me for most of my life; it is causing me much strife."

"Yeah? You are not the only one with gifts who has had trouble adjusting to them. I see, hear, and think about things none of you moronic lummoxes can possibly comprehend."

She laughed. "I see you have not changed."

"Shut up. This has been so since I was a child, but it has gotten worse in the last ten years. At times it is more curse than blessing. Maybe what we did was wrong, I don't know, but we did the best we could. Even I can't predict the future, you know."

"But why do I not remember anything about it?"

Mom shook her head. "I have no explanation for that, Aurora. I assure you it was no doing of mine; that is not within my abilities, even though I would have wanted that. The shock of you not being able to see took a terrible toll on us both—you didn't talk for over two weeks. I imagine you somehow repressed those memories."

"I know now that you are a genius, and I may have had doubts about that before, but your embellishments again stretch the truth too far—"

"Maybe once, but I was changed after *Darkkday*. Have you never wondered how I got my hearing back? With sensory perception greater than any human who has ever existed?"

She smiled. "I suppose I never thought much about it since I did not know you were Bonnie Mendoza until a few weeks ago. I guess it is fairly easy to hide things from a blind girl."

"Cut the sarcasm. My physical contact with you during the explosion saved me, but something changed in me after that. Within a day, my hearing was restored a second time, and I began to see and think things I never thought possible. I sometimes feel I am losing my mind."

She wiped tears streaming down her face. "Mom, Dad, I—I'm sorry. I should not have said that. I am just trying to process all this stuff. Not easy peasy."

Jack smiled at her. "I know you didn't, and there isn't anything you could say we wouldn't forgive you for. But just look at yourself and what you've become in a short time. What will become of you in ten years? Twenty? Many times we wished we had told you, but there never seemed to be the right time."

"I am sorry you do not approve, but it is my life to live. I guess some things in life you must find out for yourself." She gestured towards Mom. "Look at the diverse career you have had. You were thirty and still playing with magic tricks. At least I am not in a rehab center for compulsive gambling."

"Using me as an example is a very poor choice, one of the reasons I never told you." Mom got down in her face. "I played around until I was thirty and amassed a fortune wasting time in casinos, till they threw me out; the *Science Squad* intervened and sent me off to rehab, where I met other celebrities with similar problems. After I spent several years as a forensic investigator and magician, I went to Caltech and played around some more. For another thing, I didn't have the responsibility to the world that you did."

She shook her head. "I never wanted any of that!"

Her mom leaned closer. "I didn't want some of the things I got either, but I had to deal with them. That's what being an adult is all about."

"But you're still just a kid," Jack said. "New, shiny, rich relatives with fancy airplanes, clothes, two hundred thousand dollar cars, and Air Force One—it's hard to compete with all that. It would've been harder had you been younger. All I can give you is the advice a small-town preacher can, and I'm really not even one of those, as you've probably discovered."

"You are the best man I know, Dad. I am so sorry. I was out of line. I had no idea about—you know."

He nodded. "You were, it's not the first time that happened and likely won't be the last. I've come to terms with Jackie but I doubt she has, as I never saw her again."

"I am sure she has, and she must think you dead."

"You can't possibly believe that. She and Wendy clearly knew the truth long before you showed up. But don't you see why it had to be this way? Would you have been the person you are now had you been brought up with those superficial things?"

"I suppose that is one choice, but it does not mean yours was the right one." She shook her head. "You do not know everything just because you know more about the Bible than me. Just because they have money does not mean they are bad people. Give them a chance, even though they are fancy pants."

"I didn't say Bella, Nick, or even Wendy were bad, as they have all done much good for the world. But they live in a complex environment, shaped by hundreds of extraneous factors that you aren't ready to deal with yet. I assure you that those factors have shaped them, and I promise you Nick isn't the same person he once was. He and your cousin are billionaires, and you don't get that way by being nice and kind all the time, lest you think otherwise. Is that what you would've wanted?"

"None of us are the same. We are not the only people who lost loved ones on *Darkkday*. Bella lost her brother, her parents, her grandparents."

"I know all that; we don't need to repeat it. And going to Bella's house, for God's sake—there must be reporters and paparazzi around that estate all the time, not the best place to hide out—"

"Let me finish, as you do not know everything. Nick lost Marcy and their unborn child in the explosion. That child would have been your grand-nephew or niece."

He stared at her and stood up. "*What* did you say?"

"Marcy was pregnant when the plane exploded."

"Are you certain? Bella told you that?" Petra asked.

She shook her head. "No, neither Nick nor Bella said anything, they do not burden me with their problems, since I clearly have enough of my own."

"Who, then?" Petra asked.

"Fahnaz told me."

"Senator Fahnaz Saleh?" Petra paused for a moment. "The Democratic candidate for President?"

"Yes, of course. Do you know another?"

"You are on a first-name basis with such famous folks now?

Where in the world did you meet her, and why would she know that about Nick and Bella?"

She nodded. "I have met many influential people. I went to her home in Freedom City one day when I flew up there. Surely you have seen the news about the Graham Army base stuff, which I uncovered later. Fahnaz is also an old friend of Nick's."

Mom stood up and pointed at her. "I didn't know that, Aurora, and I am truly very sorry about Marcella, but those tragedies don't change things. Would it have made you happy or your life better to have grown up in a city named after you or in the White House? What kind of identity do you think you'd have had there? After the explosion, people thought you dead. How would you have wanted us to explain your survival? The government would have exploited you, made you a freak show."

She took a sip of milk and wiped it from her mouth with her right forearm. "Yeah, so what is different now, mom and pop? The world embraces me. No guys in black suits have come after me yet, so please do not fret."

"Come on, don't be such a dope. You should be smart enough to figure out why that is," Jack said.

"Why? Because of Wendy?"

"Duh. She *does* carry a bit of weight around Washington," Jack said. She grimaced as she heard her mother laugh hysterically at her dad's intentional joke. "But what's different is that you are now a legal adult. We told you that you could make your own decisions. You wanted to hollow out that cave, and we didn't force you."

"Wait one minute here. You took *Tinman's* money and helped, you know, so do not act like you were not a part of it. Neither of you is a saint. I also do not remember anyone trying to talk me out of it."

Jack laughed. "That's the stupidest thing I've ever heard. I was the furthest thing from a saint you could possibly imagine, I did worse stuff than you ever thought about doing. There is also a sordid side to Bonnie Mendoza of which you are unaware, and I don't mean the gambling."

Petra nodded sadly. "My husband speaks the truth, I have a dark and violent past."

"Yeah, we know, Mom. But I bet you never got arrested, Dad."

"Betcha you're wrong. But I did all this as the means to an end. I didn't see any other possible way for you to do those things, for you to realize your destiny. Don't you think we knew this would happen?"

"Well, I certainly did not. I want things to be the way they were two months ago."

"The moment you decided to put on that armor and save mankind, you left that world behind. There was no stopping you."

"Then why did you show it to me then, Mom? What the hell did you think would happen? Did you not anticipate a time when I would decide to go out on my own?"

"Your mother and I had a big argument after I found out about that, I didn't agree with it. But the cat was out of the bag, and the best thing I could do was try and make it into a positive."

"I wanted to adapt it so you could see, Paige. Obviously you had other plans. You wanted to be a kick-ass superhero and we had lots of talks about the pros and cons of that career choice," Petra said. "While we have some responsibility here, so do you."

She nodded. "I know."

"You saved the life of a Senator's brother and the dozens of folks aboard Air Force One," Jack said. "Including the President. But I told you weeks ago there were people you would then meet who would change your life forever."

"Yeah, but you could have told me *who*."

"And would you have believed it, that she was your own flesh and blood? I told you I had met her, and you laughed at me."

"Come on—I might have believed it if you had placed it in some type of realistic context. We were speaking hypothetically."

He shook his head. "No way. We didn't encourage this, but we also didn't want to run your life. If the armor hadn't been shattered, you'd probably still be living here. It wasn't possible for us to have anticipated that, and we had hoped for a year or two more with us; but now you've become the biggest 'rock star' ever—a lot of people think you're Christ. How did you think it was going to eventually turn out? That you could just come back here, and life would be the same as it was?"

"I guess I was too young to make that decision. Maybe I should just have been a secret agent or something." She shrugged.

"No one makes good ones all the time, and a flying secret operative wouldn't be very effective. We worried for a long while that people would reject you, but clearly, that didn't happen. Being an adult means being able to live with your decisions, good and bad, and you'll make many of both. God knows I made many crappy ones. Not that you made a bad one, because if you were going to do it, this was probably the time, while Wendy is still in the White House for four more years and the Republicans control Congress—but it is life-changing, and you couldn't even wait until graduation to do it. You're very headstrong, just like your mother. And your dad. They both nearly got themselves and me killed playing spy."

"Hey, take that back, Jack," Petra yelled as she walked out of the kitchen towards the bathroom."

"I'm sorry, I can't change what's true, you know."

"Shut up, Mom. It is not easy, fearing that people will find out that Paige and *Stella* are the same person. And should I take the name Aurora back? All tough questions to answer."

"Mom and I don't have all the answers if that's what you came back here hoping for. We don't know any more about you than we've already shared. I only hope we were able to instill some values in you to carry with you the rest of your life. I don't even know if you're at the peak of your powers yet; probably not. But you can take care of yourself. And, as opportunistic as Wendy is, she pretty much controls the world for now. She won't let anything happen to you." Jack shook his head. "It's not in her best interest. And, deep down, family means everything to her."

She opened her mouth wide. "So, this was all a master plan you and my intellectually unparalleled mother created? Thanks for letting me in on it."

"None of this was planned. I gave up my life, Paige, to come live with you and your mother, as you've heard. I just want you to know there's more about life than you and what you think you've given up. I would give anything to see Jackie or my sister Molly—Nick's mother—again. Or Nick's son Jose, whom I've never met."

"I have not met Molly yet. Jose is an extremely precocious child, and I enjoy playing with him."

"But I don't see how it's possible now to go back without freaking everyone out. Seeing Jackie again? How would that work out?"

"I—I did not think about such things."

"Of course not; you just think of yourself. I gave all that up to fake my own death after *Darkkday* after I found evidence your mom was somehow still alive and was trying to contact me."

"She was able to do that after she and I crashed? How? She does not seem to have the skills necessary to operate under the radar and do all that."

"Do not *ever* underestimate your mother."

"Your stepfather speaks the truth."

"But how did Jim die, if I may ask? Hopefully, the details are not too gory, tell me the complete story in all its ghoulish glory."

He laughed. "They are. He smashed his car into a concrete wall in San Diego, and it burst into flames and exploded. Likely intoxicated, the police report said, as there was a charred empty vodka bottle found inside, which I planted. A fitting, believable end to a guy most thought was a loser."

"Come on. There would have been a body."

"There was. I am no amateur when it comes to such things."

"You put a mannequin in there? That is not very realistic."

"Oh, how you underestimate me, for shame. It was a real guy, some homeless wino whose corpse I stole from the morgue."

"Liar, liar, pants on fire. You made that up."

"No, it's true. I can be quite resourceful when the need arises. You have your dad to thank for that, he taught me a lot of tricks back in the day."

"That was a rather elaborate scheme for Jim's tragic demise."

"Yes, it was. Your mom being a forensic scientist helped, too. There's a granite tombstone of me at South Mound Cemetery in New Castle, about six miles from Nick's house—you should go see it as I hear it's nice, but there's no whole city named after *me*. I guess they buried that hobo there. He got a better funeral than he would've gotten otherwise." He pointed at Petra. "Do you think she could've competently raised you herself?"

"Hey, I could have done so. What do you mean?"

"No, you couldn't have, Bonnie."

She walked slowly over to the sink and sat on the counter. "I understand, but I am just trying to sort things out. Can you not possibly comprehend? What did you want me to do?"

"Remember, you had a choice. No one made you into a superhero. We sat up there on that mountain weeks ago and had that conversation. You could have stayed here, gone to college, and done whatever you wanted."

"Yeah, but—I cannot stay long. I just came back to see you."

Petra stroked her hair as she walked back into the kitchen. "I am sorry, Aurora, that you grew up unable to see and that I can't see things with the simplicity that Bella can. I did the best I could."

"I know you did, Mom. I had a good childhood, I have no regrets, and being able to see would not have made it more special. At times it feels more comfortable to be blind. I know you know what that is like."

"Yes, my poor mind is now a jumbled mess of theories and mathematical formulae. I was happier when I was deaf, working for the police forensics lab and doing magic shows. It was even better after going to Caltech; by that time, the cochlear implants had ceased working due to nerve degeneration, which made it easy to shut things out and focus on what was really important to me. But life changes us. We did what was within our power to build a life for you. Know in your heart that growing up with that disability has given you compassion and humility, as I received from my deafness."

"Yeah, sure. Where the hell did all that compassion and humility go then, Mom? You sure do not have them now."

Mom shook her head. "I don't know. I wish I could go back, but I can't. For all my abilities, time travel is not one of them."

"But you are one of the world's most famous scientists. You won a Nobel Prize. Your discovery has made the United States the most powerful country in the world."

Petra snickered. "Humph. Power." Mom paused for a minute. "Yes, a mere child like you, and the puerile ones you admire in Washington and Aurora City—would see it that way. Believe that I see and understand concepts that you cannot. For once in your life, trust me."

"I am so tired of the arrogant way you talk down to everyone all the time, Mom."

"Really? Well, too bad. Take heed of my words, child, as they are wise and predictive of the woe that shall befall the materialistic beings. It is only a matter of time before they shall reap the rewards of greed and unchecked military power. The money and glory are but a mirage, don't you see? Element 119—I hate to call it mendozium as I deserve no posthumous honors—was meant to be shared with the world, not to build Aurora City; named after you, but now a memorial to capitalism, with mansions for Bella and *Tinman*, not to mention bankrolling the greatest aberration of them all."

"What?"

"What?" Mom's fist slammed down and broke the thick oak table in half. "How can you even ask? The Frankenstein's monster they now call President-for-Life, the horrendous Hippo-POTUS? She was my best friend. Now, look at her. Hah."

"I know what you gave up for me. But do not be mad at her for what she did because you could not be her. The fourth of the Seven Deadly Sins Dad talks so much about."

"What craziness are you talking about? How dare you speak to me that way?"

"Oh, do not start that again. I dare. *Envy*. You envy her, the life she leads, and I am sorry because I am the cause of it all. The President is a great person. Forgive her flaws, as you have more than your share as well. I regret you are so jealous."

Mom laughed. "What? You think I am jealous of Great Dame Fatso Mary Gwendolyn Gallinsworth Darkkin or whatever the hell her name is now? The first President with her own gravitational pull, with mindless Senators and Congressmen orbiting her in the vacuum of space that is her brain? You must be joking."

"She isn't fat anymore, just big. Her body fat is only twenty-three percent, as I understand."

"What? Does that include her big fat head? It's full of blubber instead of brains."

"You are horribly envious. Trust that I understand those things better than you."

"Humph. That is absurd."

"I know it all, Mom, the real story. Not just from her but from Bella, a fairly objective person. Wendy did a lot for you. She wasn't perfect, but neither are you. Some of the bad things you have done are beyond belief. Whatever happened between you two, can you not forgive and forget just a little bit and not throw a fit?"

Mom wiped tears from her eyes. "Maybe, in time. I'm sorry I am now so obnoxious and arrogant, but circumstances have made me into someone I don't like very well. Yet, make no mistake that Wendy has also been irreversibly changed. I will leave it to political historians to determine if it is for better or worse."

"Life changes us all, Mom. Shit happens, they say, as life is not gay and all play."

"Yeah, well, a lot of shit happened to me."

She shook her head in disgust. "It does not matter much, since you cannot count your blessings. There is a place for you back in Aurora City, New Castle, or Bonitaville if that is what you want."

"And what is it you think we would do there?" Jack asked.

"How would we possibly explain ourselves? To Molly and Stavros? Yeah, we'll just show up and hang out like nothing happened. We knew this would eventually occur, and that we'd have to stay in the background. Don't worry, we'll do okay. We've already told the high school you left to live with relatives in Indiana."

"Amazingly, that is the truth for once. I had enough credits technically to graduate. But I know that I must go back soon."

"That's right. There's nothing for you here, Paige, we knew that when we started this. Go forth and do great things."

"I never said there was nothing for me here."

"Yeah, she did, in so many words," Mom said.

"Shut up. You know it's true, Paige. I'm not being sarcastic, but merely factual."

"Can I at least stay the night? I'm tired."

"You? Really?"

"Yeah. This life wears on you."

"Maybe, if you behave. How can you be tired?"

"Emotional exhaustion. That amount of flight takes a lot out of me. It is mentally taxing and somewhat boring. The digital music selection available in my helmet also needs to be updated for my preferences."

He nodded. "Well, your bed's made upstairs. Just make sure not to make a mess in the bathroom like you usually do."

"Gotcha. I have learned a lot about my powers in the Sulphur Springs lab. Apparently, my body absorbs radar just like the suit did. Better, apparently."

"Yes, I know; I theorized as much," Petra said.

"Royce G. Bivereaux III feels that perhaps in time I will be able to absorb visible light, making me somewhat invisible."

"But how would you see anything, then?" Petra asked. "If light bends around you, how can you see it?"

"You know, I never thought of that."

"Figures. You might also run into some time dilation issues when you do that, just so you know."

"I have heard that term from Johnny Kepler as he also shares that concern, but I still am not sure what it means."

"You should not mess with forces you do not understand."

"I believe it is a bit too late for that."

• • •

It was good to spend the night in her own bed again after so many months. For some reason, she kept worrying that the paparazzi would come calling. She wasn't stupid, though. Despite Jack and her mother's precautions, it was them against the world. The way Wendy looked at her, she knew it all and had for some time. This was all kept a secret because her aunt desired it to be that way. She assumed that it would continue so, although she couldn't help feeling a bit used. She wanted to do things on her own terms, not the way others wanted.

She came down to breakfast in the house she was so familiar with. She had changed her hair color back to its non-tinted state, and she went without the visor.

"One thing puzzles me, Mom." She took a bite of cereal with milk, one of the few food items Mom couldn't ruin.

"What?"

"Why do I have no memory of any of this? Before the explosion? Did you do something to my mind?"

"No, you overestimate my capabilities; I told you that already. I don't really know, Aurora. When the explosive wave passed through you to me, it must have somehow removed your memories. You still retained your motor function and speech, unlike me when I was eleven and had meningitis. But I have to think that God somehow gave you that blessing."

"A blessing? To not remember my childhood?"

"You were six. It would have done you no good to remember those things, as those first few weeks were not pleasant. Let it go."

"That—will be difficult."

"I have no memory of anything of my childhood, either. I had met President Reagan twice after winning national spelling bees, but I have no recollection of that. Be grateful for what you have. Most have far less than we."

"I shall try and will not cry." She took a sip of milk. "But tell me about the first time you met her."

"Who are we speaking of?"

"Wendy. And no editorializing, please, as I know what your opinion of her is now. I want to know about back then."

"Oh, my. Well, I used to be deaf, as you know. I was thirteen, and she eighteen; she was volunteering at the rehab center where I was getting therapy. She had just moved here from Tennessee on a track and field scholarship at San Diego State and wanted volunteering experience because she wanted to be a doctor. I was still a little skinny kid and not yet my full height; my illness had set me back a couple of years. She knew sign language and some Spanish, so she worked with the deaf children. I idolized her. Their expectations of me were mediocre, and they decided that I should learn basic life skills, maybe go to a vocational school and learn a trade.

"But she taught me self-confidence, not to take shit off anyone, and to aim for the stars. She did much for me. With her help, I more than tripled my core strength within a year and a half. For those things, I am grateful to her."

"That's when she met Jay."

"Yes—although I had no idea they had dated in college until my mid-thirties. Marianne Gallinsworth, your grandmother, knew about it, but she was the only one."

"Did my dad know?"

"No. He and Wendy were not very close for many years, as they had a falling out after she left Oak Ridge. They reconciled after I married him."

"What happened with Wendy and Jay?"

"Jaime was a selfish, lazy, immature playboy with a short attention span and unmatched eye for the ladies. I helped him get through high school and college because of his unparalleled lethargy. As much as I complained about you, your languor cannot begin to compare to that of your uncle; he is singular in that aspect."

"What? He is eight years older than you, so how could you have helped him with his studies?"

"Simple: by age three, I was his intellectual superior."

"That does not explain what happened between them."

"Apparently, he decided to play the field, as one girl at a time was never sufficient for his limitless libido. He went out with her very attractive roommate while she was at a track meet; she came home early and found them in bed together, so he is lucky to even be alive. Understandably, she could not stand him for years. Despite his flaws, he is a good person, and it is beyond me how he could have been capable of treating someone so horribly, but there it is. Life is messy."

"And after all that drama, they are together now. That seems rather improbable."

"Yes, but catastrophes do that to you. He took a private jet to Pittsburgh immediately after the nuke blew our plane up, as that's where she was hospitalized after her cholecystectomy. She forgave him for what happened with Beth a long time ago."

"I guess I can see that. But what happened between you two?"

"I don't know, Paige. She went on to be Surgeon General, to greater fame in the Olympics, and became a national hero when she saved President Reardon and British Prime Minister John Truesdale by knocking them down and taking a chest full of ceramic bullets. I must admire her for her bravery. She did recover, and went on to become Governor of California, and, of course, President. We went our separate ways, and I left the CIA to do my research on Element 119 back in Tennessee, of all places."

"I still do not understand why you're not deaf now."

"I do not fully understand either."

"You do not understand something?"

"Hard to believe, huh?"

"I was being sarcastic, Mom."

"Oh. Well, I had some transient return of my hearing after Rita McPherson injected me with what I thought was the Ontario Lacus organism, which is responsible for our friend Juriann's abilities. But what I got clearly wasn't that. I lost that hearing after a few months, but after the *Darkkday* blast it returned, and my other senses became augmented."

"Rita. Yes, Bella told me about her."

"Bella seems to know a lot of things. I guess most of us, including me, underestimated her all these years." Jack said as she heard him pour a cup of coffee. "Do you have any friends there?"

"Well, yes—Lt. Russell Stanton, an Air Force pilot. I met him at a career fair here, actually."

"Sure," Jack said as he walked into the room. "I remember when he was here. Nice-looking guy. So, how are you and the pilot friends now, after meeting one time?"

She smiled. "Uh, not one time. I almost crashed his plane when that EMP device interfered with the electronics and I crashed into his plane; he helped me find a cave to stay in until the Aurora City cavalry arrived. He has evolved into, sort of, er—"

"Sort of what?" Jack asked in a sharp tone. "Paige?"

She sighed. "My boyfriend, okay? He was at Eielson, but now he is stationed at Wright-Patt, an hour away."

"*Boyfriend?* Do you mean Wright-Patt, as in Wright-Patterson Air Force Base?"

She nodded. "That is correct. Just outside Dayton. About an hour away from AC by motorcycle."

"You're actually dating an Air Force officer? Are you freaking kidding me?"

"Please define 'dating' more clearly."

"I don't think I need to."

"Huh. I am an adult, so the full spectrum of grownup activities is now available to me; that is how it is meant to be."

"Oh, never mind, I'm sorry I brought it up."

"If I am old enough to save crashing airplanes, I am old enough to date whomever I desire, so do not be so judgmental. I was going out with him while I was still living here, anyway."

"You dated him before you left?"

"Yeah, he was at Eielson until recently, duh. I have done a lot of stuff you do not know about. And it is not like you did not do it."

"What?" Petra asked. "That is an inappropriate comment."

"I was referring to Dad, not you, nerdy birdie."

Mom puffed out her chest. "Are you insinuating that I did not have opportunities as well for sexual congress? How insulting."

She shook her head. "No, Mom, trust that such a topic is the furthest thing from my mind, but please change the subject. This is getting too weird."

"I know, but is that wise? An Air Force officer?" He paused for a few seconds. "What am I saying? I don't want to know anything else."

"Good, because I am not telling you anything else, as it is not your business. But he is pretty cool." She paused for a few seconds. "Everything is okay, if you know what I mean."

"Everything?" Mom asked.

She nodded. "Yeah."

"Well, be sure to be careful. We do not know what cataclysmic event could happen if safety is not a prime concern."

She nodded. "Got it, Mom. Just because I understand the birds and the bees does not make me a sleaze."

Mom looked at the ground. "*Oogly* advises you to be careful as well."

"That is reassuring. I have not heard much from him lately."

"Not to change the subject, but I have an idea," Jack said. "Come with us to school and see some of the old gang."

She shook her head. "I do not think so—"

"It's okay; you didn't get to say goodbye to some of them. It's not like you have to be anywhere. We did have to concoct a back-story to explain why you didn't return after you secretly left here."

"Visiting relatives in Indiana?"

"Something like that."

"I am Nick's cousin, by the way, since you are his uncle. That is the story the White House came up with."

"That's kind of weird. It makes us relatives after all."

"Maybe not this time, but perhaps around Christmas, I could come back again. It would be good to see Bobby, Rachel, even Tommy Munson. I miss Ned Egghead the most."

"I'm sure he misses you too."

"Not. So, let us discuss this façade you engineered in greater detail. 'Jack Marshall?' Was that the most original name you could have concocted?"

"It's kind of generic, fits in, doesn't draw attention."

"Okay, but what about 'Paige?' Where did you get that?"

"From Latin *Pagius,* meaning 'young helper.' Are you not the young helper of mankind, Aurora?"

"Huh. 'Young yelper' is more like it. Yours is the worst. Petra Nureyev? A Russian? What a stereotype, like you walked over here across the Bering Strait or something."

"That old battle armor takes commands in Russian, so it was the only logical way I could explain to you why you should learn that language."

"I bet you picked the name from some stupid random name generator or something."

"Your point being?"

She shook her head. "Never mind. But I must know the answer to something, Mom."

"What?"

"When you slapped me, it hurt. Why?"

"I have the limited power, it seems, to influence your mind, to break through the invisible dark energy field that surrounds you by making you dissipate it. I can do the same with anyone else. You have surely noticed your vaccination scars."

"I suppose so."

"When I held you and calmed you as a child so your aunt could give you a shot, that was necessary."

"So you could really hurt me if you wanted?"

"*Now?* Doubtful. I caught you off guard last night. You could, of course, have retaliated, and I would be dead. I also am convinced you could resist it if you were prepared. With sophisticated drugs or weapons, then it might be different." She heard Mom get up from the kitchen chair. "There is something else you need to know if you haven't figured it out already."

"What?"

She felt the slap again, the force several times as hard.

But one thing was different.

It didn't hurt. What the hell?

"You slapped me about three times harder that time. But I did not see it coming, as I am not wearing the visor."

"Yes. It would have knocked out a few teeth in most people."

"But it didn't hurt this time. Why?"

"Because last night you had the visor on. My ability to do that apparently depends on your ability to see. I cannot do it with you in a sightless state. I figured this out after the explosion."

"So, in a way, I am stronger without sight than with it."

"That's one perspective, although to my knowledge, I'm the only one who can do it. If someone else could—well, that would be very hazardous to your health."

"Thankfully, there is no one else besides you."

"Where will you be going now?"

"Back to Aurora City, I promised to sign some autographs at a bookstore and do whatever else they have lined up for me. They wanted me to do batting practice with the Atoms. I have not decided on that one yet."

"Remember that you wanted this, Aurora. I just hope being a celebrity meets up to your expectations."

Chapter Fifty-Two

The next day *Stella* spent two hours at the autograph-signing party at Earl's Bookstore downtown and bid goodbye to dozens of onlookers as she saw a familiar figure exit a black SUV on North Darkkin Street. She had declined a later invitation to hit baseballs at the Atoms' indoor baseball complex.

"Jackie, what are you doing here? I thought you would be in Washington."

"*Stella,* the President needs to talk to you immediately. Can you get in?"

"I suppose so . . . I did not know about any of this, and is she even here now? She did not tell me of this event."

"Yes, she's in one of the M2 buildings waiting for you. It won't take long."

"Well, okay, I guess." She got in and sat in the back with Jackie. "Who are these folks? They do not look like they have sufficient growth hormone levels to be part of your staff."

"They are part of my staff I don't see very often."

The Black woman laughed as she then felt something she had just experienced two days ago for the first time: pain. Something was thrust through the suit into her left deltoid.

"What the hell?" She was becoming groggy and kicked one of the staffers out of the rear window before losing consciousness.

• • •

"You were right, Argon," van Sant said, looking at the video cameras showing her body placed inside an airtight titanium enclosure at the Cairo complex, hooked up to an oxygen mask.

"Of course I'm right. Her body is protected by some type of energy field which cannot be detected. It must shield her from all forms of toxins, including radiation. *Mantissa* fooled her into thinking she was Jacqueline Levickis, and thrust the sedative-hypnotic into her body after forcing her to drop it. Without that, her body isn't that much different from ours. It apparently dissipates when she's unconscious, but not just when she's sleeping."

"What are we going to do with her?"

"We're going to study and try to duplicate this physiology. Combining her abilities with *Mantissa's*, we can rule the world."

"I get that, Ray, but do you have any idea the power that you're trying to harness?" Tolliver asked nervously.

"Do you have any idea the consequences if we don't? No one person should have the power of a god. Do you know what could happen if she were to turn on us?"

"What the hell?" van Sant said. "You're trying to get the power for yourself, Argon, so what's different here, you hypocrite?"

"Shut up, *Santaman*. I didn't ask you, retard. You maybe have money, but you're a silent partner in this, remember that."

Six-four Reuben J. Skelton grabbed Argon, clearly not approving of how the scientist had addressed his boss. "I should draw and quarter ye for such insolent remarks, Argon. No one addresses the regal *Santaman* in that fashion unless he has a death wish."

"Okay, whatever, man, sorry. Jesus."

"Sorry shall not spare ye a horrific death next time, cretin."

"I hear you," Tolliver said. "But—she's a known entity to the government now, so they must be looking for her."

"Let them look. And don't you think they've been thinking about doing the same thing as us, Mike?"

"What do you mean by that?"

"This human being represents power supreme. If you don't think the President wants a piece of this, you're horribly naïve. But they don't have the genius I do. And we'll soon rule the world."

• • •

"Do you have any idea where Paige is?" Bella asked her husband at home in the kitchen. "She never came home from *Stella's* visit to Earl's Bookstore. She should've been back an hour ago."

"What? No, why?" Nick replied, munching on a cookie.

"I was going to take her to Ball State to visit. She needs to start thinking about her future."

"Well, she needs to graduate from high school first. But she moves pretty fast, so maybe she's already been back here and went back into town to get into trouble again like last time."

She shook her head. "None of the drivers has taken her anywhere. I've looked at surveillance footage from that time in that area and don't see anything."

"She could've gone the other way."

"Oh." She thought for a moment. "But she would've used the access tunnel, then—the computers show no evidence that the doors have been opened, so she never went or came back that way. I doubt she took off from the house. I'm really worried, the last time she went into town alone, she ended up getting rescued by *Orthoman*, like you mentioned. We really don't want that again."

"Maybe she went somewhere else, you know, like Dayton?"

"We'll see." They walked up to her bedroom and went in, opened the large clothes armoire, and found three *Stella* suits and two sapphire visors. "We only made four visors, two of them are here, and the third one was destroyed in the bank incident and hasn't been replaced yet. She didn't fly anywhere. And she said she would carry one in her bra just in case she needed it, as usual."

"So she has the one. Maybe she went somewhere with Russ."

"Doubtful, she would've told me." She found Paige's cell phone. "No way she would've left without this, but I'll find out right now." She scrolled through the list of numbers and found one for the Air Force lieutenant.

"Hey, what's up?" the male voice answered. "I'm in a meeting now, call you later."

"Russ, it's Bella. Is Paige with you?"

"No, of course not. Hold on a minute." Fifteen seconds passed. "Sorry, I needed to step outside. What did you ask me again?"

"Is she with you or at your apartment?"

"What? No, I haven't seen her in several days. She flew to North Pole to see her folks, then came back to your place yesterday."

"Yeah, she had been downtown for an event several hours ago

but never returned, and I thought she might've gone to Dayton."

"No . . . but are you telling me you don't know where she is?"

"We don't know."

"Are you going to call the police?"

She sighed. "I doubt that's a smart idea, and if something happened to her, how could the local police possibly help us find such a being? I need you to take a trip with us."

"Where?"

"Back to North Pole. I need some assistance."

"Are you clairvoyant, Bella?"

"I'm not, Lieutenant, but my uncle is. I also know no one drove her anywhere. She didn't fly, and she's not with you. Even when she went on trips with you she always called, except for the time those robbers 'kidnapped' her. There's only one solution, and it ain't good."

"What?"

"Something's happened to her."

"That's impossible, Bella."

"Is it? I know you don't know me very well, but you need to trust me on this one. If I say something is so, it probably is."

"Then, how?"

"She has an immunization scar, which you've probably seen, meaning that it's possible for her to drop this invulnerability field she has, at least temporarily. Or for someone to make her do it."

"How could anyone do that? Hypnotism? Really?"

Bella nodded. "Something like that. We'll figure it out soon. While the DSD and other big Washington brains are working, we need to do our part; for that, we need a mind way bigger than anyone on the *Science Squad* to figure it out. That mind is in North Pole. Despite all of our intense studying, no one really knows how her powers work."

"Are you saying—"

"I am. You've met some interesting folks, but get ready to meet a real living legend—if she can be located, that is. She may not appear like much these days, as I haven't seen her in over twelve years, but she's the real deal."

• • •

Jack was washing some dishes when he saw the light outside

and heard the faint hum of high-powered jets. He ran outside and saw the Stannous hovercraft land in their yard, and couldn't believe his eyes by what he saw when his wife's niece, wearing a blue aviation jumpsuit, exited the unique aircraft . He yelled at the five-five woman running toward the house as the others walked up.

"What do you want? You idiots, of all people, should've known better than to have ever come here."

"Shut the hell up. I don't give a shit about you, Jimmy Jack. We're here to help Aurora."

"I don't know why you came, then. Why would she need help? She was living with you in your fancy mansion, last I heard. She was just here a few days ago, anyway." Jack looked at the massive Juriann. "I know the others, but who in the world are you?"

"My name is Juriann Hultaar."

Jack laughed. "That doesn't help me any."

"He's Rad's son, Jimmy Jack. We also call him *Orthoman.*"

"Okay, kind of brings up some bad memories, sure."

"Look, this isn't the best time for a family squabble, Uncle Jim. We need Bonnie's help," Nick said.

"Then you've wasted your time coming here, Nick, because I don't know where she is either. Petra's been gone for three days."

"What? Where?" Bella asked.

He shook his head. "She does that sometimes. I don't know where she goes, and it's better not to ask."

"Well, we need to find the hell out. Paige has disappeared and we think there's some clone of Bonnie out there with some of her mind powers. Is that possible?" Bella asked angrily.

"What? That's preposterous. And how would I know that?"

"After all that's happened in this family, get real," she said. "One question: can Petra breach her energy field?"

He nodded. "What? Yes, but only momentarily, and only when she's *Stella* and can see; it doesn't work when she's blind. Paige can apparently do it herself, briefly, with enough concentration."

"How do you know that?"

"The old Vladimirov armor. The brain wave patterns are very weak and any electromagnetic energy other than visible light won't penetrate to her. She has to 'open it up' a little bit for it to work. It takes a great amount of concentration."

"But Petra could make her drop it. She has to be able to. Paige has an immunization scar, the shot presumably given before she developed her invulnerability."

"I don't know; that was before my involvement in all this. But Aurora could see then, of course, but was still a toddler. And Bonnie would never do that."

"No, but the evil clone might. There's evidence that one exists, project *Mantissa,* created by Ramon Argon."

"Who the hell is Ramon Argon? That last name isn't very appealing if memory serves correctly."

"Malachi's nephew, who presumably made a greatly augmented clone of Bonnie, created from old DNA from the Ontario Lacus incident. I don't have time to go into the details."

Russ came forward. "Now, who are *you?*" Jack asked.

"Air Force Lt. Russell Stanton."

"The military is involved in this now? Just fantastic."

Russ shook his head. "I'm not here in a military capacity, sir. I met Paige when she was still living with you. She would've told me if she was going somewhere."

He nodded. "Yeah, I guess so, and I remember you now from the career fair at the school. So, you're the guy?"

Russ nodded. "I am."

Jack shook his head. "Well, that's great, but like I already told you, I have no idea where Petra's at. She sometimes disappears for days at a time, you know. We do need lots of money around here."

"No, I don't know, Jimmy Jack," Bella yelled. "She doesn't even have a drivers' license; she gets lost going around the block, as I recall. How in the hell does she go anywhere?"

"She's not anything like you would remember, Bella. Petra has the power to manipulate others' perceptions of her to a great extent, so I guess she hitches rides on planes or something. After the explosion, her senses and brainpower got a quantum boost from Aurora, so she surely has done stuff we don't want to know about, like hacking into debi-stations to get cash and decapitating ruthless dictators."

"Aurora has vast physical abilities, but super-intelligence and heightened senses aren't among those."

"I don't know how, but Petra can avoid getting lost with her GPS bracelet, just like when she was younger. She'd be very hard to find, and her senses are superhuman. She could probably sense when I'm coming. She can literally smell me from miles away, and she has better hearing than any canine."

"But she wouldn't sense someone she wasn't expecting."

Jack nodded his head. "Maybe, maybe not. She also still thinks like a child and always has. If I was going to look for her, it would be in the place she knows best: San Diego."

"San Diego is a big place. If she was going to 'disguise' herself as someone, who would it be?"

"That's easy. Go to the museum, Bella. Figure it out."

"Which one? There are several with her name there."

"The big one, the *Mendoza the Miraculous* Museum. She idolized him, the greatest of magicians. You might see if a guy fitting the description of Harry Houdini is walking around the back alleys of San Diego. Or—" Jack thought for a moment.

"Or what?" Bella asked.

"Or, more specifically—Balboa Park, which is close to the museum. That's where I would go to find her if I were you. Alex said that was always her favorite place to go to think things out."

"Balboa Park is 1,200 acres. How are we going to find her?"

"I don't know," Jack said. "I guess you'd better get going, then."

Orthoman, Amp, Bella, and *Golfer* went back into the hovercraft, getting ready for the 3,400 mile trip to San Diego, while Nick, Wolf, and Biv took a trip to Washington on a chartered private jet.

• • •

White House Chief of Staff Kristina Bennett tapped her boss on the shoulder sharply as she exited the West Wing conference room. "Madam President, there are some, uh, visitors for you in the Oval Office."

Wendy looked up as she walked briskly through the West Wing. "Who? I've got a full schedule today, Kris. Why did you let them in?"

"Because the First Gentleman is in there, too. He says it's pretty important that you go in, and he canceled your morning appointments as well, Ma'am."

"Are you kidding me? He did *what?*" She walked into the Oval Office, where she usually saw important government representatives and other VIPs, not her husband in there with Nick and ancient remnants of *Dr. Wendy's Science Squad* like *Chemical Cowboy and Photraman.* Like she needed those weirdoes coming out of the woodwork now.

"What are you doing, Jay? This isn't the time."

"The hell it's not. Listen up, Wendy."

She rolled her eyes and scanned the room full of her old colleagues. "Guys, I appreciate the funky reunion here, but I really don't have time today. Can't we reschedule—"

"No, we can't, Wendy," Wolf said. "We need your help."

"What? What does that mean, *Cowboy?*"

Nick looked up at her. "*Stella* has been gone for days, and no one knows where she's at."

"Huh. Well, don't y'all think she can take care of herself? She's a big girl now."

Nick shook his head. "Like we already discussed, no one really understands how her energy powers work. There was some guy who used to work for me who also apparently was related to Malachi Argon."

She thought for a moment and walked towards the Resolute Desk. "That's very strange, and anything having to do with Malachi Argon sure isn't good, but so what?"

"If they had some way of affecting her invulnerability, it would be disastrous. Bonnie is also nowhere to be found."

"So? She's been in hiding ever since the explosion, so what is it you're getting at?"

"There were rumors that Bonnie had these weird mind powers after she got her hearing back, temporarily."

"Yes, that's true," Jay said. "She could project things into my mind that were beyond comprehension for a brief time. But those abilities disappeared after about six months, around 2011."

"I saw her vast powers, yes," Wendy said, nodding. "She killed Malachi Argon with the power of her mind. I watched her do it after I pleaded with her to stop. As evil as he was, she isn't God who gets to decide who lives and dies." She walked around the office in a circle. "They were inextricably linked to *Oogly-Googly*, the purple blob-thing, a synesthetic brain construct that, to her, was alive. But those abilities were only present when she had natural hearing, and the astral projection stuff only worked with Jay and, to a much lesser extent, Bella, it seems. She lost her hearing again months after the Ontario Lacus incident. By the time Aurora was born, she was completely deaf again. So those powers can't exist."

"We don't know that for sure. Paige said that she's able to hear. Quite well, in fact."

"Yes, my intel has told me that, although I don't have an explanation for it or if that translates into what you're proposing."

"Paige says all of her senses are greatly augmented," Biv said. We postulate that somehow the *Darkkday* blast passed through Aurora and conferred some abilities to her."

Wendy looked out the east window. "She can maybe be a little persuasive, Biv, but mind powers? That was a one-shot deal."

"It isn't that simple. We do know that Argon wanted to experiment on her. What if someone cloned Bonnie? Wouldn't a being like that have the same abilities? And couldn't those abilities be improved on somehow?" Biv asked.

"I suppose Malachi Argon or his protégé, Rita, could've done something like that; they'd probably still have her DNA from the *Ontario Lacus* incident. What do you think happened?"

"Bella visited Rita recently at her college, she claims not to know anything about any clone, although she had an idea Juriann might exist."

"What if this clone somehow did something to Paige—*Stella?*" Wolf said.

"There's a complex in Cairo, West Virginia, and it's one of Malachi Argon's old labs, we just found out," Nick said. "Malachi's nephew Ramon Argon used to work for me but got let go when we changed our corporate direction."

"Waitaminnit," Wendy said. "Another Argon scientist? Why the hell would you guys have hired *anyone* whose last name was Argon? Smith, Jones, Brown, Miller, Johnson, maybe—but *Argon?*"

Nick shook his head. "It's a big company, and I wasn't aware of him being around, and most knew nothing about this Malachi Argon guy then. All we know now, Bella got from Rita McPherson."

"Yes, because it was classified, and I've been to those labs, believe me. So, I hear you, *Tinman,* but what do y'all want from me?"

"We need the military to be on standby for what we find, but stay the hell out of our way for now, Wendy."

"Do you know what you're asking, guys? We need the military to go in there *now.*"

"No. *Orthoman, Amp,* and *Golfer* went to San Diego to find Bonnie, as she's not home, and Jack says she'd likely be there. If anyone has a shot at getting rid of Ramon Argon and this clone, it's them, Wendy, not the military. If this being is what we think, it could completely destroy your information network, with devastating consequences, and maybe already has. This demands a special skill set. I know you don't think much of them these days, but trust me on this one."

The President nodded her head. "Okay, Nick, you have my word. But you've got only forty-eight hours before we move in."

"Then we had better get going for the rendezvous."

• • •

Balboa Park
San Diego, CA

Juriann, Todd, Bella, and Johnny had arrived in the Stannous hovercraft in San Diego near the edge of Balboa Park and picked up a company car from the local M2 branch an attendant had waiting, with Bella waiting with the vehicle for when they needed to leave. Quickly, hopefully.

"Do we really think this excursion is a good use of our limited time, with *Stella* missing and the world in jeopardy?" Juriann asked as he drove the electric sedan down the road.

"Ah, chill out with the soliloquy, *Orthoman*," Kepler said, sipping a soda. "We need her help. Hell, she's responsible for you bein' here in the first place, you said, so it'll be like a reunion."

"Shut up, Kepler," Juriann yelled. "I have become very weary of your smart-ass remarks."

"Johnny has always been irritating, Juriann, but he's right," Todd said. "You think you've met smart people, but you have no idea. To fight this thing, we need—"

"*We* need?" Juriann asked. "Care to rephrase that, Todd?"

"Yes, *we* need Petra Nureyev at full thrusters, trust me, Juriann, or we have no chance, so lose the arrogance. And you need us to make this work, lest you forget that important fact."

"My apologies, it just seems like looking for a needle in a haystack, attempting to find her out here and all. Aren't we just wasting time?"

"Unless someone comes up with a better idea, no," Todd said as they pulled into the parking lot and exited the vehicle.

They walked through the park for the next twenty minutes, not sure what they would find.

"Why are we looking here?" the large man asked. "The world

really might be coming to an end, and we're foolishly wasting time out here looking for Petra, a person who may not even still exist."

"Your big ol' brain doesn't know everything. I betcha she does, *Ortho,* and we're out here because she and Todd used to hang out here in college. This was one of her favorite places to go meditate."

"What about Jim—er, Jack, or whatever he calls himself now?" Todd asked.

"She'll be avoiding him, most likely. We don't need him anyway, and Jim's no help to us anyway."

"And not avoiding us?" Juriann asked.

Kepler shook his head. "She won't be expecting me or *Amp,* and certainly not you. Jack said she must be out here somewhere. She and her two blood relatives besides Paige—Bella and Jay—she can vaguely communicate with them telepathically, somehow. It's pretty damn weird, but true."

They looked around curiously for ten more minutes and finally spied a fiftyish, dark-haired man sitting on the park bench who looked slightly out of place. "Over here, Hultaar."

The unlikely trio walked up to the odd man, who stared back at them, dark brown eyes darting nervously back and forth.

"What are you three moronic goons staring at? Don't you have anything better to do than harass one of the greatest figures in human history?"

"I just noticed how you bear a resemblance to someone I used to know," Todd said. "And I don't think that guy's up in the pantheon of world greats. You, maybe."

"Humph. Small world." The man ignored him and began shuffling a deck of cards with his right hand at incredible speed. "I am who I appear to be, nothing more, nothing less. Mostly less. Brain cells die off every day, never to return. I have lost far too many, as you can plainly see. Fortunately, I started off with exponentially more than all of you."

Juriann came up to the man. "Is this seat taken, sir?"

"Sit wherever you choose, mammoth European one. The park welcomes all visitors. It is not my place to decide otherwise."

He sat down next to him. "You know who I am, don't you, after all these years?"

The man stared at him for several minutes. "*Ja.*"

"You look like someone I have heard of. *Du heißt Ehrich, ja*? *Ehrich Weiss*? *Wie gehst du?*"

"What makes you think this weirdo speaks German?" Kepler said. "Who the hell is Eric Weiss?"

"Trust me. You know better than I."

"Es geht mir gut. Ja, ich heiße Ehrich, du bist richtig."

"Better known by your stage name. Harry. Harry Houdini."

The magician dead for over a century stared at him. *"Ja."*

Kepler looked down curiously. "You know, he *does* sort of look like Houdini. If you concentrate and want to believe it, he does even more."

"Of course I do," the dark-haired man said angrily. "I am he, in a regenerated state, you one-legged moron." He waved his hand furiously. "Now, begone, eccentric and vaguely familiar ones from a sordid past I wish to forget. I have much meditation to do, to rest my giant brain for the Herculean tasks that I will soon need to complete, once I figure out what those are."

Juriann looked closely at him and pulled on his hair. "I said 'a little bit.' When you touch her, it's not quite as good. Weird."

"Do not confuse my gender, and I did not say you could touch me. Move it or lose it, *Orthoman*."

"Sorry, Harry. This is for your own good." Juriann pulled on the beard.

The clearly displeased "Houdini" grabbed his hand. "Hey! What are you doing, you oversized aberration of humanity?"

Kepler joined in by pulling off the curly hairpiece as bystanders took a glance, then moved on, this type of weirdness being nothing extraordinary for Southern California.

Kepler laughed. "It's just a damn wig. Unlike Ramon Argon's *Mantissa*, the disguise isn't totally her manipulation of our perceptions, it has to be someone about the same build and size to pull it off, and you have to want to believe."

The fifty-two-year-old magician sneered at him. "Yeah, *Golfer*, but I can still do magic tricks. If I do one, will you leave me alone?"

Kepler shook his head and mopped sweat from his brow. "Damn, this is freakin' me out. We all thought you were dead."

"Dead?" "Houdini" squinted and pointed his right index finger at him. "*You* will be dead soon if you don't depart. I was minding my own business, and you dare to interrupt my meditation?"

Juriann came closer to her. "Excuse me, *Mein Herr*, but my friend has his doubts. So, can you prove that you are truly Ehrich Weiss with a demonstration?"

She snarled. *"Warum?"*

"Just a little show of good faith, Ehrich."

Weiss sighed. *"Naturlich."*

Juriann produced a length of rope from his pocket, which he handed to Ehrich, and he watched it transform into a pair of old handcuffs from the 1890s, he guessed. She handed them to Juriann.

"How'd she do that?" Kepler asked as he handled the heavy old manacles. "Did she always have real magical powers?"

"What do you think?" Todd said. "She's much, much more than that. She's our old friend, one of the best magicians ever. It's a mind-control trick." He handed her an old *Mendoza Milagrosa* action figure from 1996 he had carried in a backpack.

"*Was is das*?" The magician took it and studied it intensely.

"We need this person's help. Aurora needs her help."

"Houdini" shook his head as tears streamed from his eyes. *"Unmöglich. Bonita ist tot. Aurora ist tot auch. Sie heißt Paige jetzt."*

"Nein." Juriann touched the magician. *"Nicht wahr.* You know that's not true."

He then watched something miraculous indeed as she slowly morphed into the early-fiftyish white-haired woman.

Kepler stared in disbelief. "It *is* her. How did she do that?"

"Through the power of her mind. She has the limited ability to make us think she looks like someone different, but the person has to want to believe in it," Todd said. "You can suppress it if you try. She probably had some of those powers back in the day."

"If the power was more complete—it could change the world, *Amp*," Juriann said.

"Yes, and it may have already," Todd replied. "This is why Ramon Argon wanted her powers instead of *Stella's*. Argon apparently has augmented these powers to a high degree in this version of Bonnie's clone and can rule the world with the power of *Mantissa.* But now he's decided to obtain the power of dark energy in addition. He can use the money, connections, and cyber-expertise of *Santaman* and *Red Skeleton* to nuke key U.S. cities and create unprecedented chaos while he implements his plan."

Petra looked up from her trance-like state. "What is it you want me to do, intrusive idiots? Who is this *Mantissa* person you keep raving about?"

"You created me for a reason: to help with problems no one else can. Now, like I said, Aurora needs you."

Petra shook her head and stared at the ground. "She has all of you, as she is a grown woman and needs me no more. She has left Alaska, never to return. Your abilities pale when compared to hers, orthogenetic one." She yawned and lay on the bench, covering herself with old newspapers. "Now, I must sleep and rest my old cerebrum to cherish the few lucid moments I have left."

"Hey, listen up," Todd said, tapping her on the head. "Get with the program. Someone cloned you somehow and made an evil being called *Mantissa*. They did something to Aurora. It seemed to be the only way to penetrate her defenses, in a manner of speaking."

She sprung up like a jack-in-the-box emerging from its container after *Admiral Ampere's* words finally sunk in. "What? Theoretically, that would be possible, but extremely haphazard."

"Huh? You're really gonna lecture someone about 'haphazard,' Bonnie? You gotta lotta nerve, after all the unethical shit you did," Kepler said.

"Yes, I certainly do, yet I will not discuss my poor life choices with and justify them to one such as you, Kepler. Where is she, anyway? I have not sought out her presence by choice."

"Then try and find her, Petra, and stop playing Harry Houdini. Only you can do it," Todd said.

She closed her eyes and went into a trance-like state for several minutes, then stood up. "I don't know; she is not there. Has something happened to her? How can that be possible, *Amp?*"

"We don't know either. We think *Santaman* and a relative of Malachi Argon's named Ramon Argon did something with her."

She thought for a moment. "The evil Kristoff van Sant—*Santaman*—he was known to me, I thought he was in prison. You mentioned him a moment ago as playing a key role here. And Malachi Argon—an evil name I have not heard for nearly twenty years. You do know that I killed him, don't you?"

Todd frowned. "Yeah, we know, Bonnie, it was recorded on the old helmet that was damaged in the Bering Strait incident."

"I should have erased that recording. My daughter would have trouble killing, but I don't, trust me, given the proper provocation. Where do we go, and how do we get there? There are several I will surely kill if my daughter has been harmed."

"This *Mantissa* is something else, Petra. She's like a greatly augmented version of you, which could make her far more dangerous than *Stella Scura,* in many ways."

"So the hell am I, Todd. Do you for one moment doubt that?"

"Nope, not any more. Let's get going."

"You've grown a bit since I saw you last, Juriann." She turned to Kepler. "It's been a long time, *Golfer, Ampere*. Not long enough." She laughed.

"It has, Bonnie—er, Petra. But apparently they are using a lot of power, and I can help you find where they are going," Todd said.

"Is it just us going?" Juriann asked.

"Yes, just the grown-ups. Our destination is no place for *Amp, Golfer,* or *Tinman,*" she said. "But how are we getting there?"

"You'll see," Juriann said.

"Whatever takes us there had better do it quickly."

• • •

They drove in the car back to the edge of Balboa Park and saw the M2 hovercraft as Petra peered inside and frowned. "I am not certain I feel safe with this pilot, whose skills are unknown to me."

"How do you know who the pilot is? You can't see inside from this angle."

"Yes, well, I just know. Another juvenile delinquent."

They went in and saw Bella in the pilot's seat.

"Lord have mercy on us. When did they give you a pilot's license, Isabel? This is indeed frightening."

"A long time ago. Nice to see you too. Just shut the hell up and get your old butt in here." Bella put on her radio headset as they sat in the back compartment.

"About this *Mantissa*—we need the Vladimirov helmet."

"The thing got messed up by the SecDef's EMP weapon, and she hit a plane," Bella said. "It's in pieces. *Amp* was able to retrieve some data from it, like he said, but it's beyond our ability to repair, even if we had all the pieces."

Petra shook her head. "No, no, not that one, there's another entire suit down in the old Röntgen-Cave."

"The which?" Bella asked. "I guess I missed out on that one."

"Rad's old hideout in Solway, near the distillery. We shut it down and sealed it, but there's still stuff down there. I'm the only one who is aware of it; I used it as a secret lab after his death."

"But why do we need that crappy old suit?"

"Because the ability of *Mantissa* to overcome Paige, if her powers were derived from me—depends on her natural vision, and it won't work when using the suit. I discovered that by accident. She, therefore, needs the suit again to take on this *Mantissa*. And when I find this piece of shit, it's going to pay dearly, believe me."

"How did I come to be, Petra? I've pieced some things together, but no one knows for certain," Juriann asked as they flew towards Aurora City in the M2 hovercraft.

"I am the only one who knows the complete sorry tale that is your life. Do you want the truth, Juriann? It is not a pleasant story by any means. With truth comes much darkness."

"And enlightenment." Juriann laughed. "Coming from you, it should be entertaining."

"Humph. Likely not, cloned one." Petra took a sip of Negra Modelo beer from a frosty bottle she pulled from the craft's small refrigerator and ate a handful of potato chips.

"What? Do you really think you should be drinking now? Why is that even on this vehicle? Never mind, forget I asked."

"You Dutch dolt, I will do what I please; even completely intoxicated, my brain is superior to yours. I deserve it after all I've been through."

"Okay, okay, simmer down."

She chugged the rest of the bottle. "I will not 'simmer down.' A renegade lieutenant general named Brant Gallagher funded, using illicit investors, a project of Malachi Argon's designed to create super-soldiers. In the mid-2000s, Argon discovered a microorganism with fantastic regenerative powers in an ethane lake on Titan called Ontario Lacus. Through advanced technology unknown to the government, he and Rita McPherson, another geneticist of low morals, were able to resequence the DNA. This collection of proteins had the ability to regenerate tissue, and in fact cured Rita of her paralysis for a period of time."

"And he used this to create a super-soldier. Me?"

She shook her head. "No, it's far more complex than that. Argon had already experimented on you, or—rather his son Travis—to give him superhuman speed and endurance. Your father and half-sister, but not Aurora's father, carried a rare gene mutation found in certain elite strength athletes, but no one knew that then. He succeeded in partially expanding Travis' great natural strength, but the side effect was that Travis developed an aggressive form of leukemia because of the treatments he used, which interfered with normal cell regeneration and repair."

"Why did this Argon do this to me—his son?"

"He was arrogance personified, and wanted power. He also had severe Parkinson's disease and had experimented on himself, I later learned."

"What happened next?"

"He used the extremophile microorganism *Orthogeneticus titania* to try and regenerate Travis. It worked to an extent, but he needed a stem cell transplant to save him. It was at that time that things got even more complicated."

"What do you mean?"

"Argon discovered his DNA was no more similar to Travis' than a random person, so his father must've been someone else. So he set out to find a match, knowing that he had an uncommon mutation in muscle proteins that I mentioned. He and Rita put together this incredibly complex pro football drug testing operation to try and screen pro football players who might possibly be matches since some elite power athletes have the gene as well."

"I don't understand what that has to do with me."

"Patience. You asked to hear this sordid tale; thus it must be told in its entirety. My brother Jaime used to be a pro football coach in Las Vegas before he was pro football commissioner, and—the First Gentleman—so we went to visit him after he suspected some of his players were on steroids. But, fortuitously, an ex-elite power athlete who was almost a perfect bone marrow match for Travis came in right through the door, unfortunately, to the Las Vegas testing center, where my brother was the coach, as I stated."

"What? Who?"

"Who else? Can you not guess who might be a bone marrow match for you? Our illustrious Commander-in-Chief in her finest hour."

"What? But you said pro football players, and they're all men. She's a big gal, but she has many distinctive female attributes—her cup size, for example. She's too small for most positions, also."

She nodded. "Correct. But she and her brother—my late husband Alex, God rest his Appalachian soul—concocted this harebrained scheme to try and expose it. To make a long story short, she used prosthetics to pass herself off as a washed-up punter, and it worked. But they got some of her DNA, and Argon concluded that she and Travis Argon must have the same father. The rest, you can figure out."

"Why would she have done something that messed up?"

"It is based in fundamental science and was very clever, but dangerous. But, yes, that's when we found out she was bipolar, so her judgment was not sound. My late husband was similar in mental state at times. The two siblings together were not to be trusted with their outlandish ideas, when they actually got along, which wasn't often." She opened another bottle of beer and took a drink.

"Yes, I deduced as such. The colorful nuclear physicist, Dr. William Conrad Darkkin, was, therefore, my father."

She frowned. "It seems that Rad Darkkin had an affair with Argon's wife Katrina around 1971 or so, a year before Wendy was born. I killed Malachi Argon and almost killed Travis in a battle to the death. Wendy was about five weeks pregnant at the time with her second child Dione Cassandra, and Argon wanted to use Cassie's fetal cells to try and regenerate Travis. Fortunately, Rad and I prevented that from happening. Rad died in the end, or so everyone thought. Rad had received some of the protein too, in a rather reckless move on his part."

"That sounds about right. The two of you together, what a great combo that must've been."

"Yeah, and he's not buried in Oak Ridge, but we took him back to the CIA where we did actually use Cassie's bone marrow and Travis Argon's cells to regenerate Rad's cells, too. Otherwise, you are, for all practical purposes, a clone of Travis Argon. Surely some people have noticed your resemblance to Rad and Wendy."

"Right, that's exactly what the hell I thought when you walked into my office at Princeton," Kepler yelled. "Remember the Dwight Latham song, 'I'm My Own Grandpa—' I guess that's you, Hultaar. Kinda messed up. Crap, I thought this family couldn't get fucked up anymore. I was wrong."

"We're all messed up, Johnny Kepler, including you."

Kepler nodded. "You got that right, slick. That's why we're all together on this great team. My destiny, I can't escape it."

"And Aurora? How did she figure into this?" Juriann asked.

"Rita injected me with the protein too, or so I thought. Shortly after that, my hearing returned, plus sensory abilities that are simply amazing, and I inexplicably gained mass. I was deaf before, of course, but my hearing now is superior to that of the best canine, as is my smell. My visual acuity is ten times yours. The original

Ortho-Man, and you, the *Orthoman,* are a product of natural genetics and a highly evolved microorganism originally from Earth. Apparently there was something else found on Titan, with origins on Earth as well. But while *Orthogeneticus titania* had origins as primitive Earthly extremotherm *Archaeobacteria,* the other, what I possess, and what Rad injected into himself later, was surely *alien.*"

"What?"

"Genetic material from, apparently, the only other being like Aurora who ever existed. He sent his 'seed' here through some temporal vortex to hopefully be reconstituted at some later date."

"So, it appears that he was reconstituted, in a way, actually."

"I suppose that was his desired result. Whether or not that's the case, I know not."

"Was Paige normal as a child?"

She nodded. "At first, yes. She developed normally, with typical developmental milestones. She exhibited no exceptional intellectual abilities, to my disappointment. But at about age three months, we discovered it was very tough to pierce her skin. By age two, she could survive boiling water, for example. She accidentally overturned a pot of boiling spaghetti on herself and laughed about it. She was holding a kitten with her other hand which was unharmed; one on the floor was burned terribly. It was then when we realized that a living being in contact with her skin would be protected like she was."

• • •

After dropping Todd, Kepler, Nick, and Bella off at the Stannous hangar, Petra and Juriann headed next to Solway, Tennessee, near the old Darkkin distillery. Juriann was a fast learner and had gained sufficient skill to master the hovercraft, as the mission was far too dangerous for the others to tag along. Like Petra had said, this was for the big boys and girls.

They exited in the middle of a field as they headed off towards the woods. She muttered something in Latin to her left as if talking to someone.

He laughed. "There's no one out here, Petra. Who or what are you conversing with, in Latin, no less?"

She snarled at him and pointed to the ground. "I just happen to be engaging in repartee with one of the greatest minds ever, *Oogly-Googly*. I thought you knew all about the *Science Squad* and his limitless intellect, second only to my own."

"He wasn't featured very prominently on the show, except as a little kid in a purple blob suit."

"That was not a fitting homage. Yet, with a limited budget for special effects, he was all we could afford."

"You talk to an imaginary friend?"

She sighed. "Humph. I expected far better from a genetically enhanced man such as you. He is *not* imaginary; he is a synesthetic construct composed of photons representing the seven Newtonian colors and has immense intellect beyond your comprehension."

"Wow. The seven colors of the rainbow. Sounds like a better sidekick for *Photraman* than you."

"That ignorant loudmouth Royce G. Bivereaux III cannot possibly understand his greatness. Neither can you, apparently."

"An anthropomorphic blob—does he have legs and arms? How does he walk?" He went to where she was pointing and kicked the ground. "How does that feel to him?"

"Why, that was callous, *Orthoman*. Fortunately, he is composed of pure light, so your aggressive actions have no effect on him. He thinks and moves at the speed of light, too."

"Yes, whatever. As long as he doesn't get in the way."

"He will be a great asset."

They came to a clearing in the woods. "*This* is the Röntgen-Cave, Petra? Is this one of your delusions?"

"Hardly. Just because I can perceive things you cannot and my brain cell mass is not what it once was does not make them 'delusions.'" She looked at her GPS watch, which showed her precise position and direction she wanted to walk. "Towards the end of the woods is a secret passage to the old one. The improved copy of the suit I made when I was with the CIA is down there."

They opened the outer ground access door and went down the concrete steps as they came to a fortified door.

"Do I need to break this down?"

She snarled and looked at him as if he was five years old. "That is not necessary. Brain, not brawn, shall ultimately prevail here."

"How do we gain access, then?"

"Duh!" She moved up to the small panel, which looked like a temperature regulator, and pointed to it.

"You'll get in with a thermostat? That's a new one."

"Quiet." She removed the outer plastic panel, which revealed a sophisticated scanning device, and she looked into it with her right eye.

"A retinal scanner. You *have* to be kidding me."

"Do I look like I am kidding?" She scowled again. "If the wrong person looks into this, it'll explode and blow their head off."

"It's really hard to tell if you're joking or not."

"Humph. Do I look like I enjoy joking around?"

"No."

"Then shut up. Yes, I was joking; there are no explosives here, are you nuts?" A green light came on the scanner, as the massive steel door opened as they went in. "Lights on," she commanded, as the main room was suddenly engulfed in fluorescent light, and she went over to another locked case, the size of a human. She rapidly pushed a set of ten numbers on a keypad as it opened.

He looked at it and was clearly unimpressed.

"This is it? What we came for? What a pile of junk. We're wasting precious time."

"That is correct, Juriann, what did you think we were doing? Humph." She took out the lightweight metallic suit in pieces and lay it down on a table. "It may not appear like much, but there is nothing else like it on Earth. As you can see, I made some, er, anatomical modifications." The torso portion was now more rounded and clearly was meant for a female, given the breast indentations.

"Why do you need the new breastplate? For you, it obviously shouldn't matter."

"*Ortho,* I tire of a lifetime of jokes about my minuscule mammaries. It is for my daughter, lummox. I am officially retired."

"That's probably good. It still works?"

"It was kept here, in secret, far from Alaska, in case Paige ever needed it again, so I guess she does now. The plutonium-238 batteries, which power the thermal generators, have a half-life of 87.7 years, so it is fully charged, and the advanced lithium-ion polymer batteries can charge in the craft, the universal power converter can draw power from any source, or the sun." He watched as she opened it like a tin can and began putting it on.

"You sure Wendy doesn't know about this place?"

"Humph. You are too optimistic." She sputtered. "The primitive blonde *Neanderthal* that somehow became our President is of limited intellect, possessing a small, dinosaur-like, walnut-sized brain housed inside that gigantic two-inch-thick skull. The head grows larger every day while the brain shrinks from disuse."

He shoved her, almost knocking her down. "You know, I've only been around you for a few hours, but I'm already sick of your big mouth, so I can see where Paige is coming from."

She stared up at him. "Yeah? Whatcha gonna do about it, tough guy?"

"You might see in a moment. It sounds like sour grapes to me. Have a little respect for the woman, as she's done much for a lot of people."

She patted him on the arm. "I admire your loyalty, defending your sister. I cannot fault you for that, my friend, although ye surely be misguided. But it may be your undoing."

"Her being my biological half-sister has nothing to do with it. What she has, she's earned. Give her a little bit of credit."

She laughed. "Yes, 'little' is correct. But that's a fool's errand, as she doesn't know of such things which are beneath her existence."

He shook his head and laughed. "I really think you're full of crap, Petra. If it's still here, intact, it's only because she wanted it that way."

"Untrue, the greatest pure intellect in history knows better." She tapped her left index finger on her head. "But, think what you will. We have little time to debate such matters."

"Okay, I don't get it, but why do you dislike her so much? I thought you were best friends back in the day."

"The key word there is 'were.' Many things change. Yes, of course she likely knows of this place, she is not the bucolic buffoon I once thought. She has an intelligence quotient second only to my own in this family, except for maybe you. But I shall not go into the infinite reasons why I have disdain for her, and we have more important things to do." She took the remarkably flexible dark blue metallic suit from the table and put on the chest plate.

"You're going to wear it now? Why?"

"Because it is easier than carrying it, dummy. I am only slightly taller than Paige, and I am the original, after all. We may also need it for what we find."

He watched the small-breasted woman close the chest plate and put on the lower section. "At least Aurora won't need to, er, compress much to get inside this one."

"Yes. It is not an issue for me, as you have declared."

They closed up the old abandoned workshop and headed back

to the M2 fusion hovercraft, to perhaps meet their end.

• • •

"Where are we going now, Petra?"

"What? You are annoying me. Cairo, if you must know."

"Egypt? I've never been there. Sounds exciting, but do we really have time for that right now?"

She sighed. "No, imbecile—Cairo, West Virginia: the location of the old Argotech complex. About 390 miles from here."

"Oh. Paige is in there, we think. I don't know how they're holding her. Or—if she's still alive."

Petra shook her head. "If this *Mantissa* is a clone of me, it would likely be able to break down her defensive field. And it's unlikely they have found out enough about her to consider killing her, if that's even possible."

"There has to be power coming from somewhere; if we disrupt it she may be able to break out. But this looks pretty fortified."

"Luckily, we have brought plenty of items to aid us in gaining access and blowing this thing to Kingdom Come, if my daughter does not do it before us."

"There must be surveillance cameras and other security measures to keep intruders out. Why did you remove the helmet?"

She nodded. "Yes, of course. The high density of the fullerene compound coupled with other shielding does not work with my limited psionic abilities."

"'Lesser humans?' A bit arrogant, don't you think?"

"Present company possibly excepted, of course."

"Yeah, right. You killed my predecessor, I heard."

She nodded. "I did, although I had help from your father, the brilliant antihero Rad Darkkin. Rad found some type of genetic poison that was designed to kill Travis, should he ever rage out of control. He did. Without that, Travis would probably have killed me."

"So, maybe you and I going toe-to-toe might not work out so well for you."

"Yeah, so? I am older yet wiser. I have nowhere near the brain powers I had then, as Father Time is undefeated, so the outcome would not at all be certain. I do not wish to find out, though."

Juriann shrugged. "This Ramon Argon, who the hell was he?"

"He apparently is the nephew of Malachi Argon," Bonnie replied. "The world's most famous biogeneticist. Argon was the adopted father of the President's half-brother, an evil creation much like you."

"I am not evil. You created me. What happened to them?"

"I killed both of them." She stared up at him. "You ever screw around with me, Hultaar, I'll do the same to you."

"I'm my own man, don't threaten me, and you don't scare me." He stared at her. "But what was he doing? These schematics?"

"According to the files Isabel gave me from his brief tenure at M2 Research & Development, this Ramon Argon was experimenting with anti-gravity devices."

"Anti-gravity?"

"Yes, it was the *Deltaman* project, but deltonics is impractical given the power necessary to weaken gravity."

"But power is abundant now thanks to hydrogen fusion."

She shook her head. "It's still not nearly enough. Aurora's vast powers are dark energy-based. I don't know where the power comes from, as existing evidence does not support that dark energy exists near us to any great extent. According to the fragmented information from my contact with the Thonxxeronians, she channels power from a dark star."

"Dark stars."

"Maybe; dark matter is not necessarily the same as a dark star, but that's the reason for the name, *Stella Scura*. It was, nonetheless, a catchy moniker."

"Why Italian?"

"My favorite language. *Stella Scura* is also alliterative, which I knew would be appealing to her."

"If Italian is your favorite language, why did you decide to become a Russian, may I ask?"

She looked up at him. "Idiot, it seemed the most logical way to have taught Russian to Paige so that she would be able to understand the Vladimirov armor's readouts. Otherwise, she might have questioned why I was fluent in it."

"Yeah, or questioned why you had an advanced cyber-suit of exotic battle armor in the first place, just saying. Not something most teachers in rural Alaska have."

She nodded. "That too. Despite her unfortunate lack of interest in science or math, she actually is quite intelligent and is capable of analyzing many abstract concepts that I cannot. Her lack of natural vision made it much simpler to hide such things. It does seem to make for a good disguise."

• • •

Thirty minutes later, they landed about three miles from the complex, under a small hill, and exited the vehicle after covering it up with some brush. Luckily, the craft was 'stealth' with significant shielding from radar and other means of detection.

"I guess I understand why we're 'parking' a ways away, but why under this hill, Petra?"

"Who knows what's going to happen in there? We want the vehicle protected from damage."

"Assuming we are not damaged. Unlikely."

They walked a mile and a half until Petra told him of a power surge right under them.

"You're sure of this, Petra? I don't see anything."

"This helmet enhances my senses to an amazing degree, there is a steel access door right below us, trust me. Shovel off the dirt."

"Whatever. Okay, here goes." He cleared off a foot of dirt and discovered the large steel access door. "You're right. Won't some alarms or something go off if I breach this?"

"My electronics will disable the outer alarms, but in a few minutes, it won't matter. This is the main power grid."

Juriann pulled on the handles with all his might as they heard the sound of metal fatigue as the door burst open.

"What's this?" he asked as they went down into the bunker.

"Over there." She pointed to a massive electrical box. "My sensors indicate this is the main power grid. Pull out the power cables, that will disrupt the power leading to the surveillance cameras."

With a mighty heave, the world's strongest man pulled the electrical box from the concrete wall, as the room went dark.

"That's great. Now we can't see."

"Maybe *you* can't, but I sure as heck can. This helmet augments my already heightened natural senses to a degree you cannot imagine. There is a high density of titanium and other dense metals eight hundred twenty-eight meters due west; that must be where she is."

"What are we going to do now? They surely have auxiliary

power."

"I have no idea. If my hunch is correct, we have bought Paige enough time to break free, after which she will need our help again if *Mantissa* is present, and a grand melee shall ensue."

"Can this *Mantissa* hurt you?"

"I don't know what to expect. Probably, yes. My guess is, once we free Paige, the three of us will be more than a match for it. It will be a mental and physical confrontation."

"Again, I don't know if we have much of a choice. And it's possible *Mantissa* isn't here with them right now anyway."

"This is possible. I should be able to sense an intelligence like mine, and I cannot. I just hope we will survive what happens when she wakes up."

"What does that mean?"

"The influx of massive amounts of dark energy may not be pleasant and may create a nuclear-level event."

"No, you're kidding."

She shook her head. "I never kid about things like destruction."

• • •

The feeling was bizarre, yet not unpleasant. Where was she? She floated through what she imagined was space, without a body. How was this possible? Emptiness of space, and the faint glimmer of stars. Things she had never imagined seeing before.

She then heard a deep voice, which was impossible, because she seemed to have no corporeal substance, and she knew even with her limited scientific abilities that sound couldn't travel in space. Was this what death felt like? Where was this coming from? It was not at all like her mother's voice.

She then saw it: a silvery face appeared in her visual field, shimmering against the starlit background. What the hell was this?

"The one known as the Dark Star: come to me. It is only through this near-death experience that we can communicate. Someone of immense strength has sufficiently disrupted the forces that hold you dormant so that you can achieve a basal level of consciousness. Soon, this opportunity will pass, and we likely shall never communicate again."

It wasn't true vision like with the Russian helmet or sapphire visor, but instead was like something was projected into her brain.

"Where am I? Who are you?"

"I am of a race of beings composed entirely of dark matter and whose essence is made of dark energy. My name would be unintelligible to you lower beings, but you can refer to me as Gart-Monn."

"Gart-Monn. I am sorry, but that name means nothing to me. Are you God? Is this Heaven? Or the other place?"

"I am not the Almighty whom you believe in, unfortunately."

"Wait a minute. I never said I believed in Him; I just asked you if you were Him. It is not the same query at all."

"That statement seems contradictory. However, unlike you, I am not composed of conventional matter, but a kind called 'dark matter,' which you or your primitive human instrumentation cannot even detect except in a most rudimentary manner. Therefore, being made of pure energy, I am virtually immortal. But even I will perish someday, eons from now."

"Thanks for the pejorative comments to one composed of plain old blue-collar 'matter.' So, is there a God, if you are not Him?"

"Alas, this I do not know, even I am not all-knowing."

"Well, who the hell am I, then? Am I immortal?"

"You are a metahuman born of a human father and a mother who received, through a unique chain of events, the genetic material from one of the only other beings like you to ever exist. Know that most of your abilities come from this genetic material initially discovered on the giant moon of Saturn and later recovered from Earth by the genetic scientist Rita McPherson."

"You said 'most.' Who are the others, and who did they come from?"

"The ability to control them comes from the great natural gifts your mother's genetics passed on to you. The others like you have long since passed. Tens of millions of years ago, as you measure time."

"I am afraid I do not understand."

"There is no other human who could control your abilities, for you have absolute control over the muscles of your body with extreme precision. That is the gift from your mother that allows you to control it. But your energy is also tied to the flesh and blood of your body. While your lifespan may exceed a normal human's, you are indeed capable of passing on to death. This, you are near."

"I do not understand. If the genetic material of this 'other being' is within my mother, why does she not she have my powers?"

"The bonding of the dark energy field to a human appears to require the genetic recombination process you call meiosis, so a new being must be born. That unique being is you. She does have moderately augmented strength and durability, as well as exceptional sensory perception, but nowhere near the incredible power you possess. Yet, she has unique abilities that may prove useful to you one day."

"What abilities are those?"

"I cannot discuss them here, as they are only theoretical."

"Huh. Many have prophesized that, in 2029—the coming year of our calendar—the Christ child shall come again. I have wondered many times if I am that child, as others also surely have in the last two months. A city was built in my honor by my cousin years ago."

"We who have seen the entire passage of your civilization know that the child Jesus of Nazareth possessed amazing abilities, as he was known to us, but rest assured that he was certainly *not* one of us. We know not of your God. But he seemingly had the power to heal, to restore life, to do things that are far beyond even our powers. While you possess great abilities of energy manipulation, they cannot transcend the physical or restore mortal life. The coming year being 2029, as you measure time, seems merely a coincidence, the prophecies merely ravings of those who worship what their small minds are incapable of understanding."

"How did all this happen? My mother says she does not know."

"She knows some of it, but not all, so she speaks the truth. You must surely know she is incapable of lying."

"I believe that, for the most part." Except hiding from her about really being Bonnie Mendoza.

"Genetic experimentation by the egotistical scientist named Dr. Malachi Argon resulted in many woes to your race. The remnants of the being once known as Tharr-Kann Axoon, destroyed by us, ended up on your Earth. We learned that he had placed those seeds there with the intent of somehow replicating his 'race' and restoring his corporeal body after we destroyed him."

"Who was this being who gave me my powers?"

"Tharr was once like us, a being of pure energy, when he discovered the humans of your time period."

"Did he send that genetic material with the intent of creating me, a hero for mankind?"

"No, Aurora Darkkin, such is an overly idealistic view, as he patterned himself after humans. He shared the flaw that is present in many of your beings—greed and evil. He did that for only one reason, as I said—to recreate his body millions of years later, to become king of this planet. You are a unique byproduct that could not have been foreseen. He would destroy you and the entire Earth's population in an instant if he were here and would have no remorse over doing it."

"I bet not. Is he going to come back in some fashion?"

"Nothing is impossible, but it would seem unlikely, as the scant amount of original DNA has been destroyed."

"I guess it is fortunate I am here, then."

"That remains to be seen. Tharr wanted to experience their emotions and created synthetic beings like the humans, using dark matter manipulation to create a planet known as Thonxxeron, in the distant past."

"In the past? You are saying this individual could time-travel?"

"Yes, as can we. The ability to manipulate gravity brings with it unique properties of time dilation."

"Should anyone? The danger that could present is enormous."

"Perhaps, but the dilution of the deoxyribonucleic acid content by contributions from your mother and father do not allow you all of our abilities."

"Maybe that is a good thing. So he was not a great hero of this planet Thonxxeron, it seems?"

"No, Aurora Darkkin. Why would we have destroyed him if that had been the case?"

"I do not know your agenda, sorry, Charlie."

"He was evil personified, a heinous one who destroyed most of those beings as he saw fit. We finally put an end to it by condemning him to near-complete destruction."

"Huh. 'Near-complete destruction' does not sound very final."

"He is one of us, in essence. It was not possible to completely obliterate him from existence."

"Great—sounds reassuring. But you say 'most of them'—again, does this mean there are some still alive on Thonxxeron? Beings like me?"

"Some Thonxxeronians with abilities like yours survived, but that was millions of years in the past, as I described; they do not exist today. Tharr did reproduce on that planet, and his offspring, while limited in power, were collectively able to resist his destruction. But they are all gone now and have been so for thousands of millennia, as you measure time."

"How far away is this fancy place, ace?"

"Hundreds of light-years away, in this galaxy, actually. But Tharr dispatched a vessel carrying his DNA to your planet seventy million Earth years ago. A meteor we sent destroyed the dinosaurs on Earth and sent the DNA of Tharr-Kann to space."

"You killed the dinosaurs? Get out of town."

"I do not understand your statement. I am not in any town."

"Never mind. But you have these great powers, yet you sent a mere meteor to destroy his DNA? Why did you not just obliterate it with your big-ass mind or something?"

"It is not that simple, as we must do things according to our plan. We are not omnipotent."

"Yikes, who designed your plan, man? Rube Goldberg?"

"I am sorry, I am unfamiliar with that individual."

"Aww, forget it."

"That is enough of this inane idiomatic banter, simple being. Regardless, the force of the meteor was such that some of the matter expelled from Earth landed on the large moon of your solar system's sixth planet—you call it Titan. The evil human known as Malachi Argon discovered material which contained an evolved microorganism, and also Tharr-Kann's genetic material—two distinct entities—although he didn't know what the second one was. We directed the scientist known as Rita McPherson to return to Mexico, where scant amounts of the original material remained; she, with direction from me, refined it into a serum that was placed into your mother's body. We had chosen the vessel most suitable, one whose mind we had encountered years earlier."

"You actually spoke to my mother? So her rantings about talking to aliens were real?"

"Yes. She is the one human we have encountered who could master our language, who had the ability to project her consciousness as I am doing now, albeit in very limited fashion."

"So, this was how she developed her amazing theories—she obtained them from you."

Gart-Monn paused. "No, this is untrue, Aurora. We have no use for primitive nuclear fusion, as our energy is self-sustaining and far more advanced than that, which functions with a fraction of the efficiency of the conversion of dark matter to pure energy. What she developed, she did on her own. Your mother has an amazing creative intellect. Know that much of your uniqueness comes from her."

"That does not entirely answer my question. What kind of being am I? The term 'metahuman' does not mean a lot to me, as I am neither scientist nor philosopher."

"You carry with you a part of Tharr-Kann's powers—that of the most abundant force in the universe, dark energy. While your ability to manipulate the dark energy is a fraction of ours, it is easily sufficient for you to easily rule over the humans, should that be your goal. They need guidance, as you must surely realize by now."

"But, where does my power come from? That is one of many things that puzzles me."

"It comes from the dark matter and energy that is around us, but much of your vast power comes from the dark star Thargis in the Delta Quadrant. Dark stars utilize matter-antimatter reactions to convert one hundred percent dark matter to pure energy."

"Yeah. Dark energy, that is what my mom speaks of." She finally realized that she had no corporeal form, yet was communicating with Gart-Monn. "And I do not desire to *rule* over anyone; I want to *lead* them because they want me to be their leader. I desire to be elected President when I am old enough."

"That is indeed a difficult path, Aurora. There are many other paths awaiting you in your quest that may be more fruitful."

"It is mine to take. I am not interested in what was planned or what others want for me."

"Understood. But, if successful, then you can be the benefactor of your race. We did hope this—to remedy the wrong that was Tharr-Kann. The one we could have stopped but did not until it was too late. We, therefore, vowed never to interfere again. It would have been within our power to restore your sight to how it was before the explosion. Would that be something you desire?"

"To have my sight restored?" She thought for a minute. "This may sound strange to you, but . . . no, I do not. While it is a handicap, having this disability has made me who I am and keeps me close to humanity. I understand rejection and humility and would have been a totally different person without this problem. I have enough abilities, I do not want or need more. In a way, I feel more comfortable in that state."

"That is what I thought you would say."

"Yes, but while I may not have the status of an energy being, I am also not stupid. Is interfering not what you are doing now?"

"Perhaps, but in this state, you can freely communicate with us, and we are not acting, just giving information to you. Courageous beings, including your mother, are attempting to assist you as we speak."

"About her: my mother is a noble and good person who has suffered much in her life. *She* should have the powers, not me. Think of what she could do with her intelligence."

"No, Aurora, your mother's destiny is something different and has served another purpose on your world, although she still has much yet to accomplish. While of great intellect, perhaps in certain areas the finest we have touched, and brave, she lacks many of the fundamental qualities that will make you a great hero. In other ways, she lacks the judgment of even a small child and is therefore ill-suited for that destiny. But she has a power some would call even greater than yours, one that many shall covet."

"What?"

"The power, in an enhanced state, to alter perception and to manipulate minds; the ability to overcome even you. Know that she has killed with this power before, she has a dark side as well of which you are unaware."

"My mother, kill? Yes, I had learned this unfortunate fact from my aunt, as well as recorded video of an event that occurred a year before I was born."

"Realize that she surely *is* capable of such deeds. She has killed with her bare hands as well; rest assured that capability exists within you also."

"The gifts I have I was born with. What right have I earned to possess them? Compared to many, I am nothing."

"You underestimate your intelligence, and you surely must understand what your mother or most other beings cannot. One who does is your President, who has surely told you this: it is not your physical gifts that may make you the great leader of your land, but your ability to lead others, with the compassion and humility that have made you who you are. You don't need your dark energy powers to accomplish this."

"Gart-Monn, I am very confused. If I have the powers but do

not need them to be great, what is the purpose of having them at all, then? To be an entertainer who does party tricks? Is this all I am destined to become?"

"Why? You know this, as you have answered your own question numerous times: because you have a choice on a level that no one else can possibly comprehend. Most of your people would use such abilities to gain immense wealth or power, so therein lies your uniqueness. Do not underestimate that many will try to manipulate you to learn this secret and use your powers for personal gain. It is the human way."

"You said 'may be the great leader of your land.' As if there is some doubt about that."

"Fate is not always predestined, as you may not even survive beyond this encounter. It is the fact that you possess almost limitless power, but may choose freely not to use it in your governance, that will possibly make you the foremost leader of your people. The only way to accomplish this is to be elected like any other official."

"Yeah, I get that, as I ain't no dummy. But can I assume this astral form again at will? Why have I not been able to before?"

"No. It is only that you are near death that you can do this, because you lack your mother's powers of limited astral projection. Once your mortal body dies the dark energy that binds you to it will cease to exist, like Tharr-Kann."

"I wish I could go back through time, to prevent some of the greatest disasters in history. The assassinations of Lincoln, John and Robert Kennedy, Graham, and Martin Luther King? I could go back, kill Hitler, and prevent the Holocaust. I could stop Pearl Harbor and the planes that crashed into the World Trade Center on 9/11. Finally, I could have stopped *Darkkday*."

"No, you are not capable of those things. And altering history is not that simple, as there are repercussions for all actions. Killing Hitler and stopping the Pearl Harbor attack might have prevented United States entry into World War II and saved many lives, but then your country would not have developed the technology necessary to harness the power of the atom."

"Huh. Given who my grandpa was, maybe that would have been way better for everyone."

"No, things are not so simple. And if John Fitzgerald Kennedy had not been assassinated, your world might not have developed the technology to reach your satellite."

"I still say we would be better off."

"Unlikely, as another country could then have developed those technologies and used them for evil ends. Finally, you would not have evolved into the being you are now were it not for the event you call *Darkkday*."

"That might be a good thing. I ask you again a more morbid, yet practical question, given my recent, rather reckless lifestyle: shall I ever die, guy?"

"There is a dark energy field which has its own life, as you would call it, although it is nothing like your biological form. It protects your living cells from harm and is a sentient being in its own right; it will filter your air of toxins, your food of poisons, your air from deadly radiation. It was this, the greatest of your native abilities, that shielded you and your mother from destruction twelve of your years ago and absorbed most of the radiation that would have killed millions. While you know of these powers, you undoubtedly cannot explain them. The energy was dissipated into the dark energy field from which you draw energy.

"But your physical body, while more robust than normal, is certainly capable of being annihilated by even the most primitive of conventional weapons. Your protective aura prevents this, but you can dissipate this field if you wish, albeit with great effort; it is this power of your mother to manipulate thoughts that accounts for your only weakness. This was exploited by those who created an evil clone of your mother, called *Mantissa,* to do this, which has left you in this state. It also does not function if you are rendered unconscious, although it works during normal sleep. Surely you must know this after eighteen of your Earth years.

"A warning, however: there exist weapons on your planet, created by your own kin, which may test even your immense resources. Soon you may indeed encounter these. But, although I have been forbidden to do so, events will soon happen that can restore your consciousness so that you feel pain. But I give you a warning that the sensation will be most unpleasant."

"Yeah, well, I would rather do that than die."

"Then it shall be so. Never shall I interfere again."

"That will be the day; you have promised that several times, you said. But, is there a heaven? With my father, my cousins, and others killed in *Darkkday* up there?"

"Alas, female known as Aurora Darkkin, while I know much, that even I cannot ascertain. This is something you must have faith in because there is a higher power than mine. Go forth with this gift, but remember that, with the dark energy powers you possess, great things can be accomplished. While you are not the Savior whom your society's religious books claim is coming, you can nevertheless do much for your people, decades from now."

"*Decades from now*? That is too long for me to wait."

"You have the impatience of adolescence and must instead look towards the distant picture where greater rewards await, rather than the temptation of immediate gratification. This is what was hoped."

While she was initially in awe of this guy—or whatever the hell he was—his rambling was becoming as irritating as her mom's. She was tired of this crap, even from an omnipotent being of pure energy that might even be a hallucination.

"Good to know you had a plan for me. So, what happens now, Gart? Let us get on with this, as I do not like being manipulated by anyone, not even you. I appreciate the info but I need to get on with my life, or death, or whatever the hell it is."

"*What?* You dare to speak to me in this way, impatient child, to one who was old before your planet even existed?"

"What a stupid question. Hell, yes, I dare. What does you being Gart the old fart have to do with it? You think you are better than me because you are ancient and made of dark energy?"

"Silence. You *dare* compare me to flatus, a mere waste gas expelled from the anus? Is that truly your meaning?"

"Sorry. It is just a saying, I tend to speak in alliteration and rhymes, they say, but take it any way you like. You said I was almost dead, so what do I have to lose now? I will go out of this world the way I came in—kicking and screaming. I answer to no one except maybe God Almighty, if he's really there. By your admission, you ain't him. Sucking up to people, even omnipotent beings of pure energy, is not in my nature. So *shut the hell up* and let whatever is going to happen to me happen, just spare me the soporific soliloquy."

Silence for what seemed like an eternity.

"Well, Gart-Monn? That all you got, big shot?"

"I am impressed, yet this strong attitude was not unanticipated. You are one of great will and strength which belies your years."

"Fantastic. Not to hurt your feelings, since you probably do not have any, but I do not really care what you think, in case you have not determined that already."

"I know, this is obvious. Not many would have the fortitude to say that to one many times as powerful."

"I bet my aunt would; in the brief time I have known her, she has taught me much about that. She has her problems, but she is definitely not the narcissistic megalomaniac my mother claims she is."

"Agreed. Therefore, I am confident that you shall not succumb to the multiple petty grievances you will encounter in your life. And I do have feelings for other lower beings, despite what you may think."

"Awww. So refreshing to this 'lower being' to know all that."

"But, a warning, young Aurora Darkkin: know now that, while you believe yourself to be a force of benevolence, the potential for great violence and destruction also courses through your veins."

"Yeah, yeah, whatever. Heard it before. I believe it, too. I might have taken out Brant Gallagher if it were not for Aunt Wendy."

"Yet, this fundamental fact cannot be altered. Momentarily you will unleash unprecedented fundamental physical forces that even you cannot comprehend. In this, we are unable to interfere, as such force is the very power that composes us. Your world, beware of the Dark Star."

"Yes, you told me about my mom—and I was told this by my aunt, that we both share the blood of one who at times was less than moral. Heard it before, how Gramps Darkkin drank, chased after women, made nuclear warheads, experimented with LSD and other mood-elevating substances—"

"No, this is not a mortal being your President would be aware of, not one with petty human foibles. I speak not of her father—your grandfather—he who passed many years ago. While a horribly flawed man, he represented greatness in his own strange way, despite his obsession for creating nuclear weapons which may yet reduce you and your society to dust."

"Huh? Who, then?"

"Have you learned nothing from our discussion? I speak of the great evil of Tharr-Kann Axoon, he who destroyed a whole civilization, as I mentioned before. The one whose genetics you carry within you. It is something you need to be the hero you strive to be."

"Why would I desire a part of darkness within me? What good can possibly come from it?"

"Because Tharr is a part of you, just like your mother, father, grandfather, and all others in your ancestry, and you can't alter that fact. Without that essence, you would not be complete and have the desire to strive, to be better than you are. As the heroic being you strive to be, you would be ineffective."

"But I believe myself to be more a product of my upbringing rather than my genetics, as magnificent as they may be."

"This is true, that under different circumstances, you might have turned out badly. Your uncle Juriann Hultaar is a clone of one who was very evil and met his death at the hand of your mother and grandfather. However, he also possesses some DNA of your cousin Dione Cassandra, who died in the event you call *Darkkday*.

"But Hultaar has the essence of a heroic being, and you share that common bond. He learned that from his adoptive parents, whom your mother sought out when he was but an infant. But know that every heroic individual needs the darkness sometimes. Although you do not realize it, soon you will have to confront this. and learn that you are very capable of violent acts you cannot even yet imagine."

"Despite my big mouth, I cannot ever be violent. I almost went down that path recently when I wanted to kill Brant Gallagher, but that was a terrible mistake. I cannot lead the people through example by acting in that manner any longer."

"Alas, if you cannot, then you will surely perish. It is impossible to defeat the evil that is in your new adversary unless you confront this and release power you never thought possible. There may be much evil you will need to confront later, as well."

"You said I might be reduced to dust by Grandpa Rad's weapons, yes?"

"That is correct. The deranged being known as *Santaman* will be sending what you call hellfire down onto your greatest city. It is he you must also confront soon, near here."

"The being who did this to me is a clone of my mother."

"Yes, another mistake of genetic manipulation created to exploit her cerebral abilities: *Mantissa*."

"Will I ever be able to remember what happened before the *Darkkday* blast?"

"You can remember whatever you choose, Aurora Darkkin. You only have to desire it hard enough, as it has always been within your power to do so."

"It was not some mind trick of my mother's? She told me no, but I am not sure I believe her."

"No. You surely must know by now that your mother is incapable of lying outright; it is one of her most endearing qualities. Such a feat is also not within the scope of her abilities. But remembering may not be pleasant."

"Not telling me who I was for most of my life? That is not lying? Do you have another definition?"

"She did what she felt she had to do, although I am sure it caused her much distress."

I will try to look back, although it will be difficult. And perhaps not what I want at all. But I will never know unless I try.

I am going back to the beginning, somehow. I am now six years old.

The next moment, she was sitting on her mother's lap, their arms intertwined. She looked at the handsome man next to her. Her father? A few other people vaguely familiar from old photos, others not. The colors, so brilliant.

Is this how normal people see? How wonderful.

I wish I could stay back in this time for a while.

A slight turbulence, so she was in a jet.

She then saw the blast, an incredibly bright light, as everything around them vaporized. It didn't hurt a bit. Sight, then nothing.

But Mom and I are moving and falling . . . very fast.

I will never see as a normal person again.

Yet, today I am reborn into something greater—this event will make me who I am.

I am as I once was, and so much more.

There is no going back now. Much is to be done to correct things.

Where were they? She remembered falling for what seemed like an eternity, her mother holding her the entire time. They were both naked, and she reached up to feel her hair, which was gone, as was their clothing. After several minutes they hit the ground, but were unharmed. They rolled down a mountain for what seemed like miles. They were over the ocean, but now on mountains. How many hundred miles had they traveled, and how?

She then heard her mother's distinctive voice, telling her that life would be hard for a very long time but not to worry because they still had each other; and to the rest of the world, they must remain dead.

She was able to see, at some point in her existence. But not after. The familiar feeling of sightlessness had now returned to her.

I feel the pain, like my flesh burning off. Where am I?

The peacefulness of my unconsciousness has disappeared.

Tired, so tired, yet I seem to be feeling stronger each second. What is happening to me?

Pain going away, but I cannot move my arms or legs; no, something is holding them.

Huh. Not for long.

I cannot describe the feeling of the energy returning to me.

It is both exhilarating and unnerving.

Now I know how Russell felt that night we did it.

I am going to find you fucking sons of bitches.

And, then, may God have mercy on your souls.

For now I know I am not divine.

Gart-Monn was right. I am not called the Dark Star for nothing.

It was a cold October day after school. The eight-year-old girl came in, sobbing, and jumped into her father's lap as he waited at the school exit on the bench, getting ready to take her home.

"What's wrong, honey?" Jack asked.

"The kids, they make fun of me, Daddy, because I cannot see and I talk funny. I cannot help those things."

She felt his hand brush her hair. "I know, Paige. I wish I could make it better, but I can't."

"Well, heck, cannot God do it?"

"God can do anything, honey."

"Then why does he not fix me easily? Your boss I do not understand; therefore he must not be all that grand."

"I don't either, Paige, but we don't know how He decides to do things. We must only trust that His plan for us is the best."

"Huh. I am not sure I believe in God, then, if he does not want to help. He is not a true friend, or me he would want to mend."

"Don't say that, Paige, you must always have faith in Him."

"I thought you were a minister. Why not just talk to God, then? You talk all the time about how 'all-powerful' He is. Prove it!"

"It doesn't work that way, dear. I wish it was that simple. That's what having faith is all about."

"I do not mind not seeing like you and Mom can, but why do they ridicule me? They must, therefore, be evil. Mom tells me of the many evil beings out there."

"Of course you mind seeing, Paige; you wouldn't be human if you didn't want to be like everybody else. And Mom exaggerates. Most people are good at heart, but they're just being obnoxious, thoughtless kids. They don't really mean you any harm."

She cried and nodded. "I guess at times I do mind, but I cannot do anything about it, so I make the best of what I have. Is that not what you taught me to do?"

"Yes. No one has everything, and you have more than most. But, no, the other kids aren't evil, honey; they just don't understand. People tend to strike out against those who are different. Children can be especially mean. Some grow up, but a very few continue that behavior into adulthood."

"Do they know I am different, Daddy? Other than not seeing, I mean? I fell off the top of the jungle gym today, and it did not hurt a bit. It never does. Why is that?"

"Paige, what in the world were you doing up there? I told you never to do things like that."

"I want to play games like them, but I cannot see, so I missed the bar when I jumped. The teacher was upset because she thought I was hurt, but I was fine; she did not see me climb up there. I wish sometimes I would get cuts or bruises like the other kids get when they play, but I never do. I am sorry. I cannot help that either."

"You have to be careful. I know you're only eight, but you need to keep the things you can do a secret."

"Why? Why can I not just show them what I can do? I am way stronger than any grownup now. That would fix them and all their mayhem."

"Really? You mean strike out at them as they do you? Be a bully like them? Would that make it all better?"

"It might, at that. Makes sense. Does the Bible not say, '*an eye for an eye, and a tooth for a tooth?'"*

"That's the book of Matthew, and you conveniently omitted the remainder of the verse, which you would know if you didn't selectively interpret the Bible. *'But I say unto you, that ye resist not evil: but whosoever shall smite thee on thy right cheek, turn to him the other.'"*

"Dumb, stupid Bible. Those ancient guys did not have to deal with what I do at school, where everyone is a fool and a tool."

"I think not, Paige. But no one controls you, and the choice is, and will always be, yours. Someday you will need to decide for yourself, as we won't always be around."

She smiled. "That means I can do it if I want?"

"Like I said, you decide yourself if that's a good idea because I don't think we could stop you. But choose carefully. Some actions can never be undone."

The small blind girl shook her head after thinking pensively for a few minutes.

"Well? What have you decided, Paige?"

"No, I suppose not—that would not be fair. Retaliating would make me no better than them. I have to be better than them, to be an example."

"Good for you, Paige. I'm proud of you." He gave her a hug and a kiss on the cheek.

"But what can I do, then, Daddy? How can I get respect if I do not stand up to them?"

"There are other ways. You can beat them at something that doesn't require special abilities but can still be persuasive. Something that will serve you and mankind the rest of your life."

She wiped the tears from her eyes. "What would that possibly be?"

"Another of your gifts. Something I do often because I'm a minister, but I'm not naturally gifted at like you. Words."

"Words? How so?"

"You have an astounding vocabulary for a child, and it will only get better as you mature. Learn to beat them by arguing and proving your point, not by pummeling them with your fists. You can have the power to persuade people with your voice, not your strength, and someday lead this nation by that alone. In time they will admire you."

She shook her head. "They will too admire me for my strength. I will be famous and live in a big mansion, with lots of toys and new clothes and cookies and other such fancy things, and I shall never invite them to parties, the big smarties."

"So, you'll be alone at those parties?"

"Yes! All for me."

"How are you going to pay for all these things?"

"Why, I could just make myself rich."

"How would you become rich? By stealing money?"

"Yes, I could! All there is."

"Would that be a good thing to do?"

"I believe not, as that would be wrong. But I could be a famous athlete or something and make money that way, what about that?"

"Do you think that would be fair?"

She chewed on her lip. "No—of course not. But I can do it with my mouth, is that what you are saying?"

"Yes. You can use your mouth to your heart's content, Paige. Figuratively, that is. You can't bite anyone."

"I shall be the biggest mouth the world ever had!"

"Atta girl. Just play fair, now. That's the riddle you have yet to understand. If they admire you because of your powers and because you live in a mansion, it will only be because they think you can do something for them, or because they are scared of you, and neither quality is desirable, as they are not about *you* as a *person*."

"Well, I do not care."

"No, you can be an inspiration to others in other ways, and then they will admire you because of the other things that you are. I know you don't understand, but you will, in time."

The memories—so many. Where have you been? Is this real, or just a dream?

No time for them now, though. There are other tasks at hand.

I grow stronger every moment. What is happening to me?

I feel my heart rate accelerating.

"Again, Paige. You disappoint me with your pathetic laziness."

The twelve-year-old girl was fatigued—not physically, but emotionally. "I have held myself on one hand for over an hour; surely that is enough to satisfy even you."

"Surely it is not. You'll do it again until I tell you when enough is. You know little about dedication, goldbrick."

"You bore me to death every time I take a breath."

"Slowly. Think it through. Pull just hard enough. The chain is the weak link."

She pulled on the heavy metal chain encircling her wrists, trying to slowly break it at the chain. She frowned as they pulled apart, sending metal shrapnel likely hundreds of feet through the air, her mother apparently safely behind a large rock. "Like that?"

"No, not like that. Are you insane?"

"I am not, but you are. Who cares how I break them? What is the point of all this? This is surely not bliss."

She felt Mom grab her. "Listen, Paige. This is about you and your lazy ass controlling your strength with uncanny accuracy, not your 'bliss.' You now have a degree of strength fifty times that of a normal human, yet you must live in our world. It may increase even more; we do not know how much. There will be times when controlling that strength with utmost precision may save a life, like a surgeon who saves lives with his magic touch. Do you want to crush someone's hand when you shake it? Just one slip-up could be devastating."

"No. I will try harder. But everyone makes mistakes, so you do not have to be so mean."

"Maybe you think me mean, but I have no choice. You can take it." She felt her mom shove her. "Trying is not enough. Unlike me or others, you cannot afford to make mistakes, *ever*. Lord knows I have made many that cannot be rectified. You could easily kill someone without trying. One thing you cannot do is raise the dead."

• • •

That was enough reminiscing about her childhood. She was smart enough to figure out what had happened after that, and there was no time to live in the past—not now, not ever. All this had really pissed her off, and someone was going to pay dearly.

She was grown up now. And she was done taking advice from some stinking non-corporeal being, even though he was fairly bright and might be a relative of some sort.

She was getting tired of all the new relatives.

Gart-Monn said that there was much evil within her, and it was a necessary component for all leaders. Some of that was finally bubbling to the surface.

The main lights went off in the complex.

"Ray. Alpha wave brain activity starting. There's a huge power loss, don't know why. *Shit*."

"What happened? No alarms went off."

"I don't know; it's like something just destroyed the power input somehow. How that happened, I have no idea. We should have been fortified enough to survive any natural catastrophe."

"Get it back up, Tolliver. I thought you had the anesthesia on the highest setting."

"That's just it, Ray. We're assuming normal human physiology, but she isn't completely human. And something's disrupting the power grid, as I said—I'm trying to compensate."

"Get the tissue now, then. Extract her bone marrow. I'll put it into the damn bio-matrix for genetic regeneration. It's a lot sooner than I had desired, but we'll work with it."

My eyes are now wide open, yet I cannot see.
Any other person would panic. Yet—
This means things are as they should be. Back to normal.
Good for me.
Not very good for whoever the hell did this.
The power is flowing back into me.
Like drinking water from a fire hose.
It is now mine to wield once more.
Not yours, for you are not deserving, lowly insect.
I am not in a forgiving mood. So—
You are deserving of something else.
Know now the wrath of the Dark Star, for she rises once more.
You are surely going to pay.

Tolliver stood up and threw his hands in the air. "The algorithms aren't anywhere near ready, Ray. It'll take months, maybe years, to even begin to figure out the DNA, even with our quantum computers. You saw how that aberration *Mantissa* turned out. This—this is going to kill us all, you dumb fucking bastard!"

"*Mantissa* is a great first step, and I'll disintegrate its sorry bones once this is done and work on a new one, as it is near the end of its life expectancy. I thought that ability was more than raw power. I think differently now, after having seen it."

"My God, it's a horribly disfigured entity, not deserving of life. You know it only assumes a normal 'appearance' by some type of mental manipulation."

"Shut up, Tolliver. Now, or we won't have a chance."

Tolliver looked at the instrumentation, which had come back to life. "The backup generators are back up, so whatever caused the transient power loss is irrelevant now." Tolliver activated the controls on the robotic arms as the carbon nanorod drill bits ground against her body.

Those bits were the hardest substance in existence, several times harder than diamond.

They could drill through anything.

Or so Tolliver had thought.

"Okay, then, let's get going. Once we have the stem cells, we won't need her anymore."

Tolliver began sweating as he read the screen, with a message he definitely didn't need right now:

MALFUNCTION
CRITICAL DEVICE FAILURE
ARMATURE OVERHEATING

"We—we can't do it, Ray. The drills won't penetrate her skin. The diamond nanorod bits are breaking under the force. and the goddamn motors have burned out."

"Harder, then, dammit! What do the scans show?"

He turned on the CT scanner as his face turned white. "Blank."

"Well, you know that can't be right. Get the power back up."

"Power isn't the problem any longer, as the scanners are working fine—it's because the X-rays can't penetrate her body now."

"What's wrong with the scanners? You're wrong; get the power back up as that must be the problem."

"Again, it *is* back up, Ray." The overweight Tolliver wiped the perspiration streaming from his forehead with a white cotton towel. "Oh, holy shit."

"What does that primitive utterance mean?"

Tolliver threw the towel at him. "Figure it out, genius. It means we're going to die unless she's a forgiving sort, but I sure as hell wouldn't be."

• • •

She was now half-awake, immersed in some type of goop, whatever that was for. Didn't care. Without the visor, she couldn't see anyway.

Big deal. She had been blind for almost all the life she remembered, and she could take care of herself. How? Simple: she would just smash and destroy stuff until something broke.

Low-tech, but effective.

She shattered the heavy chains with almost no effort and pulled the mask off her face as she demolished the containment pod into a thousand pieces and pulled assorted tubes out of her body. *Someone* was going to pay for this. As bad as she felt, it might take a few minutes, though.

That was okay. As long as it took was fine with her.

• • •

Tolliver watched the monitor as her eyes opened wide, and the three technicians monitoring the equipment turned around and stared at him with more fear in their eyes than he had ever seen.

"Holy crap, Ray, she's awake."

"You think? I can see that, Mike."

"Then we're fucking screwed. Look at what she did to the containment pod already."

Argon shook his head and, while visibly nervous, did manage a faint smile. "Don't overreact. I said she can't see anything, so how are we in imminent danger? Those walls are solid titanium alloy, two feet thick, so chill. They could hold King Kong. She isn't going anywhere."

Tolliver shook his head in panic. "I think not, Ray—you may be a world expert in biochemistry and molecular genetics, but you must not know jack shit about physics. A typical biologist with minimal respect for the fundamental forces of nature."

"I know enough to know I'm not afraid of her."

"Yeah? Based on my calculations, she can likely generate energy in the yottawatt range, maybe even higher."

"Not right now she can't."

"Likely a mere fraction of that, certainly."

"So? That's not so much, compared to a—"

"*Really?* That's equal to a small star, which is a hell of a lot more than a trillion King Kongs, you damn dumb ass. I would've *never* done this had I thought the power might fail." They watched as she broke out of the thick titanium cylinder as if was made of cardboard and groped for the walls.

"What's she trying to find?" Argon asked. "A way out?"

"I don't think she's worried about that now. She's thinking." The monitor showed the scowling, naked female apparently planning her next move. "Now she looks pretty pissed off, so I imagine she's searching for something—"

"What?"

"Clearly, you fucking idiot, it is—us."

He shrugged. "Dumb blind chick, she can't see squat. No one could; that area is impregnable."

"She may be blind, but she's certainly not dumb, and she doesn't need to see us to destroy us. Even if she's at a fraction of her power, it ain't good. I don't know and don't care. I think I want to get the hell out of here."

"Power from where?"

"It's dark energy, Ray, you dumb-ass geneticist; you can't see it. But once she converts it to something else, we're dead meat."

"Tolliver—I think you're exaggerating. She can't go from unconscious to that level of threat in only a few minutes."

"Doesn't matter if you agree or not, Ray. We're gonna die, it's too late. However fast we can run, it isn't fast enough. She likely won't be anywhere near peak power for a while, but that won't matter. As the saying goes, you can't outrun a nuke."

She pounded on the walls, still naked. Rage—she had never succumbed to it, but perhaps it was time. Woozy—a hundred times worse than when she landed Air Force One. But likely enough strength was at her disposal to do her intended task. Slowly she could feel the tough metal walls caving in.

"Whoever you are, I am coming to find you," she screamed. "If God exists, may he protect you from me because no one else will."

"She's almost here. Let's get out of here, Ray!" his assistant exclaimed. "She fricking landed a two million pound airplane. Do you have any idea the energy that requires?"

He pushed on the exit door and met resistance. "We can't, Mike. Something has disrupted the power supply and computer system and the electronic locks won't open. Shit, it isn't gonna matter."

• • •

I have had enough.

I know why I have not expressed anger to this degree now. Forgive me for what I do, because I cannot help myself.

I am not a goddess. I am merely human, with human frailties and emotions.

One emotion I have suppressed for so long is surfacing.

I want to yell so badly. Heaven help me.

Run as fast as you like. It will not matter.

Unless you are faster than sound, you are going to die. And now . . .

Now I am become Death, the destroyer of worlds.

The angry, very tired young woman let out an Earth-shattering roar as she smashed through the titanium walls, disintegrating them with ease into particles less than a millimeter in diameter. Argon and the others instantly ceased to exist as they were crushed into dust by tons of metal and the massive shock wave.

What have I done?

I have touched no one.

Yet, I sense something catastrophic has happened.

There is no going back now. I have changed forever.

• • •

Thirty seconds earlier, Petra somehow sensed something distinctly unfamiliar and heard the shock wave three seconds before Juriann did as she pushed him down.

"Oh, my Lord. Get over me, Juriann. Incoming!"

"What? I don't sense anything—"

The lightly armored figure pushed him to the ground. "Get down *now*, or even you won't survive the shock wave. We may be dead anyway."

"Petra, you're nuts, I don't hear any—"

"Get down in the crawl space, idiot! Bert the Turtle says duck and cover!"

"Turtle? What the hell are you rambling about—"

"Didn't you watch your atomic propaganda commercials when you were a kid in the Netherlands? Rad Darkkin was your dad, for

God's sake."

"Come on. I didn't know any of that as a child."

"Shut up." Petra was startled as she heard the high-pitched roar oscillate through the building. They hid underneath a reinforced metal depression as they felt debris hurtling overhead, a 400-mph shock wave strong enough to level an entire city.

Several minutes later, Juriann pushed aside the debris and climbed out. "What the hell was that?"

"Hell hath no fury," she said.

"What does that mean?"

"She blew her stack; what did you think, idiot? It was bound to happen sooner or later. Yow! That hurt my sensitive hearing."

He looked into the distance and only saw vast nothingness.

"Good Lord, Petra. Everything is gone. It looks like what I'd imagine the aftermath of a thermonuclear explosion would look like. Hiroshima or Nagasaki."

She nodded. "Yes, it is exactly like that, except there is no radiation, of course."

"Are you certain of that? There are surely limits on the amount of gamma radiation even I can withstand."

"Wimp." She shook her helmeted head. "No, there exists only background radiation; I assure you the instrumentation in my suit is accurate. Yet, there have been many fatalities, I am certain."

"I didn't know this was possible."

She nodded. "I always did, unfortunately. She is not one to be easily angered, but when she is—let me simply declare that we are fortunate the world is still in one piece. She is theoretically capable of acts more violent than you can possibly imagine. At full power, we would surely have perished."

"I've never seen anything like this ever in my life."

"I merely hope this never happens again, or we likely shall not live through it."

• • •

Dexter Slabb picked up his Tekphone and smiled.

"Yeah, Lori. What's up?"

"Dex, there's been what appears to be a Level I nuclear event in eastern West Virginia. An entire industrial complex has been leveled, and everything within a one-mile radius has been destroyed."

"I don't believe that; who set it off? How is that possible? We surely would have known about that—"

"It wasn't one of our nukes, nor was it anyone else's."

"But it's impossible."

"There's also no detectable ionizing radiation of any type."

"A nuclear level event in an unpopulated area, without any nukes? That makes absolutely no sense."

She nodded. "Yes, it could, when it's accompanied by a massive sonic wave of frequency 231 Hertz."

"231 Hertz?" He paused for a moment as he remembered the average adult female's vocal pitch. "Wait, are you saying, Lori, that it's *her*, and she—"

"Yes. We detected a mighty big female yell, accompanied by a massive release of what had to be gravitational force, creating a titanic shock wave through the area, which, from the spectroscopic signature, reduced massive amounts of hyperdense metallic and concrete structures to particles. We've been wondering where she's been, and I guess now we know."

He rubbed his eyes. "My God. What the hell was she doing out there, and what happened?"

"Don't know, but we're indeed fortunate that it wasn't in a populated area but up in the rural West Virginia mountains."

"Seriously, what would happen to if she had a temper tantrum in a populated area? We'd have no defense against that."

"You think? Let's hope she never does."

"We'd better get a cover story for this, as we can't be the only people who've detected the event, Dex."

• • •

Juriann then curiously spied, two hundred feet east of them, a naked young female figure wandering through the seemingly endless mist of crushed rubble, like a modern-day magical princess walking through a desert, minus the dress and tiara.

She appeared to be in no hurry, as befitting a deity clearly in command of her somewhat dusty environment.

Petra looked at her daughter's facial expression; she had never seen anything like it before. It was possible she didn't know they were here, but it was as if they were beneath her existence, from one who had transcended into another state of being.

"Is—is she okay?" Juriann asked. "She looks unharmed."

"She looks like Moses coming down from Mount Sinai, except that Moses probably was clothed. I know she has now seen some things I have, and surely many I have not."

"Moses? Mount Sinai?" He shook his head. "I don't get it."

"Duh!" Petra sighed. "The Ten Commandments, with Charlton Heston and Yul Brynner? Yvonne De Carlo—Lily Munster?"

He shook his head. "Never heard of that movie."

"What? Scored by the famous Elmer Bernstein, who also composed the score for Robot Monster, one of the greatest films of all time? Don't they have good movies in the Netherlands?"

"I guess I missed that one."

"It describes the few survivors of a post-apocalyptic Earth, which has been destroyed by atomic bombs, sort of like here."

"All that stuff happens in The Ten Commandments? Come on, the first atomic bomb wasn't even developed until the mid-1940s."

"No, Robot Monster, dunce. It is in the Bible, after all."

"Robot Monster is in the Bible? That's a lie. You made that up."

She punched him in the arm. "Yikes, you primitive pre-Cambrian haploid—the Ten Commandments. Are you even vaguely familiar with them?"

"Not as much as I should be, unfortunately."

"Yes, unfortunate, as you can use all the help you can get. But my original statement refers to someone who has seen the supernatural—the Almighty—and has thusly been enlightened. So, she shall never be the same again."

"Why?"

"Look at her expression, sonny. She is no longer one of us."

"I don't think she ever was."

Paige stopped thirty feet from them. "I am right here, Mom and Juriann. Do not talk to me in the third person. I have taken about enough from everybody, and here you are rambling on about inane trivia. There is nothing wrong with my hearing."

"Are you okay?" he asked.

She paused for ten seconds. "No, not really. I feel weak like you cannot imagine. At the same time, I also somehow feel stronger than ever before, if that makes any sense. I also feel like I have aged about twenty years." She stopped and bent over, hands on knees. "I heard what you said—that I will never be the same again."

"Are you? The same, I mean?" Juriann asked.

She shook her head. "No. I cannot describe in detail how I have changed, yet I know I have, substantially, as I now recall everything in my past. However, I want to find out one thing first."

"What?"

"Who the hell—did this to me?"

"I don't think we'll find out now, as you pretty much leveled the whole place and everything within a one-mile radius," Petra said. "We think it's some guy named Ramon Argon. His uncle's wife was Travis Argon's—Juriann's—mother."

"What happened to him and the other horrific beings who did this? For them, it shall not be bliss."

"They're vaporized," Petra said. "Good riddance."

"They are what?" she exclaimed. "I sense much dust, and there seems to be no structures or vegetation remaining, although we are outside. Are we in a desert?"

"No, Aurora. We're in West Virginia," Petra said.

"Did my illustrious aunt drop a thermonuclear weapon on them? How did you survive if that is the case? Why are you out here with no shielding?"

"No, *you* did this, in a manner of speaking," Petra said. "After Juriann disrupted the power, you broke that holding area apart and leveled the control room, and also converted everything in a six-mile radius into a parking lot. Damn lucky you did not kill us, we barely escaped destruction by falling into an underground bunker."

"Huh?" She scratched her dust-filled hair. "I did what?"

"I said it looks like Hiroshima out here," Petra said. "Minus the radiation, of course. And that's with you at a fraction of full power, apparently."

"What did I do? I just remember being *really* pissed off, yelling, and wanting to pound something. I yelled some more. Then, I hear lots of loud stuff and lots of wind blowing. Finally, I am out in the open air, and here I am, and here you are."

"Yes—well, you, in your angered state, created a massive shock wave that reduced everything to dust, equivalent to a low-yield thermonuclear weapon."

"How?"

"How else? Child, you surely know the answer to your query: *with the power of your mind.* You have the potential for unimaginable destructive forces you do not yet understand."

She shook her head. "I was so angry, and I killed. I vaguely remember thinking of J. Robert Oppenheimer's ominous quote from The Shrimad Bhavagad Gita. What have I become?"

"As you just said, the destroyer of worlds. Killing Argons seems to be in our blood. I killed two, you one. Hopefully, they are all gone by now. Sorry, Juriann, present company excluded. Like Aurora, you do have some Gallinsworth blood in you, unlike your predecessor, so there is at least some normalcy."

"Thanks."

"Yet, I had no idea what they were doing, as naturally I could not see. The walls were thick—I just let loose with more than I ever have before. I was not sure I could do anything like that."

"I can see the look on your face; surely you have seen them, or however you perceive things—those of pure energy who have no name, and you now know you are capable of such deeds."

"I have seen and conversed with them, the ones composed of elemental energy, but I had no concept I could do this."

"I am sure they must have told you otherwise."

"Yes. I was told that I had the potential for great destruction."

Petra patted her on the shoulder. "I knew it was within you. They deserved to die for what they did. Let us be thankful that you were weak; otherwise, the whole state might have been destroyed."

"What the hell?" She shook her head in disgust and shoved Petra away. "This is all because of my anger."

"How can you say that, Aurora? I—"

"Shut up, Mom. I regret I am not sorry they are dead, but I did not know I could do such a thing." She thought for a moment and realized something else as she felt the skin of her breasts. "Waitaminnit. Is there light out here, Juriann?"

"Yes, of course there is; we're outside, it's daylight and kind of dusty in the aftermath, but so what?"

"Why do you say, 'of course'?" She lifted Petra up like a rag doll and put her between herself and Juriann. "I am naked, you perverted, genetically-modified voyeur!"

"*That* you surely are, nothing I can do about that." She felt him hand her a piece of cloth, which seemed to be a towel he had kept from the underground area. "Don't worry. I've seen it all before."

"Huh, not mine, you have not! I am not one of your little Dutch girlfriends." She put up her fists and shook them at him angrily. "I will punch your lights out, lout."

"No, you aren't, at that. But we're related—I guess it's all right."

She pushed her mom away and smacked him on the shoulder, knocking him over. "It certainly is *not* all right, and I wish we knew how we are related, you oversized, hirsute, ridiculous lummox! I should kick your butt for that, we will indeed have quite a spat."

"Sorry, Paige, I can't help that you're naked—"

"No, but you could at least look the other way, I must say!"

"How do you know I'm not?"

"The direction of your voice. I can easily tell whether someone speaking is facing me or not, as your spot tells me a lot."

"Well, my eyes could be closed, and no way can you tell that."

She balled her left hand into a fist again. "They will soon be so swollen they will definitely be closed, *that* I promise you."

"Listen up, both of you: we have way more to worry about than how much of a lummox Uncle *Orthoman* is, although the amount is clearly substantial." She felt her mother hand her something familiar but curiously different. "Is this what I think it is?"

"Of course, I have secretly been working on this, and the prototype has been in storage in Tennessee. Since we have no garments for you other than some spare underwear I brought, and you have pretty much destroyed this area beyond repair, it would be wise to put it on. I have recalibrated the sensors for your brain wave patterns from the previous records."

She felt the breast indentations, which clearly hadn't been part of the original version, which was designed for a somewhat less than average-sized Soviet male. "This is styled a bit differently than the old one."

"It was created months ago to approximate your size and build. I pretty much nailed it, I think."

"Huh." She put it on, as she had done many times before (except she had no clothes on this time, only underwear her mom had brought), as the magnetic latches sealed her inside; it was about a sixth the weight of the old one. She put the helmet on, powered it up, and noticed the vivid synthetic vision she had last experienced right before she went out of control and struck Russ's plane. "The boot-up and response time is definitely much improved."

"It has about seventy times the processing speed and memory access time of the first model; it had better, for what it cost."

"Where did the money come from?"

"Humph. Some from Nick; the rest, you do not want to know."

"The visual acuity is amazing, Mom." The voice was also different than the other one. "It sounds like me now, not Rad the Grand-Dad. What is the deal?"

"This one isn't broken." Petra tapped her on the head. "It has something else, too."

"What?"

"Tell it to 'activate wings.'"

"Okay. *Activate wings!*" Nothing happened. "Hey, what a gyp."

Petra laughed. "No, in Russian."

"If it is new, why did you program it in Russian again? That seems pretty dumb, Nureyev."

"Why not? Is there something wrong with Russian? Next to Latin and Italian, it is my favorite language."

"Oh, all right, I do not desire to argue with you." She sighed. "*Активироватькрыльями.*" She heard the hardened fullerene wings spread from her back, and a small fuselage emerged from the helmet. "Hey, cool."

"One problem with the other one was that it wasn't very aerodynamic. This process should allow you to significantly boost your velocity, perhaps even to Mach 9 or 10. The limit of your flight speed isn't only your power—it's your shape, which produces aerodynamic drag." Mom tapped on the helmet. "Another thing is different, too. Bend your head down."

She did so, eyes pointed to the ground, and noticed she still saw straight ahead. "What the heck is this?"

"It is like swimming—your head being up creates more drag, so this one sees out of the top of your head, if you want. You can change it with a simple command."

"That is fantastic; but if we had another suit, why did you let me talk like that with the other one? And these advances could have done me much good."

"Well, I had planned to give you this if you hadn't gone off to the Bering Strait to do stupid stuff. But it's not as if you used it that much, anyway—the fullerene skeleton in the old one was far stronger, which I thought necessary for your flight around the world to Taraq; but I don't think it makes much difference now, and that voice was scary, in a way, to strike fear in your foes."

"What? It was pretty damn idiotic; that statement sounds like something from one of your comic books."

"Yes. Your point being?"

"I sounded like some dumb-ass hillbilly and not at all frilly."

"Hey, listen here: your grandfather was indeed a hillbilly but never *stupid*. Like me, he had periods where he was very enlightened. He liked to experiment with mind-enhancing drugs. I, on the other hand, did not require those."

"So I heard, great to know."

"Plus, it is broken now and not worth repairing, with Russian Federation replacement parts hard to come by these days. As I said, I was going to get it for you on my next 'trip,' but you had your 'accident' with Ashburn's EMP device, and we didn't see you for a while. I had hoped we wouldn't need this, but we do."

"Where to now?"

"Likely to Kentucky. I have a feeling we are not done yet."

"Kentucky? Not a place I was planning on visiting. And I think you saved this suit for yourself, not for me. You're lying."

"No comment."

"It certainly is not your cup size. Anyway, was this *Mantissa* in the building when I destroyed this complex?"

"How do you know its name?"

"I know many things now, Mom. Some I wish I did not. Yet, what is done is done."

"No, I don't think it's gone, as I surely would have sensed the destruction of a powerful mind greater than my own."

"Great. I was also told something cryptic about nuclear destruction from Grandpa Rad's missiles at the hand of *Santaman*."

"Kristoff van Sant? Are you certain?"

"Yes, why? Sounds like a character from your comics."

Petra shook her head. "There is a bunker near here, in eastern Kentucky, which fits the bill; *The Red Skeleton* is sufficiently skilled at cyber-attacks to defeat our defenses, and *Mantissa* likely had the ability to hack into the system as well with its vast mental abilities. No one would detect someone would infiltrate from within. Let's get our sorry asses going. And there's nothing comical about him."

• • •

Twenty minutes later, the trio landed in the M2 hovercraft outside the military control center that her mother said had once contained old DARC missiles from the 1980s, which were probably still functional, knowing who the President was. Petra had also sensed as they drew closer that *Mantissa* was within the building.

Juriann burst into the room and saw Kristoff van Sant in the control room along with Reuben J. Skelton and several other men and watched in awe as one of the men morphed into a duplicate of him and rapidly approached.

"I took you down once, *Stella Scura*. What makes you think the outcome will be any different this time?"

"Because I brought my family this time, and I am prepared. We are all going to kick your ass."

"Are you kidding? I'll knock all of your heads from here back to Fairbanks."

"You think so?" Petra looked at her clone, easily thirty years her junior. "You think all you are is your genetics, you hideous freak. But what made me was not just that, but my experiences, just like *Stella* here. I earned them, unlike you."

"A soliloquy isn't going to save you." *Mantissa* picked up Petra with one hand and threw her against the wall. "Anybody else?"

"I have figured most of it out, Juriann. The powers require visual imagery to be effective. So, in the darkness, her powers will be ineffective."

"So what?"

"So—you know someone who can function in the blackness of dark better than anyone else. In the dark, the odds are turned in my favor. If her powers are derived from Mom, they cannot work when I am sightless. Be useful and get the power off."

"May all your guesses be right." Juriann knocked out the power supply by ripping the control box from the wall. Darkness, after a blinding flash of electricity.

"Let us see how you work in the dark, evil creation."

"It won't matter. I beat you once, and I'll beat you again."

"You won't beat all three of us," Juriann said.

"Now it is my turn." As Mom predicted, she couldn't be hurt without her natural vision, as their previous encounter was with the sapphire goggles, but she still left the visual enhancements off in the darkened room. The rest of the suit was just for show. "I was unprepared once, but never again. Welcome to my world, so take your best shot." *Mantissa* had already knocked down Juriann and her mom a couple of times. But she could tell her adversary was getting tired as she felt the hand grab her. "Touch me all you want, freak—it will not matter."

"You come back for seconds. Do you think this wise, girl?" The creature had now adopted the voice of her mother and grabbed her neck.

"I do. Gee whiz, it is not working, is it?" she said as she kicked the creature across the room. "From what I guess, you are about two years old, with the maturity of a one-year-old. Prepare to get your ass whipped."

"You would not kill your own mother?" *Mantissa* laughed.

"Is this a debate? If so, you are surely outmatched. Why would you not use your gifts to help mankind?"

"I don't need your existential rants. Why would you be such a dumb ass to not use your power for your own purposes?"

"Thank you."

"For what, idiot?"

"For making this decision easier. No, I would not kill my mother." *Stella* let out a shrill cry, took her left fist, rammed it through its thorax, and pulled out its heart, feeling blood spewing everywhere. "You, on the other hand, are neither my mother nor a human being, but a horrible aberration of science created by a madman. Join him and go back to the ashes from whence you came."

She rose up, covered in blood; Juriann had found the backup power and the lights returned, as she switched the helmet back on, holding the quivering heart in her left hand. A warrior born. And now reborn in this defining moment.

Juriann looked at the hideous being that had once looked like Bonnie Mendoza when she was young. Gray skin, blood vessels showing. "Oh, my Lord. What a terrible creature. Is that what she, it—really looked like?"

"It would appear so," Petra said. "It looked that way to me, so it was puzzling why you lesser mortals thought she looked like me. She may have had some of my moves, but she did not have my looks. A terrifying aberration of genetic manipulation."

"Like me?" Juriann asked sadly.

"Like all of us," Petra said dramatically. "I am no different now, the metahumans we have now all become—."

"OMG! The verbose melodrama is too much." She scowled, still holding *Mantissa's* beating heart in her hand. "Mom, shut up. And you, Uncle *Orth:* grow a pair of damn balls and get some self-esteem," she said, as she looked up into his eyes with the eerie helmet. "You were created to help society, not destroy it like your predecessor was. We cannot go back and change the past, you know, but we can go forward. Be thankful you are alive and cease all the sulking, although you are hulking."

"Sorry. I guess you're right, Paige."

"Damn straight, great of massive weight. We are all creations of something; it may or may not be God, but we are more beneficial alive than dead. You are one of us, Juriann."

"So she manipulated our perceptions to appear different?"

"Yes," Petra said. "Just as your perception of me as Ehrich Weiss was not as it seems. That required some cooperation on your part, but *Mantissa's* powers were far greater."

"I never thought you could've killed," Juriann said, gasping. "That was pretty much over the top."

"You saw what I did to Argon's lab and am uncertain if I can kill? Seriously?" She looked at him with astonishment as she put the visor back on. "But *did* I kill just now? How can one kill what was never truly alive? A deep philosophical matter to ponder at a later time. Yet, I saw no other way, Juriann. Was there any chance its power could have been benevolent to mankind?"

"I certainly don't think so, but before today I didn't know you were capable of that kind of violence."

"You know now that I am. It is what the energy being told me when I was still in clouded consciousness."

"Um, who told you what, Paige?" he asked.

"Never mind, I have seen things even my mother cannot comprehend. Even now, it all seems like a wild dream."

"While I would normally doubt that, I believe you completely."

"Huh. Nevertheless, it should therefore be clear to you that I am *not* the daughter of God. For a moment, there was a darkness within me that I have never known before. Let us pray it never surfaces again."

Juriann looked at her. "We all have it, *Stella*. It was necessary for you to confront that in order to face your future."

"Yes, yes, I was told all that by Gart-Monn. Now that we have agreed on something, what now?" she asked.

"We get the hell out of here," Petra said. "It isn't over yet."

"What do you mean by that?" she asked.

"I mean that there is likely more death and destruction on the way, my fantastic heuristic brain has predicted."

"Hey, in case anyone noticed, where the hell did *Santaman* and *Red Skeleton* go?" Juriann asked, looking around.

"There is an auxiliary complex, I believe, Juriann, and we need to get there immediately. We have stupidly spent far too much time philophisizing like true comic book heroes would. *Stella?*"

She looked around and read the Russian readouts. "Oddly, there is an energy surge about five miles from here. The sensors indicate radioactive material—Pu-239, it says. I am not sure I understand what all that means, but the sensors going off in this new helmet cannot be good. I do not think Pu-239 is one of your healthiest elements, although I am no expert. I think my old suit contained Pu-238."

"There is a hell of a difference between the two. Is the plutonium source moving?" Petra asked.

She shook her head. "No, it is stationary."

"You and Juriann need to get your butts out there, then. The end of the world is near, daughter, just as I had predicted."

"What about you, Petra?" he asked. "You can't pilot the hovercraft, as that would be more dangerous than this entire mission."

"Do not concern yourselves with me, I will survive, somehow. I always will."

"Well, I guess we're flying there the hard way. Get on my back, Juriann, and shut up."

Juriann climbed on her back as they took off; Petra heard the first sonic boom as they hit Mach 1 in about ten seconds. She couldn't open the wings with him on the back, but they weren't far away from the missile launch control center.

• • •

Less than a minute later, they arrived at the auxiliary complex, which Petra claimed was a backup launch facility, in case the other one was damaged. *Orthoman* burst through the fortified steel doors with ease after she had detected two moving forms inside, one twice as heavy as the other.

"Be careful, Juriann. I do not think I need to tell you that."

"I will, but remember that you already had your fight. This one's all mine, *Stella*." He saw the two men running towards him.

"The incredible *Orthoman*. We finally meet," van Sant said, laughing. "I heard of you but thought you were long dead, killed by that freak Mendoza. Merry Christmas to you and your new adopted country, which will soon be in pieces. Glorious it shall be!"

"I'm very much alive, van Sant. First I'm going to kick your butt. Then, I'm going to kill you."

"Ye must first go through me, inhuman bulk, and ye soon shall be reduced to mere atoms," Reuben J. Skelton yelled loudly.

"Shut up, *Skeleton.*" He picked him up with one hand and knocked him into the wall, unconscious. "Loser. Now I'm coming after you, van Sant. And you're going to die."

"Really? How are you going to do that?"

"Like this." He went over, grabbed the spindly man, and threw him across the room. "Does that work for you?"

"Juriann—" she went near him. "Do not kill him. You are better than that."

He gaped at her and laughed. "*You're* going to stop me? I'm not afraid of you. Take your best shot, *Stella.*"

"Are you daft? I can easily stop you."

"Maybe you *can*. But you *won't*."

She nodded. "No, I will not, and I know, like your sister, you are not really afraid of me, as the worst I could do is kill you."

"And like her, I don't care about that."

She nodded. "I believe you. But, like the pregnant lady I saved from shooting herself and jumping off a window ledge in my police training, you have to make that decision for yourself—whether or not to take certain actions. Know that certain cerebral ruination from which there is no return lay waiting for you if you destroy the *Santaman*."

"Look who's talking. You've gotten awfully high and mighty after talking to your big energy being. You blew up Argon's lab, killed everyone there, and damn near killed your mom and me, so shut the hell up, *Stella*."

She shook her head. "I did not fully know where I was or what I was doing, I had just essentially emerged from a medically induced coma, and it has nothing to do with Gart-Monn. But recently I almost did what you are planning on doing to the person who killed my family, but someone stopped me."

"Who?"

"The genetic link between us, but does it matter? The point is, had I not listened to my aunt, I would never have been the same.

Please listen to what I say."

Van Sant got up wearily. "I like her idea better, *Orthoman*. You resemble your predecessor—you're a lot like him."

"I may look like him and have some genetics in common, but know I'm nothing like him, except for the part that might have killed. Shoi-Ming tried to destroy Washington; how did that work out for him? Not very well, I estimate."

"The power we could've had together, *Orthoman*. You don't care that we could've ruled the world. Those Argon fools, they wanted too much; I am not as greedy. But if I can't rule the world, I'm going to, yes, wait for it—destroy it. And you as well!"

He threw van Sant across the room again. "What do you mean?"

"In less than two minutes, there will be a DARC thermonuclear missile sent off from this complex towards New York City. It will vaporize the entire city, and not even your vaunted strength can do anything about it."

He laughed. "You're crazy. Air Command will shoot it down."

Van Sant shook his oddly-shaped skinny head. "I don't think so. *Red Skeleton's* cyber-worms coupled with *Mantissa's* reprogramming of the entire defense system has infiltrated their computers; there's no way their anti-missile systems can be activated with sufficient accuracy to do so, and it's all over for the great U.S. of A."

"Can I ask—why this would be done?" he asked.

"You obviously think me crazy or demented. I assure you I am neither. The world is at a crossroads, perhaps it does not deserve to exist, *Orthoman*. Wasted opportunities. Our civilization needs to start over with the few that survive. The destruction of New York will plunge the world into financial chaos, leaving you and I, for example, the superior beings, to go on."

"Yeah? You think your crappy computer will work well now?" She picked up the two-ton Rigel supercomputer like a toy and threw it against the wall, smashing it and the wall into a hundred pieces. "How 'bout them apples, *Antisanta?"*

"Idiot girl!" The spindly man laughed and shook his head. "It doesn't matter; it's too late. Those things are on automated countdown, and your smashing my computer won't help. This time *Darkkday* will *really* happen."

"You're wrong, *Santaman*. There's one way." He looked at *Stella*.

"I see she has suited up for the occasion with her shiny new duds. Well, she might have survived *Darkkday*, but that one was nothing compared to this. On Christmas Eve, your Savior is going to die, how fitting. Their sensors will think it was fired from Beijing, the computers will retaliate, and there will be hellfire reigning down as you cannot imagine. What blissful nuclear destruction."

"The President wouldn't start a war with China," Juriann said.

Van Sant shook his head. "Not willingly, no, but she won't have a choice, as the computers will make it for her. And I escaped from prison once, I'll do it again, you freak."

"No, you won't."

"Why's that?"

Juriann took van Sant, lifted him over his head, and threw him head-first into the computer bank. "That's how, fellow freak."

She scanned him with her biometric. "Just so you know, he is merely unconscious."

"Yes, of course, if I had intended to kill him, he'd be dead. But hadn't you better get going? He said two minutes."

"Hey, you are the one who wasted two whole minutes arguing with stupid *Santaman.*" Juriann was right; she fired up the radio and lifted off. "*Stella* to *Tinman*. We have a problem. Get every resource you know about DARC missiles. What? You heard me." She then called the personal number of the President. "Hey, listen up, Dame, things here are rather lame. One of Grandpa's missiles is headed for Manhattan in about one minute. Better get out of there. I am going after it. Yes, you heard me. Thankfully, I have a new suit now."

Continued in:

Book Six
A Child Once More

Book Six:
A Child Once More

"Forget them, Wendy. Forget them all. Come with me where you'll never, never have to worry about grown up things again."

—Sir James Matthew (J.M.) Barrie, from "Peter & Wendy"

Chapter Fifty-Three

The White House
Situation Room

Joint Chiefs of Staff Chairman Gen. Lawrence Kriger's face turned white as he looked towards the President.

"Ma'am, we've confirmed *Stella's* statement: a DARC-Ranger 9000 is headed from Beijing to New York City."

"I know, but we don't really think the Chinese fired it, do we?"

Kriger cautiously shook his head. "Part of our defenses have been hacked, so, no, of course not, but she says it came from eastern Kentucky. Beijing denies any knowledge, which is correct since they didn't do it. They are mighty nervous now as well."

She scowled at him. "How could've that been possible? And can't we just shoot it down with our defense grid?"

Kriger shook his head again. "Normally, yes, but there's been a massive computer breach and our countermeasures aren't responding. It's as if some incredible advanced cyber-intelligence has completely reprogrammed everything."

"Yes, it's all making sense now. The *Squad* told me of a clone of Bonnie Mendoza with exponentially augmented mind powers, which would have the ability to do that."

"Holy crap. It's just like *Darkkday*, Ma'am, except that a hell of a lot more people will die this time when it hits, and the computers will retaliate by bombing China. It's unlikely that this one will malfunction like it did then."

"Right." She secretly knew it had not malfunctioned before,

only that Aurora had saved the city by absorbing the blast. But she looked at him and realized that she had failed the country. Despite all her efforts to wipe out Communism and other hostile threats, there still was this one that had slipped through.

Damn you, Rad Darkkin, you stupid, rotten bastard, for creating this monstrous thing. Three hundred megatons. Why did we need this?

No, damn me for being my father's daughter. I could have gotten rid of your toys. Did we really need them anymore? Hell, no.

But I didn't dispose of them when it was within my power to do so. I would've never used them, but I needed the threat to be real. Our enemies would've known if they were gone.

"Do we have any evidence of *Stella Scura* in the vicinity?"

He nodded. "There's a small mass traveling at Mach 9.0 towards New York, but it has a different spectroscopic signature than before. Less buckminsterfullerene composition."

"Mach 9.0, is that what you said? I didn't know she could even go past Mach 6."

"She is still accelerating and will break Mach 10 momentarily. It looks like she's headed on a course to intercept the missile."

"Will she make it in time?"

He nodded. "Yes, at the rate she's traveling, we project she will easily intercept it before it gets to the city; she wasn't that far from it when it launched. What happens when she gets there is another story entirely."

So maybe there was still hope, but experience had taught her to always prepare for the worst. She looked towards Admiral Juan Carlos Ramirez Garcia, Chief of Naval Operations.

"Admiral Ramirez, get me a Navy medical hovercraft within the next fifteen minutes."

Ramirez looked up, startled by the request. "Fifteen minutes? Are you kidding, Ma'am?"

"Do I usually kid about such things?"

"Madam President, where are you going?"

"Where do you think? I'm going to New York. If she survives, she may need help. I'll be dammed if I'm not going to be there."

"You can't, Ma'am. You could die if you go out there."

She nodded. "Probably. But you know now that I'm not afraid to die. There are bigger things than me."

"Yes, Ma'am." Adm. Ramirez got on the phone. "Get Navy One here on the double and land it on the lawn. What? You heard me."

• • •

"You have about ten minutes to reach it, *Stella,*" Nick said from the M2 hovercraft, as she heard the transmission clearly through the helmet. Russ had now joined them in the craft.

"He's right," Russ said. "It's still ascending but will soon begin its midcourse path down from sub-Earth elliptical orbit."

"What do I do when I get to it? Might be nice to know."

"You need to dig your hands into the side of the body and move it skyward, as high as you can go. It'll likely go off before you get to your theorized maximum altitude."

"I could just punch it, or throw it out of the atmosphere."

"No," Russ said. "If you try to disassemble it, tamper with it in any way, or strike it with any impact, it will likely go off, so leave it alone; it would do more damage that way. It has its own propulsion, so you trying to throw it into space will be very unpredictable. Just direct it away from here, ideally as high as you can get."

"I do not know where it is yet, and I am beginning to fret."

"The new helmet has heat sensors similar to the old one, I imagine, but about a thousand times more sensitive. You'll be able to see it in a moment, as it descends. Good luck, *Stella.*"

"I shall see you again, Russ. Maybe not in this life, but perhaps in another, if you believe in reincarnation." She ended the call.

"This ICBM can destroy an entire small country and has a yield of one-third gigaton—seventy times the yield of the one that hit her plane on *Darkkday,*" Russ said. It's not possible that anything survives that, not even her. My God."

"She doesn't know that, Russ, and neither do we," Nick said. "What good would telling her that have done?"

"Nothing, I guess. I suppose that information would be of no use to her, she doesn't know much of such technical things. Nor would it deter her from doing it."

"She's a living star; remember that, son," Bella said.

Russ nodded. "I know, but some stars do indeed reach end of life, Bella. I just hope it isn't the end of hers."

• • •

She had been heading towards the Atlantic Ocean, where Air Command said it would be coming down on its way to New York.

It was traveling towards the East Coast, hitting over 5,000 kilometers per hour. She had never really pushed past that velocity. She deployed the new wings, heading due northeast. While she didn't particularly like science, she wasn't stupid, and she knew this might be her last few minutes on Earth. She didn't care.

She pushed as hard as she could and noticed in the virtual display that her speed had now exceeded 11,600 kilometers per hour, roughly Mach 9.4. She finally reached a cruising speed of Mach 10.2, or 12,594 kilometers per hour.

Russ was skilled in weapons technology and had taught her a lot about the missiles her grandfather had engineered.

Since *Stella Scura* was truly born in the aftermath of a nuclear explosion, it was only fitting that she would die in one. She'd already nearly died and survived. If the life of one could save fifteen million people, that was a pretty good deal, she surmised.

She asked herself if she feared death. She didn't.

But she didn't want to die. Not yet, anyway.

What she wanted didn't matter.

She had to get at least to 50,000 feet to completely assure lack of damage to the Earth's surface, according to *Tinman*; that would be easy, as she'd been higher than that before. She knew she could function for at least several hours without air, as she didn't seem to require it for her energy needs. Her powers seemed to work fine on Armstrong City and in space, which disputed any theories that her powers depended on the actual manipulation of Earth's gravitational field, and the further away she got from it, the weaker her powers might get. That's what Kepler thought. Yet, she had been to Armstrong City without any perceived loss of abilities.

She hadn't really been put to the test there, though.

A bigger problem was that the visor would ice over when she got too high. If so, she would be dependent on the helmet sensors. Which really wasn't an issue since she was flying with her head down, anyway.

The biggest problem was yet to come, however, when she caught the damn thing, which would be very soon.

• • •

The missile of destruction was now on its way down; she was confident she could get to it in time, but the trick was properly redirecting it. If it hit, it would cause instant annihilation of New York City's five boroughs and the surrounding areas, and then the computers would automatically retaliate against China, unless the military experts were able to reprogram in time, thanks to *Santaman, Red Skeleton*, and, of course, *Mantissa*. The latter wouldn't be bothering anyone again.

She was adjusting her trajectory according to the onboard computer, now displaying a velocity of over 13,500 km/hr (Mach 11.0). Her mom was a mathematical genius, who likely had programmed such a scenario into the new electronics; the armor's predecessor was, of course, created during the Cold War, so it was natural to assume that the suit's wearer might encounter intercontinental ballistic missiles (ICBMs) (although neither suit could actually fly, of course), so that was a really dumb thought.

She could fly much faster than it could now, and her onboard computer could help calculate the trajectory. The missile had expended most of its fuel going into near space, then used gravity to accelerate downwards, Russ had said. She could take advantage of that.

There it was, about two miles in front of her, descending. The new helmet provided artificial vision far better than her own through the sapphire visor and about ten orders of magnitude better than any human. She was still a shade over Mach 11 when she came up next to it and touched its smooth surface, the Manhattan skyline visible about two miles in the distance. She punctured the outer casing with her hands to get a better grip.

She had the power to steer it off its course, naturally. That was easier than she thought. She hadn't even begun to realize how much energy was at her disposal. But, like Air Force One, the missile still had mass and inertia. It was easier to steer than a plane because it was vastly smaller, but the hard part was yet to come.

It would likely explode before she was clear of the populated area, and she didn't have the technical expertise to try and disarm it, if it was even possible to do that safely while it was moving. She now barely remembered the first time, in 2016; she hoped she would live to remember this. Mom's new suit was to have a very short life, but that was of little consequence now.

She thought about her life and the last time this happened in Washington. She didn't remember any of that except for a brief recollection during her visit with Gart-Monn, who said it was within her power to recall those things, but she chose not to—because life wasn't about living in the past. Without her, millions would have no future. The future was what she needed to focus on now.

She remembered all the people who had helped her and she realized again that she would be nothing without them and the help she had been given. Wendy almost gave her life for her President. She would gladly give hers for the thirty million people in the NYC metro area. She had experienced a good life, more than any human being deserved. It would be a shame not to reach the goals she wanted, but if that's how it had to be, it would be okay.

However, dying would have to wait for another day; she'd been here before and survived, albeit with a much less powerful weapon, per the historical archives. As her mother had told her repeatedly: they were both survivors. Now she had to prove it.

But what a way to spend Christmas Eve, right before the year many thought Christ would return.

She closed her eyes as she went skyward, her hardened carbon armor-encased hands embedded in the sides of the missile, with as much power as she could muster. She was still very tired and woozy, and didn't know if she could survive this. 25,000 meters, or 82,000 feet. 15.5 miles high. That should be enough.

Then, a strange feeling. Not painful, but just a little bit warm. She had closed her eyes for the burst, which lasted only a few seconds as she felt the armored suit, helmet, and her hair disappear. Not enough air for the sound to conduct. Brightness, then the darkness that she always had been accustomed to. Warm. Not painful.

Energy, more than she had ever felt. She wondered where the energy she absorbed went, as she vaguely recalled Mom's mutterings that energy could neither be created nor destroyed. She assumed it was somehow converted into dark energy and went to wherever her energy was stored; according to Gart-Monn, it was the dark star Thargis. There was something more important to attend to now than wondering about that.

Survival.

Flying blind, the helmet, as well as her uniform and all of her hair—vaporized. The ionizing radiation had been absorbed, most likely; her body should not be contaminated, based on Nick's prior experiments; but that was with less than a trillionth of this radiation source. But she was tired, very tired, dizzy, and wanted to sleep forever.

She tried to think back to her childhood, and the nursery rhymes and childhood prayers her mother said that were soothing. She closed her eyes again and sung to herself softly:

"Now I lay me down to sleep,
I pray the Lord my soul to keep,
His Love to guard me through the night,
And wake me in the morning's light."

"Now I lay me down to sleep,
I pray the Lord my soul to keep,
Thy angels watch me through the night,
And keep me safe till morning's light."

Landing Air Force One was nothing next to this. All she knew to do was fall to Earth as she peacefully went to sleep. Was this what death was like? She should've died while she was being experimented on by Ramon Argon. Everyone has to die sometime.

Like the little girl she wanted to be again, it was time to go to sleep. Maybe for good. That would be okay because she would die doing what she wanted to do. No regrets.

• • •

"She did it, *Tinman,*" Bella said from the hovercraft. "It exploded, then collapsed upon itself like a black hole."

"Yeah, but at what cost?"

"Possibly the ultimate one—she knew that going in. A true hero knows that. Ask Wendy."

"Yeah, speaking of Wendy—" Nick looked at the incoming military call on the readout and activated his microphone. "Hey, I kinda have some good news and some bad news. Which one do you want first, Prez?"

"What? Good first, I guess."

"There is an object of approximate mass seventy kilograms falling towards Earth at terminal velocity."

"I know, that's good, Nick," Wendy said over the com-link. "It means she survived the blast in one piece. But, I know what the bad news is."

"Yes, the fact we can detect her with radar means she's not absorbing the radio waves, which is indeed bad. If that part of her powers has disappeared, the rest might. She's obviously lost flight or is unconscious, or both. She may not even be alive."

"It looks like she's headed towards the Atlantic Ocean."

"Yeah. About fifty miles off the coast. We're about two miles from you, we'll intercept and join you. You might need us."

• • •

The military air vehicles couldn't fly as fast as the M2 hovercraft, but the latter was fairly small and didn't have a medical suite. Therefore, Dr. Roy C. Bivereaux (who had unique medical knowledge of *Stella*) and Juriann had joined the President and other staff as they flew on Navy One towards where the object hit the ocean.

"She hit about there, I'm told," Wendy said, pointing down.

"Where is she, then?" Juriann asked.

"Not sure. She can survive indefinitely without oxygen, Biv?"

Biv nodded. "Right, Wendy, but we don't know for how long, but at least several days under optimal conditions, maybe forever. Oxygen is only necessary to provide energy for cellular respiration, and she can apparently generate her own.

"But she's likely unconscious now and unable to do so. We don't know much about this dark energy field that apparently can do that for her, so all bets are off. In a de-powered state she's likely just like you and me, we pretty much saw that at Sulphur Springs."

Juriann put on the bulky scuba gear. "Then there's only one solution: I'm going in. No way can the diver drones do something like this as quickly as I can."

"Wait. If you go, I'm going with you," Wendy said.

He laughed, shook his head, and put his hand on her shoulder. "Forget it. Even thirty years ago you would've been an abysmally poor choice for such a mission; you're an even worse one now. This demands special physical and tactical skills; you clearly lack both."

"I *said* I'm going." She stared deeply into his blue eyes, but his glance was equally as piercing. "Don't you dare argue with me."

"And I say you're *not.* You're used to giving orders, but where *Orthoman* goes, he must go alone."

She slapped her left cheek with her left hand. "Oh, that is so tacky. Who told you to say that? Our sister-in-law?"

He poked her in the chest. "Listen up, big sister. You're pushing sixty years old, with one functional lung. How long do you think you or even the best Navy Seal would survive down there in that freezing water? Not even five minutes. You're not even a certified diver. So get your tail over there and be quiet so I can do the job I was born to do. You would only be a hindrance."

Wendy pointed at him angrily. "Don't you dare tell me to be quiet. You think I, of all people, care about dying, you oversized oaf? I know we don't know each other very well, but get real."

He shook his head. "I know you don't, which is clearly the main problem here. Your courage is immense, as any other President would be a thousand miles away by now; yet you're in the thick of the action, with no concern for your own safety. But even Petra wouldn't survive it, so I won't let you go on a fool's errand."

"You won't *let* me? Are you kidding?"

"No. I'll strap you into that chair if I need to, and now *I'm* not kidding. Even I may not survive this. Save your strength for what I find down there, as we'll need you in other ways. Whatever happens, this country needs its President. And, we might just need another physician."

"There might be some of her blood at Argon's lab, and it's possible Aurora and I are ABO and HLA compatible. I could transfuse some of it into myself."

"She reduced his lab to dust, but what the hell for?"

"My theory is, contact with her living cells, even in blood, will confer some limited invulnerability to me."

"That's rather reckless and not a theory we're going to try out now even if we could, Wendy," he said. "Even then, you wouldn't have the strength to function at that depth. There also isn't time for that, given the situation at hand. Those powers require a unique genetic composition and years of practice to control properly."

Wendy nodded slowly. "How are you even going to find her?"

"I have no idea," he said. I brought *Tinman* and Bella's sophisticated instruments for finding deep-sea fish hundreds of feet underwater, so I am confident we can prevail." He put his hand on her shoulder again. "My sister, I haven't known you very long and never knew our father, of course, but I know he was a brave man who died saving your life. There's a part of his greatness in both of us and in Aurora Darkkin."

She put her head down sadly. "But I've failed. The very weapons our father made, I kept because I thought we needed them—

and now it could mean her life. All this is ultimately my fault."

"It isn't yours." He put his hand on her shoulder.

She stood up angrily. "But it is, Juriann. I am the President, I had years to take a different direction, but I didn't. I'm also a physician, for God's sake, yet I diverted trillions into weapons development rather than population health, new pharmaceuticals, and helping cure debilitating diseases. What the hell kind of terrible person have I become? They wanted me in office four more years when I probably shouldn't have been in the White House or California Governor's mansion at all. I *am* responsible, and I don't ever run from responsibility."

"You can't change the past, Wendy. You did what you felt you had to in order to stabilize the country. And, as I recall, my predecessor didn't do much to endear himself to our family. I, therefore, hope for redemption to an extent you cannot possibly envision. So please remember my short life if this doesn't work out well."

"Juriann?"

"Yeah, what is it now, Wendy?"

She pointed at him. "Don't you *dare* come back here without *Stella*. You might as well just stay down there."

The large bearded young man nodded. "It's a promise."

He put on his gear and dove in, knowing this was his destiny and what he'd been searching for all along: to save the greatest force the world had ever known or die trying. He could hardly see at all but used the photoamplifier helmet to visualize the area. Intelligent sensors had mapped out the projected trajectory of where *Stella* had hit and where she was likely to be, based on the physical properties of a 160-pound human being in water.

A minute later he was at one hundred ninety feet. He didn't know a lot about diving, but knew this was the limit for normal people. His native body was far stronger than *Stella's* but he didn't know what he would find.

After about three more minutes of floating around, he finally found an object on his sonar with the approximate mass of *Stella*. That determination was a mixed blessing; while it was fortuitous to have found her, the fact the sonar waves were reflected and not absorbed meant that the dark energy field wasn't functioning properly, and she was probably unconscious if she was even still alive.

He was likely immune to decompression sickness, at least at this depth, and hoped she was too. He found her floating, about three hundred ninety feet below, according to his digital divers' watch. Lord, how could anyone still be alive in this? He picked up the limp, bruised, hairless naked body and attached his oxygen mask to her face, adjusting the straps, as her head was much smaller than his. He could probably make it to the surface with no oxygen, and even if he couldn't, she was more important. But he was getting dizzy. Four hundred feet was too much even for him, as he gradually made it up to the surface, barely conscious.

He still had *Stella* in his grasp and he felt several people grab for him. The Seals were in there to get him. Plus, one other, unmistakable female voice that he heard among the commotion.

She had jumped in after him after all, despite his harsh warnings. It wasn't hard to recognize her, even in a wetsuit. Like she said, she was used to giving orders, not taking them. And she was no coward, that was for sure. If there was a commotion, she would definitely be in the thick of it.

• • •

Juriann lifted her up to the deck of Navy One and saw several other military craft were there as well, keeping the news aircraft out of the way.

"My God," Biv said as he saw her, completely hairless and looking like someone with the worst sunburn he had ever seen. "Is she alive?" he asked Wendy as they loaded her into the medevac craft. "She looks like she's been beaten to death."

"She hit freezing saltwater at terminal velocity and was down there for over twenty minutes, so it's amazing she's alive at all, Biv." Wendy put a stethoscope on her chest. "She has faint respirations. Heart rate is only about twenty."

"How could the blast have burned her or bruised her like that?"

"It didn't," Nick said. "Remember your trick with the torch, Biv? The outer layer of epidermis is merely dead skin, so the blast just removed that. It'll grow back."

"Assuming she makes it."

"Hey, she will. Don't be so negative." Wendy took the fourteen-gauge IV needle. "Get out of the way, Biv. Let a real doctor in there. She must be terribly dehydrated, which can happen at temperatures over one million degrees. We have no idea what the hell a nuclear blast of that magnitude did to her."

"Is she contaminated?"

The counters registered only background radiation. "No, apparently she absorbed all the energy, which is over a quintillion joules, and it went wherever her energy is stored. The gauges would be going crazy if she was radioactive. She absorbed all of it."

Biv shook his head as she attempted brachial venipuncture. "Wendy, that won't work, are you kid—"

"Shut up, Biv." The IV slid in without hesitation into the reddish skin as she hooked up the IV. "You were saying?"

"I will be quiet now," the shorter physician said quietly.

They flew her in the specialized military medical craft to a secret underground medical facility in Virginia, designed during the Reardon administration for Presidential and other VIP medical care after Andrew Graham's assassination attempt. Very few people knew it existed and no one would likely find them.

She had kept it going but had adapted it for a different purpose—one she hoped would never arise. She was wrong.

The complex was one hundred feet straight down in solid bedrock in northern Virginia. They carried her 160-pound body on the gurney down the hall and put her in the main shock room, designed to take care of any emergency the President might encounter. They certainly had never anticipated one like this, she surmised.

Commander Leonard Gelkis, a forty-year-old trauma surgeon, came out of the lounge area wearing scrubs and stared at his new patient.

"Oh, my God," he said as he stared at the hairless naked figure, skin reddened but intact, limbs and face blue and black, as he clearly realized who was pushing the gurney, and then, apparently, the famous yet unrecognizable figure on it. "Ma'am, is that really—"

Wendy nodded. "Yes, Commander. She saved the lives of thirty million people. Now it's our duty to save hers."

The surgeon looked at her body as the rest of the team took her into the shock room. "I never thought that I'd be doing something like this on Christmas Eve, Madam President. Chest injuries, spinal cord trauma, and gunshot wounds I can take care of, but this—" He shook his head. "I'm in way over my head."

"I know, we all are. There's not a lot we can do but wait. And it looks like she has a number of conventional injuries."

"But, Ma'am, her physiology—"

"Is something we don't fully understand and probably never

will." She put her arm on the taller officer's shoulder. "Do what you can the best way you can, Commander; that's all America and I can ask of you. You are the best trauma surgeon around, that's why you're here, and you have my utmost trust. She didn't come with a textbook of medicine. All I know, I have told you. Dr. Bivereaux here may have some additional information."

Biv shook his head as the nurses and junior physicians wheeled her into the shock room. "Not much. It would take years to get this figured out. For what it's worth, her basic body chemistry seems to be normal. Organ placement is conventional by physical examination, although scanning her body's been impossible by any known means, even ultrasound. She seems, for all practical purposes, to be a fairly normal young woman who commands an aura of immense imperceptible energy that augments her strength and confers indestructibility. It isn't that her body's natively that strong."

"Well, then," Gelkis said. "I'm happy to help in any way, which probably isn't much."

She watched as they walked into the shock room as she picked up the secure line phone and dialed a number she had kept on file, just in case. A familiar male voice answered five rings later.

"Yeah."

"Jimmy."

A pause for twenty seconds. "You have the wrong number."

"Don't you *dare* hang up on me, Krakowski. This is important. A matter of life or death."

"Who the hell is this?"

"I don't have time for joking around, and you know who the hell it is. Listen up and pay attention, mister."

Another pause, ten seconds. "How did you get this number?"

"What? I can get any damn thing I want, are you stupid?"

"Where are you?"

"You know I can't tell you that. I just wanted you to know that we have *Stella* in a secret medical compound, and we're doing all we can to save her."

"I saw it on the news. Is—is she alive?"

"Yes, but critically injured. *Orthoman* rescued her from the ocean; the blast burned off all her hair, but she has weak vital signs. Not breathing on her own, which isn't encouraging. She appears to have multiple fractures and possible internal bleeding, not from the bomb blast but from hitting the ocean at terminal velocity. There's no evidence of radiation damage, so she absorbed it all before she flamed out. Brain scan shows normal perfusion."

"That alone isn't good, Wendy—if you can scan her with known technology, then she's in danger. You shouldn't be able to do that."

"Of course I know that. Our hope is that those powers return soon, which may hasten her healing. There's just so much we don't understand about her."

"Yeah, tell me something I don't know. So, what now?"

"I don't really know, I'm being honest. The best trauma folks in the country are right here, but we truly are at a place where medical science has never been before. I wish you could be here, but your presence would raise all kinds of questions. Where is Bonnie?"

"I really don't know, Wendy; she hasn't come back. It's not uncommon, as she sometimes goes away for days on end without any communication, these disappearances are typical. She may be in San Diego, or—"

"Or what?"

"Or she could be there with you."

"Where, here? This is a highly secure classified military location, so don't be ridiculous."

"Don't underestimate her, she could be there, and you'd never know it, trust me. She isn't the same person you remember."

"I doubt it, but thanks for the tip, and I'll let you know of any developments. I wish you could be here, but there's no way that could work out. If we can't find Petra, then Will is the most compatible donor if she needs a transfusion or something."

"Take care of her; she's the most important thing in our lives."

"I will. I'll give you an update soon. She's my family, too. And important to America as well. And, one more thing."

"What?"

"Thanks."

"Huh? For what?"

"For raising such a wonderful daughter. I'm sure it wasn't easy with all you had to go through."

"It had its challenges, Wendy. But it was worth it, as the end result was obvious. And, for what it's worth, you did a hell of a job too with everything."

"Thanks, Jimmy. That's worth a lot. I'd like to say 'I'll see you soon', but for obvious reasons, that's not possible."

"Understood."

Chapter Fifty-Four

They watched patiently for the next thirty-six hours, her heart rate still about forty, and she still wasn't spontaneously breathing. The blistered appearance of her skin had improved as her outer epidermal layer had largely regenerated, but she was still receiving intravenous fluids and antibiotics.

Gelkis came out to the makeshift Presidential office, where she was looking at some paperwork while sitting on the sofa. She was wearing dark blue scrubs as she looked up at him sleepily.

"Len? What's up? Anything wrong?"

"That depends on your perspective. There's something of extreme importance you need to know, Ma'am."

"About *Stella?"*

"Yes." He handed her the digi-record on the tablet. "This is the lab report from when she came in. It wasn't relevant until we knew if she would survive, as we had more urgent issues to attend to, but now that she's improved somewhat, you need to know about it."

She looked at the report and opened her eyes wide. "My Lord. Her β-human chorionic gonadotropin level is 152,000 units per milliliter—I don't believe it."

He nodded. "That is indeed correct."

"But why would you have even measured this?"

"You're a physician also, Ma'am. We learn early on to expect the unexpected, isn't that so? It's standard protocol for a female her age, which you know, of course."

She opened her mouth wide. "Is—is there any unusual aspect of her physiology that would give another explanation for this extremely high value?"

He shook his head. "No, Ma'am. You must remember the old saying from medical school: 'when you hear hoofbeats, think horses, not zebras.'"

"Of course." She nodded. "But unexpected, that's for damn sure. I never would've thought in a million years—I assume you've re-checked this result?"

He held up three fingers of his right hand. "Three times. It's real, Ma'am."

"Is the β-hCG structure entirely normal?"

He shook his head. "While it's detected on the human assay, the α–subunit of her version differs by seven amino acids from native β-hCG. It's therefore not entirely a human protein. 230 of the 237 are the same. Checked that twice. Interestingly, the β–subunit is identical."

"I guess we don't know what those DNA differences mean, either, other than it confirms she's not one of us."

He nodded again. "Yes, as if there was any doubt of that. There was a vaginal discharge when she came in, and we didn't expect this, but—"

"I didn't, either, and didn't even know it was possible."

"I assume you want us to keep the tissue."

She nodded. "Yes, we may need it later for something, but I have no idea what. I just don't know how to break it to her."

"*If* she wakes up. We don't know if that will happen."

"I do, Commander."

"I admire your faith, Ma'am. Another thing to bring up, actually, Director Slabb brought it up, is that—"

"Yes?" she asked as if she already knew his query.

"It is obviously possible now to put a microchip into a bone or subcutaneous tissue in order to track *Stella's* location in the future."

"Huh. For her own safety, of course."

"That's one way of looking at it, Ma'am."

She laughed. "Right. What did you say?"

"I told him the ethics of that were questionable, but it would ultimately be your decision. He wasn't very happy about that."

"I imagine not. Commander, I may be a lot of things people don't like, but an underhanded government sneak I'm not; what you see is what you get. And I don't really give a damn what makes Slabb happy."

He laughed. "I thought you would have that opinion."

"And is there any medical indication for such a procedure?"

He shook his head. "No, Ma'am, of course not."

"Well, then, while her destiny may be different than what I had hoped, it's her decision, assuming she survives this at all. I would never do something like that or allow anyone to; I would die first. Yet, I fully expected something like that from Dexter."

Gelkis smiled. "I understand."

"Do you even know why this complex exists in the first place?"

"I can only assume it was prepared for this very moment, given that I've had literally nothing to do during my three-month stint here, nor have any of my predecessors. On the other hand, I've gotten really good at bridge and the latest video games."

She nodded. "Yes. And do you know why I feel that way about not manipulating *Stella*?"

He sat down next to her on the sofa and smiled. "I believe it's because we share a common trait, Ma'am. In the end, we're both physicians. While you have pursued another path, you can't ever take that away. No one can really understand that but us."

She nodded. "Yes, just like you can't take the manipulative lawyer out of Slabb. If he or anyone else has any other great ideas on the girl in there, have them talk to me first."

"Absolutely." He stared at her face.

"You're the best, or we wouldn't have selected you to be here. So you must have something else to tell me, correct? You said it was my decision about *Stella* because I'm the President?"

"That is Mr. Slabb's perspective, yes. It is not up to me to correct him; however, like you, I don't really care what he thinks."

"But you have another viewpoint, surely."

He nodded slowly. "I do. Slabb thinks one way, but your being President is irrelevant to any decision-making regarding her medical care."

"You told Slabb that?"

"No, Ma'am. My opinion is not relevant to him, either."

"If we were in a traditional hospital, where the customary legal chain of command would apply."

"Yes. The closest relative in presence should make decisions, in the absence of prior directives. Mr. Slabb is also an attorney, as you mentioned, he likely is aware of such."

"I see. Go on."

"It may not be my place, Ma'am, but after a cursory examination of her rather complex and unusual DNA, there, remarkably, seems to be a close biological relative in the vicinity, an event of extremely low random probability."

She put her right hand on her chin and smiled. "Interesting theory. And you have identified who that person is?"

He nodded. "I have. Any cross-references have been destroyed and no one will know but me."

She paused for several seconds and smiled. "Yes, the truth finally comes out after all these years. I had hoped it would be under better circumstances and not this soon."

"It isn't my business; you don't have to go on, Ma'am."

"It is, and I do. As you've deduced, she's my biological niece, Len, as much as she can be with whatever else is in her genome. No one in the government besides Jackie knows that, not even Slabb or Robby."

"Yes, I thought she was Aurora. But Dexter's no dummy. He will figure it out, or perhaps he already has. Either way, he does have immense respect for you."

"I know. But you, therefore, realize the reason I care so much about her."

"Yes. But we both know someday you won't be President."

"Correct, but she'll be twenty-two by then. I don't know what her future is; if she lives she may decide to tell the world one day, or not. It is not mine to decide that either."

"I understand. No one else will get that information; you have my word." He touched her on the shoulder. "But, if I may say so, Ma'am, you look very tired. Lost weight."

"Of course I am, Len, what else is new? Very stressed. I could stand to lose a few pounds."

He shook his head. "This way isn't healthy, and you don't look so good. I would recommend seeing your personal physician as soon as possible. As you know, even the President can have medical problems."

She nodded. "Yeah, know that I am one of the worst patients ever to walk this Earth, and I may be needing a new physician, since I haven't seen the old one in some time. I should have a physical, at that. We seem to have some time on our hands."

"I agree. Happy to oblige my Commander-in-Chief. I will make the arrangements."

• • •

Russ waited in his east suburban Dayton apartment with his parents. Nothing to do but wait as the world waited to see if *Stella Scura* was still alive or not. But he didn't care that much about *Stella.*

It was Paige Marshall he really cared about.

"I'm so sorry, Russ," Becky Stanton said. "I know you cared for her. She is a wonderful girl and saved many millions of lives."

"I just wish I could be there, Mom, wherever she is if she's even alive. No one knows anything about what happened."

"Isn't there any way?"

He shook his head. "No, I don't see how. *Stella* is probably at some super-secret complex somewhere, if she's alive, which is doubtful. No one even knows I exist. Even if they did, they couldn't call me. I'm a nobody."

"The Lord will find a way, son."

"Yeah, right, how trite. Crap, I'm even starting to sound like her now, and I may never see her again."

"You just have to believe, Russ."

"Sure, Mom. I know you're only trying to help."

No sooner than Becky finished her sentence, his Tekphone rang. He first thought to ignore it, but for some reason, he looked at the display, which read "The White House." Yeah, like he wanted to be bothered by someone pulling a joke. After five rings, for some unknown reason, he decided to answer it.

"Hello?" he said sharply.

"Is this Lt. Russell Stanton?" The low-pitched female drawl gave him the shivers.

"Uh—yes, it is." If this was a joke, he would kill whoever did it, especially *now*.

"Lieutenant, this is Wendy Mendoza."

He paused for five seconds. "Yes, Madam President." He watched as his parents' eyes and mouths suddenly opened wide. "Thank you for calling."

"I know I've never really met you, but I felt I owed you a phone call. Sorry for the delay, but it's been kind of busy."

It was no joke.

"Yes, Ma'am, I certainly understand. What can you tell me?"

"*Stella* did survive the nuclear blast, although she took an enormous hit, at least five thousand Gray, which would have been enough radiation to wipe out the whole New York City area. *Orthoman* was able to rescue her from the Atlantic Ocean after she hit, and we have her in a special secret medical facility now."

"Please tell me—is she going to make it?"

"Son, I'm being perfectly honest in telling you that I really have no idea. Her vitals seem stable at this point, and her electroencephalogram indicates normal brain function, although what's 'normal' for her isn't entirely known. The fact that we could measure any of that or put in IVs and such means that whatever controls her invulnerability isn't working."

"Other injuries?"

"They're extensive but not life-threatening at this time. She has a fractured right tibia and shattered left femur, a broken pelvis, seven broken ribs, and a broken left radius. There doesn't seem to be any evidence of spinal cord injury or internal damage, other than a lot of bruising. We thought we might have to remove her spleen, but that event has passed. Her hair, nails, and outer epidermal layer were vaporized, so she looks pretty bad, but they'll grow back in a few days, per my understanding.

"She's fortunate to be alive at all, hitting the ocean at terminal velocity from that height. She was submerged in freezing water for a while before Juriann found her."

"Will those things heal?"

"If she was a normal person, then I would say they are things that should heal in time. But healing does not always mean returning to the original state. Her orthopedic injuries are extensive, so she may never walk normally again. That is if she wakes up and has no permanent neurological damage. On the positive side, she seems to heal somewhat faster than normal."

"So it's just touch and go right now."

"Yes. Whether she'll wake up or be like this for a long time or even permanently, we don't know. She is also on multiple antibiotics for possible infection, as it's uncertain what the state of her immune system is, and we don't know what she has actually been exposed to in her life. She is in a sterile environment, but even innocuous bacteria we encounter every day should be life-threatening to her. However, she does, surprisingly, have a conventional population of slightly variant human immunoglobulins, or antibodies, in her serum, suggesting a recent exposure to foreign antigens within the last few weeks, with a compensatory immunoregulatory response."

"Exposure to foreign antigens?"

"Yes. That exposure may have saved her life."

"How would that have been possible?"

"We have only one theory how that could have happened, which we have you to thank for, it would seem. It's the only thing that makes any sense."

He paused for a moment. "Um, okay. But she's a brave young woman, Ma'am. She did things her way, without fear for herself."

"I know, Russ. Thirty million people owe their lives to her."

"I appreciate the call, Ma'am, but how in the world did you know to call me?"

"Well, you two are in a relationship, correct?"

"Yes, that's true."

"So I thought it only proper. Paige talks about you all the time. I know you're someone who means a lot to her. We're all she has, Russ."

"I know."

"I also hope to meet you soon. I'm sure you're a fine young officer of good character with a bright future."

"Thank you, Madam President, for everything."

"She trusted you with her greatest secret, and I promise I'll let you know if anything changes, good or bad. I also know you are very important to her."

"I just wish I could be there."

"Well, if you want to be, I can make that happen, Russ."

"Excuse me . . . what did you say, Ma'am?"

"I can have a DSD official at your apartment in Huber Heights, Ohio within the hour, and she can bring you here. I can arrange any time off you might require, but doing so might raise red flags on your relationship."

"I don't care about that, Ma'am. She's my first priority."

"Well then, we'll see you in a couple of hours, maybe sooner."

"Yes, Madam President."

He hung up the phone, with his mouth wide open.

Becky came up to him. "That was really the President? How

did she know to call you and how did she get your number?"

"She's the President, Mom, get real."

"Tell me about it, Russ." She put her arm on his shoulder.

He sat down. "Mom, it's a long story, one that I can't ever tell you. Right now, all I care about is Paige. And, one more thing."

"What?"

"The President is sending someone for me to take me to her within the hour. Help me get packed, as I have no idea what to bring or how long I'll be there."

• • •

Fifty minutes later, the doorbell to his apartment rang. He opened the door to see the tall, mid-thirtyish brunette woman.

"Lt. Russell Stanton? I'm DSD Deputy Director Loretta Baxter," she said, showing her credentials.

"Ma'am." She came into the living room of the small apartment. "These are my parents, Tim and Becky Stanton."

"Mr. and Mrs. Stanton, nice to meet you."

"Ms. Baxter, I wasn't sure what to take. I packed a bag with some clothes. I didn't know the process."

"That's fine, Lt. Stanton. Call me Lori. You are authorized by the President to stay as long as you like. The way it is going, it could be a while. Anything else you need, we can get."

"But, my commanding officer, shouldn't I talk to him?"

She shook her head. "No, that will all be taken care of. It'll be explained as a special mission, as you are on 'loan' to the DSD. No one is to ever know about this or that this facility even exists."

"Understood. How will we get there?"

"We'll drive a short distance to a special hoverjet that will take us to The Vault in eastern Virginia."

"At the Wright-Patt air hangar?"

She laughed. "No, this is well above the pay grade of anyone in the Air Force, Lieutenant."

• • •

Seventy minutes later, he was brought through the maze of high security at The Vault, given an ID badge, and rode with Lori

Baxter on the elevator down to the medical complex level.

"What *is* this place? I had heard rumors some place like this might exist. Is it solely for the President in case of emergency, like a nuclear or biological attack?"

"At one time, yes. While I can't go into the details, the President has separate facilities designated for that now. The existence of this complex, rather, was adapted to serve one specific purpose."

"I suppose I can speculate what that 'purpose' is."

She nodded. "Correct." She showed him to his "quarters," a small room with a bed, lounge chair, and desk, about the size of a dormitory room, with an attached bathroom and shower. He was then taken to a small conference room down a secured hallway after putting down his gear.

"Thank you so much, Lori. I had no idea you all were thinking of me and that the Deputy Director of DSD would make a trip herself to bring me here."

"That's my job, Russ. I'm here to serve. Anyway, there's coffee and other refreshments in the kitchen down the hall. There's a small dining area as well which serves meals to the staff and guests; they can accommodate any special dietary needs you might have."

"None, thanks. Anything you have will be fine."

"Very good. She will be in shortly to talk to you."

"What? 'She,' Lori?"

She nodded. "Yes, the President will be in to see you momentarily. She wanted to be notified immediately upon your arrival."

He walked to the kitchen two doors down and made himself an espresso from the machine as he turned around to meet someone of roughly equal height and weight, wearing a navy sweatsuit.

"Russell, it's nice to meet you, finally." Wendy extended her arms and embraced him.

"I sure wish it could be under better circumstances, Madam President. She talks about you all the time."

She looked at the Glycine Airman watch on her right wrist. "We can go see her in about thirty minutes. I assume you want to do that." They sat down as he took a sip of his coffee.

"Yes, of course. Is there a reason I wouldn't?"

"She's in pretty bad shape, as I said. It's not pretty."

"This isn't about me, Ma'am; it's about Paige. Whatever has happened, I can accept. I do have some questions for you, though, before we see her."

She nodded. "Of course. Ask me anything."

"I guess I'm not sure who knows what around here, and I don't want to let something slip. As you can imagine, I've known her since the 'start' of her career and know pretty much everything."

"So we're on the same page, can you tell me what 'everything' means to you?"

"That she's Aurora Darkkin and you're her biological aunt, among other things."

She nodded. "They only know the young woman named Cheryl Paige Marshall is *Stella Scura*. I have gone to great lengths over the years to hide the fact that Paige is actually Aurora. The DSD and the staff here don't know that, although with all the tests being done, someone will eventually figure it out. But I don't care about that right now."

"You don't?"

"No. I've known about her powers almost since she was born and knew there would be a day when everything came out into the open. I just didn't think it would happen like this."

"You've known about her being in Alaska all this time?"

She nodded. "Yes. I left them alone and tried to make sure that no one else tried to find her. Paige's stepfather was an elite computer hacker, so he helped keep her off the grid as well."

"I guess nothing could stop Paige from going out and doing all this stuff herself, as she's pretty stubborn."

"It would seem we all should be thankful for that."

• • •

"She looks worse than I thought," he said as they walked into Paige's room twenty-five minutes later. "My God."

"Actually, she looks better today than yesterday. It's just the outer skin that's burned, and that's nearly healed. The fractures, weeks. For hitting the freezing ocean at terminal velocity and being several hundred feet underwater, I'd say she's in amazing shape."

"Does she have a brain injury, since she's unconscious?"

"We don't know, Russ. She seems to have normal brain wave activity, although what's 'normal' for her is unknown. She's exhibited no spontaneous motor movement. None of this is unusual for an injury like this."

Wendy looked at the adjoining medication prep room and saw

the tall, thirtyish Hispanic nurse with two gold bars on her blue scrub uniform fumbling through the med cart. Someone with that rank should seem a bit more comfortable with her environment, she thought, as the nurse walked into the room.

"I don't remember seeing you before, Lieutenant." She stared at the unfamiliar woman, somehow feeling something wasn't right.

"Humph. I am relatively new here. This is only my third shift."

"Right." Wendy looked at her name tag. "Mendes. First name?"

"Betty." The nurse stared at her intently. "I have seen you before, though."

"Really? When did we meet?"

"It was a very long time ago."

Wendy laughed. "It couldn't be that long ago, because you aren't that old, Lt. Mendes."

"I am older than you think. It does not matter now, Madam President. All that matters now is *Stella Scura*."

"Yes, but she isn't doing as well as we had hoped."

"I know. But maybe there is something another can do."

She looked at the tall, dark-haired nurse, puzzled. "What does that mean, Lt. Mendes?"

"Nothing. Never mind."

She shook her head. "I don't believe it, after all these years. Like seeing a ghost. Couldn't you have picked a person with a less obvious name?"

"I'm sorry, Madam President?"

"You're damn good, I must admit. However, it's hard to overlook the cynical facial expression when you look at me and the obvious sarcasm in your voice. That, and the fact you have no idea what the hell you're doing."

"Ma'am, I don't understand."

Wendy grabbed the IV bag from her hand. "This is D_5W. Water with five percent glucose. This wouldn't be used right now for anything. What an idiot! She's already mildly hyponatremic due to head trauma and syndrome of inappropriate antidiuretic hormone, or SIADH. Did you *really* think you could fool me?"

"What do you mean?"

"Come in the staff room over here. Russell, please excuse 'Lt. Mendes' and I for a while." They went into the room and sat down as she closed the blinds and locked the door. "You look so damn real. How'd you get in here?"

"Humph, the cat is out of the bag, it seems. It was not difficult to fool the mindless humans."

"Where is the real Betty Mendes?"

"She is away for the weekend. I altered the work schedule by hacking into the Vault computer; it was so simple."

"That is impressive. The other way would've been for you to just ask as we would've let you in, but being excessively complex is definitely your *modus operandi.*"

"Humph. I will do what I like, I did not feel like asking for permission to see my daughter who is near death. What kind of a parent do you believe me to be? Should I not go see her now?"

"We can, in a little bit. The respiratory therapists are working with her now. If you were really Lt. Mendes, you'd know that, you irresponsible dunce."

"*Dunce?* My intellect far exceeds yours or that of any other mortal being. My IQ is over 300 now, well beyond human ken."

She laughed. "I don't think a score that high is even possible, but whatever. Even you can't fake medical knowledge, and I know your speech patterns and mannerisms too well, even after all these years. It was you who always underestimated *my* abilities."

"Spare me the stupid clichés, Wendy, as I don't need this dramatic horseshit from you. I expended a lot of energy to come out here. And you may be the boss of everyone else, but not of me. Neither my daughter nor I voted for you."

"Oh, please. This has nothing to do with my office or your political preferences, but you and I as people."

"I am no longer that person, dummy."

"Yeah? Well, I'm not, either, if you think someone can be the same after what I've gone through. Why did you let everyone think you were dead for so long?" Wendy threw down her hands and cried. "Would someone *please* explain that to me?"

"Why? Because I made a choice, the best one I could."

Wendy nodded. "Yes. To be a martyr."

"That is a comment I would expect from you, one who serves herself above all others. I don't expect you to understand higher-level thoughts."

"*Whaaat?*" Wendy poked her in the chest and shoved her back. "After all I've done for you over the years, helping to build your self-esteem—I resent that, you egotistical, arrogant ass. I'm done taking lip from you."

"Who is calling whom egotistical? Look at what you have done with your opportunities: squandered them on superficial things, conquering multiple countries and even the Moon, strutting your stuff like the obese peahen you are—"

"Be quiet, you obnoxious nincompoop. You always tried to be superior to me, and I let you think that, because of all you went through as a child, because you were then, as now, incompetent at doing ninety-nine percent of things in the world, including simple activities of daily living a five-year-old child could master." She tapped her left index finger on the shorter woman's forehead. "That IQ of 300 workin' for you okay there?"

"Hey, waitaminnit, are any of those things my fault? Have a little understanding, given what has happened to me."

"Shut up. Maybe you deserved those concessions then, but certainly not now. *Dr. Wendy's Science Squad*: I created that whole thing for you, simpleton. Show at least a morsel of gratitude."

"What are you talking about? That was your brainchild, to fulfill your colossal ego, which knows no bounds."

"Oh, finally something you don't know. I created that group because I wanted the world to admire those with disabilities, those who were different—and because I thought it would help your socialization."

"Well, congratulations, it was *such* a great success. Sorry you lost all that money promoting it."

"I didn't care about the damn money, and that was never important to you either. I had a family and a whole freaking country to lead after *Darkkday*. I couldn't go live in the Alaskan Frontier like you and Jimmy Jack."

"Yeah, well, do you think raising Aurora was easy?" Petra sputtered. "You have no idea the ulcers that girl gave me."

"You decided to have a child, they aren't a cakewalk, and surely you had some idea after Ontario Lacus that Aurora might not be the typical offspring."

She nodded. "Yes, and in some ways, I am more capable; in others, far less. It is hard to relate, being such a superior being."

"Well, goody for you, so deal with it. I also knew Aurora was unique, not the least of which is that she has a rather strong personality. I know you gave up a lot. But look at it from my perspective for a moment—you have no damn idea how hard it is to go on and run a country after your kids get blown to smithereens. Whatever you think you've endured, such as losing your husband and parents, you have no idea what *that's* like."

Petra cried. "I don't, Wendy, you are right. I try to forget that. I know having William does not replace the ones you lost."

"He helps because he is the best of both Jay and me, you know. In many ways, he's more mature than both of us combined. He has vast intellectual and leadership potential."

"And, let me guess: he wants no part of politics, correct?"

"For once, you are right on the money."

"That does not change the direction of your life."

"Sure, I definitely wasted my life. I only had to do real work without the luxury you had of disappearing while I used immense resources to allow you that little luxury."

"You didn't 'allow' me anything! A superior being such as I does as she desires, when she desires. It has always been so."

"Oh, really. How arrogant, but typical. Like you thought you could just wander stealthily into the Vault complex without my knowledge. You may have been able to fake Betty Mendes' appearance and hack into the computer so you knew she'd be off this day, but you can't duplicate her nursing expertise, despite your 'superior intellect.' I can find anyone I want at any time. I left you alone and made sure others did, too, at the cost of a crapload of political favors and ordering the DSD—an agency I created for one purpose—to threaten the hell out of anyone who had any ideas about approaching the Marshall family. So don't you *ever* get on your high horse with me, peewee. What I have, I have earned, and I have given much to others, including you."

"Humph. Am I truly a martyr? No, I care nothing about being such a thing, to have people remember me. I hope I am forgotten, actually, as I am not deserving of remembrance since I ultimately shall be responsible for the eventual ruination of mankind."

"Oh, spare me the trite self-deprecating crap, please." Wendy slapped herself in the face.

"Shut up. Others erected a memorial to my daughter in Indiana, of all places. Not much I could do about that, as she is far more deserving than my sorry butt. But I had to make a choice to raise my daughter the best way I knew how. I had no idea what to expect.

"Aurora was sitting in my lap when it happened, and I had no idea that she could survive something of that magnitude, but she apparently can, and worse. All I know is that, after the explosion in Washington, we somehow ended up in Virginia after hitting the ground at terminal velocity, without clothing, naked as the day we were born, hair and outer skin burned off. I used my superior intellect to steal from others and to survive until I could rendezvous with James—Jack—the only I thought I could contact, the one who used his illicit abilities to help me engineer new lives for us, in Fairbanks North Star Borough. It was not easy, with my lack of direction sense and inability to tell left from right. But he gave up his life to help us."

She shook her head and cried. "You could've called me, Bonnie; I would've been there for you. You can't ever say I wasn't."

"Yes, I do sincerely believe that, Wendy, but what could you have done to help? You were in the hospital and had your own terrible losses to deal with."

"At least you acknowledge that."

"Shut up and stop interrupting. While I am sorry for the loss of your children and my husband, *everything* you do is larger than life and to excess, and I didn't want your exalted talents. The things I gave the world had to go on, as I was more beneficial to the world dead than alive, it seemed. Bella had the ability to make my dreams into practical applications, so the world didn't need me any longer. I didn't want Aurora to be exploited, so I waited until she was fully grown. She was my first priority."

"And you think I didn't know all along and that she wasn't *my* priority, too? I helped, too, and stayed away, and would have destroyed anyone who tried to mess with you. You made a decision for her. Like you ever had any substantial wisdom, what a laugh."

"I made the decision I had to, as she was a child. We can debate the wisdom of one child making decisions for another, but I had little choice. And, yes, James helped, as we could not have made it without him. We all make decisions for our children. But I let her make this one. She did not go on to that mission until she was eighteen."

She shook her head in disgust. "What? Is eighteen some magical age when you know everything? I know I'd be plastered all over downtown Aurora City if she hadn't been around that day, so I'm definitely grateful, but give me a break."

"I seem to remember, long ago, meeting a wide-eyed eighteen-year-old from Tennessee, full of ideas, who wanted to change the world. I looked up to that girl once. Remember her?"

Wendy shook her head angrily. "Not really, that person is gone, too, just like Bonnie Mendoza. And that person sure didn't have it all together. You're not the only one who's changed. You think I wanted to be President for a third term? Or at all, for that matter?"

"What an inane question. You only wanted to be President because of your colossal ego. Why, *Oogly-Googly* even said so long ago, he cannot possibly be in error."

She pushed Petra back and shook her head violently. "Wrong, dumbo, you and your imbecilic purple synesthetic construct don't know everything. I get so sick of your bullshit. There is *one* reason and one reason only I became President: to provide the best possible options for *Stella*. I can continue to provide the protection she needs from those who might have unsavory motives until she is powerful enough to stand on her own two feet."

"How very magnanimous of you, Queen Mary Gwendolyn. I forgot that I am in the company of royalty. I apologize to Your Highness, Dame Commander of the British Empire." Petra bowed sarcastically. "May I kiss your ring?"

Wendy slapped her face angrily. "Don't ever make fun of me, you pompous jerk. What now? Stay in obscurity? Do you realize what you could still give the world? Studying the physics of dark energy? Realizing the possibility of interstellar flight?"

Petra shook her head and laughed. "I have given almost everything I have, so I don't know what else I have left to give. You, on the other hand, are one of the most influential figures in recent human history. There are many more poor people in the world now, Wendy, because of what you have done."

"Because of what *I* have done? Yeah, North Korea is sure way worse off now than before I came along. Listen, pal, mendozium isn't named after *me*, you know."

"I wanted it shared with the world, which includes places like Taraq and the rest of the Middle East that is not a U.S. state—I wanted no posthumous glory, how egotistical."

"There you go: you say you're not egotistical, yet over the years, you became the most arrogant person I've ever met, and one of the most violent, too."

"Humph. Yes, I regret how I acted, Wendy. It got worse after the explosion."

"You deserve good things after all you've been through. But one thing you never understood is that the world doesn't revolve around you. All this doesn't change the here and now, Bonnie."

"Yes, and the 'here and now' is that the innocent citizens of those countries do not deserve to starve because the one national resource they have is now worthless; this was not my intent."

"Of course not—you never could think anything through and the economic impact of those things on society, as you had to be given an allowance at age twenty-five because you were so irresponsible with money."

Petra shrugged. "Such trivialities are beneath my existence. One such as I should not be bothered with such mundane things as mere money."

"How ironic they put your face on U.S currency. You have no practical sense at all, what a space cadet—it took Bella years to work out the details of your theories; without her, there would be nothing but piles of paper, a result of the disorganized mess that is your mind. You can recite π to a thousand digits—"

"A hundred thousand now. Get it right, Wendy."

"Whatever, what an accomplishment—but you could barely get to the grocery and back without getting lost. You sure had no trouble finding the casinos, though, even though you never understood or cared about money. But why did you invent mendozium, then, if not to get rid of fossil fuel emissions?"

"It was *not* to make those countries poor."

"Yeah, you know a lot about politics. What the hell did you think would happen, moron? It's not my energy company, you know. I sold all my interest in it well before the 2020 election, and it was just starting out then. Talk to Bella and *Tinman* about that. They like to spend money way more than I do."

"Yes, rest assured that I shall pay those spoiled children a visit when I leave this place. But do you all not have enough wealth? And we do not need more energy. We need cures for disease, solving the population explosion, helping the disabled, etc."

"Huh. Maybe so, and I guess you can help figure out how we're going to have this perfect world with even part of your great mind, as such a task should be child's play for you."

"Likely not, funny one. Speaking of child's play, you helped so many sick and disabled children back in the day."

"Including you, if you remember."

She nodded. "Yes, including me, no one knows better."

"Maybe I can again, someday. But are you going to be around, or will you still be hanging out in Balboa Park doing card tricks? What the hell good is that to the world?"

"I will be somewhere; you can count on that. While we have come to a departure in our idealism, if you ever need anything, I will try and be there for you, although I need time to adjust."

She shrugged. "I believe you would. But there are things I need you can't provide. No one can."

"What? Something the colossal Great Dame cannot provide for herself? Heaven forbid! What could *that* possibly be?"

She shook her head. "I can't say. I'm working on a novel solution which probably won't work, and then no one will have to worry about old Wendy screwing up the world any longer."

"What the hell does that mean?"

"Figure it out, genius. I am being quite literal."

"Humph. Cryptic. But, yes, it is fortuitous to have me as an ally, as you would rather have me as friend than foe."

"Sure, whatever. Same here. It's great to end on such a positive note with you incessantly talking about yourself. I'll make sure we get you out of here as soon as we can."

"Can we go for what we came for now?"

Wendy looked at her watch. "Sure, I guess so. You're biologically cleared, Lt. Mendes."

Petra gave her a hug. "I am sorry for what I have become, my sister, it is not something I am proud of. I had turned my back on the humility that made me who I was, and had become arrogance personified. Maybe this can be a new beginning for me, somehow."

"Again, always about you, isn't it? How arrogant."

"Let me finish if you are capable of that. I was happy being deaf. I didn't want to be injected with alien DNA by Rita McPherson, be in the *Darkkday* explosion, and develop augmented senses. By some miracle, I am normal again, or as normal as I can be. I only wish I could do the same for Aurora, as I know the burden she carries."

"Wishing doesn't make it so, Bonnie."

"Maybe wishes do come true, sometimes."

They ended their long conversation and returned slowly to the room as Cdr. Gelkis looked at "Betty" curiously.

"Lt. Mendes, where have you been?"

"Humph. Talking to your big boss here, what else? Duh."

"That's not an appropriate way to address the President, or me,

Lieutenant. This is stressful for all of us, but get a grip."

"It is better than some things I could say. So like it or lump it." She looked at Russ. "Who the hell are you?"

"Air Force First Lieutenant Russell Stanton, Ma'am."

"*Ma'am?* Huh? I am a nurse but no ma'am."

He shrugged. "You're one rank above me, Lieutenant."

"Oh, yeah. Navy Lieutenant is higher, I guess."

"Russ, witness the phenomenal IQ of 300 in action." Wendy looked towards him and shook her head. "Len. Look carefully. She isn't who she appears to be."

"What? She's Betty Mendes, she may be fairly new here, but I worked with her at Walter Reed, I'd know her anywhere."

"Yeah, then ask her a medical question, and I bet you'll think differently."

Gelkis stared at the tall brunette nurse for half a minute as she went over and put her hand on her daughter's shoulder.

"Mendes, what are you doing?"

"What I must, primitive physician."

"What the hell does that mean?"

I look at you and see my complicated life pass before my eyes.

What has happened?

You have given much to me.

Perhaps now it is time for me to give back what I have borrowed to you. In the end, it is all for the best.

Whatever happens to me is of no consequence.

She put her hands over Paige's face as a brilliant light—first red, then orange, yellow, and all through the spectrum, ending in violet, changing color each half-second—filled the room and a shock wave threw them all against the far wall, as a half-dozen security personnel entered the room, shattered window glass all over the place.

"What the hell just happened?" Wendy said, rubbing her head as she rose up off the floor several minutes later.

"Are you all right, Ma'am?" Russ said.

"Yeah, I think so, but something's wrong."

Wendy, Russ, Gelkis, and the other staff picked themselves off the floor as they saw Lt. Mendes with her hands still on her face.

She turned towards 'Betty.' "What did you do to her?"

"I just gave her back something she gave me over twelve years ago. I tried to tell you that, but you never listen to me."

"Hold that thought." Wendy shook her head calmly as she took her pulse and temporarily paused the ventilator. "Look, she's now breathing spontaneously, and she has a strong pulse rate of 104, despite the monitor reading asystole now. Len, do you concur?"

"Yes, you're correct. The heart monitor suddenly went flat line because the electrical impulses won't conduct through her skin anymore, which is probably good. In her normal state, she has almost infinite electrical resistance, Bivereaux said, thus the reason for 'asystole.'" The IV then popped out as two more nurses entered and rushed to the bedside.

"And then, that. So what's going on, Russ? You should be able to figure it out."

"She's regaining her powers, of course, Ma'am. Her invulnerability has returned, at least partially, resulting in non-conduction of electricity and the IV being ejected."

They looked as another alarm went off.

"What? Why is that alarm going off?" Wendy asked.

Gelkis looked at it intently. "It's a weight alarm; it sounds when a patient's weight changes by a certain amount, possibly indicating an excess of fluid. Or a decrease, by getting out of bed."

"Yeah, I know what it is, but excess fluid is clearly not the case. How much extra mass are we talking here?"

"It increased by approximately twenty kilograms—in about *ten seconds*. It must be an instrumentation error."

"Or from gravitational field flux," Russ said.

"Maybe. I would imagine worse to have happened in here if that was the case," she said. "Like us being obliterated."

Then, they watched as 'Betty' suddenly collapsed to the floor, blood running from her nose.

"Again, who the hell is that?" Gelkis said. "She may look and sound like Betty, but it's not her. She talks differently, as you said."

"I think we both know." They watched as the scrubs-wearing Navy nurse assumed the form of a white-haired Hispanic woman in her early fifties over the next fifteen seconds.

"Holy crap," Russ said. "I don't believe it. Is that really—"

"Yes, Lieutenant, it sure is. Time to meet your girl's mom."

"How—is that possible?" Gelkis asked.

"Commander, you might have just witnessed a genuine miracle, one you will likely never encounter again."

• • •

They put the breathing but unconscious "Betty Mendes" in another room as she came to thirty minutes later. Wendy watched as her old friend slowly came out of consciousness.

"Bonnie. Wake up."

She suddenly became completely alert as she saw the large blonde woman's face come into focus.

"Are you okay?"

She looked around, puzzled. "I don't know, I suppose so. Why am I in a bed that is not mine? *Staphylococci*, that's it."

"Staph? You don't have a staph infection, so why would you say something random like that?"

"Humph. That was the winning word at the 1987 Scripps National Spelling Bee at the Capital Hilton, that's why. Don't you know that, lady? Where have you been?"

"Interesting that you remember that from so long ago. I wasn't aware you could recall events back that far."

"Long ago? Huh?" She looked around the room for several seconds. "I have two initial questions. Where am I, in a clinic or hospital? I do not like doctors, as they are all stupid."

Wendy nodded. "Sort of, yes. What's your second question?"

"Who—are you?"

"Come on. You don't know?"

"If I did, I wouldn't ask, would I? Duh!"

Wendy smiled. "I'm an old friend, and my name is Wendy."

"Wendy—I don't know any Wendy. I have an eidetic memory, I would remember that."

"Do you know your name?"

She crossed her arms. "Of course I know my name, it is Bonita Maria Mendoza Flores, what a stupid question, gal."

"That's correct. What is your birthday?"

"Humph." She took a few sips of water from a glass on the bedside table. "What is this dumb old place again?"

"As you astutely observed, you're in a hospital."

"Well, why am I here? Was I in an accident? I don't hurt anywhere."

Wendy nodded. "Sort of. Kind of hard to explain."

"Not a very coherent answer. Are you a doctor? Wearing a crummy sweatshirt instead of scrubs?"

She laughed. "I am, although that's not what I do now."

"Did you get fired? I have a reject as my doctor?"

"I said I was *a* doctor, not *your* doctor."

She sighed. "Thank goodness. Anyway, my birthday is August 6, 1976. Happy?"

"That's correct. Which would make you how old now?"

"It is September 1987, I said that already, so I am eleven years old. Can't you count, or is the simple subtraction of integers beyond your limited intellect?"

"You really believe that?

"That you have limited intellect?" She nodded. "Absolutely."

Wendy laughed. "No, that you are eleven."

"Of course, what else?" She looked at her hands. "Hey, I can't see my hands; they're blurry! I'm going blind! What's wrong with me? Did I stupidly drink aftershave and get methanol poisoning? Have I had a stroke? I knew living life on the edge would have consequences."

"You aren't going blind." Wendy smiled and handed her a pair of +2.00 diopter reading glasses. "Here, you might need these."

She frowned and pushed her hand away. "I don't need any stupid old glasses. I have perfect vision."

"Not any more you don't, it seems."

"Barf me out." She reluctantly put the large glasses on.

"Well? Is that better?"

"No, it's worse! I can now see my hands, but what's happened to them? I'm wrinkled—old. But now you and the rest of the room are blurry." She thought for a moment. "Get me a mirror."

"Sure. Knock yourself out." The large blonde woman handed her a small mirror from the dresser.

She looked at the light gray-haired woman in the reflection and gasped. "What has happened to me? I am an old woman, I must have somehow developed progeria! How can this be?"

"Bonnie, you're fifty-two years old, and you don't have progeria. You're not old, but definitely not eleven."

"What is wrong with my eyes, then?"

She sighed. "At your age, you have moderate presbyopia, so your eyes can no longer focus on close objects. It's a natural milestone of aging, so get used to it."

"What happened to me?"

"You had an—incident that seems to have affected your cortical function. You really believe it's 1987?"

"Of course it is, I am the world's greatest speller, I just won that bee four months ago. Two years in a row."

"And who is the President?"

"Humph, I just had lunch with him two weeks ago—Ronald Wilson Reagan, of course; how can you ask such an inane question? I have heard of you wild Appalachian people, and you are as uneducated as I would have imagined. I did not know your kind even wore shoes!"

Wendy shook her head and stuck out her left foot, clad in a vintage Adidas Superstar sneaker. "No, dear. *I* am the President, and I *do* wear shoes. Ladies size thirteen, to be exact."

"Huh? The president of what? A moonshine company?"

Wendy laughed again. "No, that would've been my grandfather, Dirk T. Darkkin, but that's another story. I am, rather, the current President of the United States. It is January 2029."

"Liar, you said you were a doctor."

"I was. I have a different job now, as I said."

She laughed hysterically. "A hillbilly President? Gag me with a spoon. America could not possibly have come to this."

"It's true. I'm only half hillbilly, though. The other half is upper crust British aristocrat."

"Huh, you sure don't sound like it. Anyway, why would the President be in a hospital room with me? That is illogical."

"You just said you knew Reagan."

She nodded. "This is true. You are a far cry from him."

"Granted. I'm also one of your oldest friends. We met when you were thirteen, which appears to explain why you don't remember me now, as that event hasn't happened yet for you."

"I am sorry that I have never seen you before. I assure you that I would remember seeing someone as weird as you."

"The other reason I'm here is because we're family. My name is Wendy Mendoza."

She studied the freckled white blonde woman's build and features and smiled. "Not even! We cannot possibly be related."

"Not biologically, of course. I am your sister-in-law."

"You are married to Miguel, then?"

"No—Jay."

She squinted. "*Jaime?* Impossible! I cannot imagine that boy being married; it is beyond mortal comprehension. You must've been desperate, as he cheated on all his girlfriends."

Wendy laughed. "Yeah, tell me about it."

"So where is my lethargic, dullard brother, then?"

"He's on his way. It will take him about an hour to get here."

"Is he old, too?" she asked sarcastically.

"Yes, he is eight years older than you, this you know. You were also my sister-in-law when you were married to my brother."

"Your brother? I was married?"

"You were. He died, I'm sorry."

She took a drink of water. "My husband? I don't remember him, so I regret I feel no remorse, but I'm sorry for your loss. Did we have children?"

Wendy nodded. "Yes. More on that in a moment."

"Where is Jaime coming from?"

"The White House with our son. He is, er, your age, eleven."

"Miguel, Mom, Dad, and the others? When are they coming?"

"We don't need to discuss them now."

She grabbed Wendy's left wrist with her right hand. "You had better tell me now."

Wendy sighed and sat down next to her bed. "Okay, but this won't be easy, Bonnie. Most of your living relatives are dead. They died in an act of terrorism in 2016. A small nuclear missile was fired at the plane several miles from Washington."

"Plane? What was its destination?"

"Sweden. Going there for your Nobel Prize."

"Nobel Prize? Me? No, I don't believe that."

Wendy nodded. "You were to be awarded the Nobel Prize in physics. You're one of the greatest theoretical physicists of all time and discovered a unique transuranium element that changed the world. I will be happy to show you all the proof you need."

"But where was I? Why was I not on that plane?"

Wendy squeezed her right hand. "You *were* on it, dear. You and your daughter were the only survivors."

"I have a daughter? I am eleven years old. Girls may become moms at that age where you come from, but not me."

"You're fifty-two."

"Oh, yeah, I had better get used to that." She looked around the room and thought for several seconds. "Everyone else is dead?"

She squeezed Bonnie's right hand. "Yes, Bonnie, I'm sorry."

"I am speechless, and this will take a long time to register. How old is my daughter now?"

"She's eighteen."

"But it's impossible that I could have been on that plane. We would've been vaporized if it had been hit by a nuclear device."

"No, it's possible with a daughter who is basically a demigoddess—an incredibly powerful metahuman capable of withstanding even a nuclear explosion. She has done it twice."

Bonnie laughed. "You are either delusional or joking."

"I'm not, Bonnie. I know all this is hard to grasp, but please bear with me."

She stared at Wendy. "None of that is possible. I may be eleven, but I am likely smarter than you."

"Possibly. I can give you a run for your money, though."

"Even if it's true she could survive that, how did I?"

"She can absorb vast amounts of energy of any form, and her indestructibility is transferred to anyone in direct contact with her skin, hence why you're here."

"I don't believe it. Then where is this amazing being who supposedly is my incredible daughter?"

"She's in the next room; she absorbed the energy from a much larger warhead this time and saved New York City. She had lost her powers and was near death, and you showed up and did some kind of mind-meld, at which point some of her powers returned, and she is rapidly improving. This left you in this state."

"I don't believe that either."

"Believe it, Bonnie. You and I had a long talk before we could go see her."

"*Demigoddess?* Come on—even if that's true, I am clearly the human portion, so who is the other?"

Wendy shook her head. "No. You were the one with the special abilities, apparently from a race of beings comprised completely of dark energy. Trust me, it's a *very* long story."

She snickered. "Dark energy beings? I assume you have met and seen these divine entities?"

"No, of course not, but *you* claimed to have talked to them. Your daughter has as well."

"How ludicrous. I am no goddess."

"Not now, but a lot of stuff happened to you in your thirties and forties. Whatever special abilities you had must have been eliminated in the 'event' that resulted in your current situation."

"What is her name?"

"Aurora Angelica. You named her after the Roman goddess of dawn and an angel. It will take me a long time to explain, but she has almost complete invincibility and the ability to warp gravitational fields to propel herself at supersonic speeds and lift objects of enormous mass. She would've fared better after the explosion had she not absorbed all the energy, but then NYC and its population would have been destroyed or seriously damaged."

"So your brother was this girl's father?"

"Yes, he was your first husband and he died in the explosion. All that is left are me, Jaime, Mike's daughter Isabel, and our son William."

"I have a second husband, at age eleven? *Please* tell me I don't have a third."

"He was your husband's best friend and came to your aid after the explosion. As I mentioned, it's rather complicated, but you and Aurora went to live in North Pole, Alaska, and took on different identities as the world thought you dead. She goes by the name Paige Marshall."

"Why would we have done that?"

"Because the girl we are about to see was the world's greatest secret, and she needed time to grow in a simple, humble existence before transforming into what she is today."

"Enough of this malarkey. Let's go see her."

"Okay, but she doesn't look real great."

• • •

They walked into Paige's new room, as they were still cleaning up and repairing the one down the hall that had been damaged in the prior 'incident.' Russ was sitting in a lounge chair.

"Who are you?" Bonnie asked.

"I'm Russell Stanton, Paige's friend."

The fifty-two-year-old preteen stared at him for several seconds. "Friend? As in boyfriend?"

He nodded. "Yes, Ma'am, that's about it."

"Oh, brother. Don't call an eleven-year-old girl 'Ma'am.'"

"Sorry. I guess you aren't my superior officer any longer."

"Hey, you weren't kidding, Wendy; she looks very bad."

"She's taken a pretty severe beating, but one interesting thing about her is that her nonliving cells, or her outer epidermal layer and hair, can be destroyed. The outer skin has largely regenerated; the hair will take longer. Inside, she's much better now."

"If she's better, why does she have a cast on her arm and both legs, then?"

"She absorbed a three hundred megaton nuke. If she'd just let the wave pass around her instead of absorbing it all, then she might have come out less damaged, but then New York City would have been destroyed, even ten miles above it."

"She will presumably recover?"

"We believe so now, thanks in great part to you. You did some kind of 'mind-meld' that somehow infused her with energy, which revived her, but seems to have left you in this unique state. She does have one peculiar preexisting characteristic for which we have no great explanation."

"What?"

"She's been blind ever since the first nuclear explosion in 2016. We can't determine why, as there appears to be no physical damage to her eyes, but the best theory going is that the blast overloaded her retinas with light and her brain shut off as a kind of protective mechanism."

"Can—she see at all?"

Wendy nodded. "Not normally, but she can see with the aid of a special sapphire visor which filters out specific wavelengths of visual light. Her acuity is excellent, but her color perception is limited, something we are working on. But, without it—nothing. This device was created by Isabel—Miguel's daughter—who would be your niece."

"This Isabel, is she like me?"

Wendy shook her head. "Not really, other than she has dark hair and eyes like you and has a Nobel Prize as well. She is substantially shorter than you and has a very rare talent."

"What is that?"

"She has the power of parsimony—to see through all extraneous information to solve a problem in the fastest and most efficient way possible, even one she's never seen before. You'll meet Bella soon. She is a rather interesting person."

"But, President Wendy, Aurora has no intravenous tubing or

anything. What kind of a backwoods hospital can this be?"

"It is probably the most advanced medical facility in the world. She's getting fluids through the nasogastric tube, which is all she currently needs. It isn't possible to start an IV."

Bonnie turned her head sideways. "Well, why not?"

Wendy removed a large-bore IV catheter from the tray, took off the sheath, and plunged it into her abdomen, where she met resistance. "Because she's now regained her invulnerability, and the hardest diamond drill in existence couldn't penetrate her skin."

"How the heck did she catch a nuclear missile?"

"She has the ability to manipulate dark energy and convert it to gravitational and kinetic energy. You know what dark energy is?"

"Of course I do, what a stupid question, but that still doesn't answer my query."

"She has the native ability of supersonic flight."

"Supersonic? Impossible. Mach 1? 2?"

"She's hit nearly 10, with the assistance of a special aerodynamic suit that diminishes air friction. Without it, she's limited to about Mach 6 or 7."

"Do her powers work in space?"

"Yes."

"How do you know this?"

"She's flown to Luna on a shuttle and has made multiple lunar orbits similar to the paths of the Apollo missions."

"A moon shuttle? For tourists? Why would anyone go there?"

"It's a state, for one reason."

"Why would any idiot make that stupid desolate rock a state?"

Wendy smiled. "The idiot would be me because the far side contains vast amounts of helium-3, used in cold fusion, facilitated by the element you discovered—Element 119, or mendozium."

"Humph, there is much I need to learn about myself and the advancement of the world. So, what do we do now?"

"We wait, and we need to keep our eye on you, too. Since we appear to have some time on our hands, I have another old friend of yours who's on her way."

"Who is that?"

"You'll see, she'll arrive momentarily. You could use her help. Probably me, too. I need all I can get."

Chapter Fifty-Five

The diminutive elderly woman, sporting a long floral print dress straight from 1972 and thick, waist-length white hair, entered the conference room after a three-hour meeting with her most fascinating patient. She sat down and smiled at Wendy, another person she had known for decades.

"Bobbi, thanks again for coming on such short notice. I didn't know who else to call as this is quite an unusual problem, above the level of anyone here. Other than Jay, you're the one person she would remember."

Dr. Roberta Elsevier, the seventy-six-year-old well-known retired medical school professor and personal psychiatrist of Bonita Mendoza Flores and several other celebrities, looked at her in amazement.

"I'm happy to be here, Wendy, although I was somewhat taken aback when the DSD arrived at my door in Tarpon Springs and told me I needed to do an urgent consult on an old patient of mine in a secret military complex, but wouldn't tell me *who*. I, like pretty much everyone else, thought she was long dead. Like you, I came very close to being on that plane."

"I know. Did she recognize you?"

Bobbi nodded and took a sip of coffee. "Not by my appearance, of course, which is over forty years older than she remembers me, but by my voice, sure, given her ability of absolute pitch."

"Yeah, we all look different, for sure. What do you think?"

"Know that I haven't had time to do more than cursory intelligence tests. However, this version of Bonnie is clearly profoundly gifted. Her eidetic memory recalls events back to about age two or three, but nothing after eleven, although she's absorbed an enormous amount of information already in the time it took me to get here, as you've given her access to the Internet and various media.

"While she hadn't learned much magic at that age, her celebratory cipher skills are clearly present, as are her verbal abilities. In addition to her native English and Spanish, she speaks and writes Italian, Latin, French, Greek, German, and Portuguese fluently, but not Russian yet—ironically, the language she taught Aurora. She correctly recalls the current events of the time in detail, as well as the family pets—the beagle Pythagoras and the Maine Coon Euclid—and she is in fall 1987, as she says. She is, of course, a high-level grapheme-color synesthete who is clearly on the autism spectrum, although we didn't know nearly as much about it then as we do now. These factors match my records of her at that age. Interestingly, there's no mention of the intangible synesthetic construct known only as *Oogly-Googly*."

"She's forgotten about him?"

Bobbi shook her head. "It's unclear, but I don't think so. Rather, she seems not to care. She tried to summon it without success, but she then moved on to something else, given her typical short attention span for things she's uninterested in. Given that her hearing is fully intact, seeing him should have been simple to do."

"That's probably for the best, as he was nothing but trouble. Of note, when she touched Aurora, there was a blinding flash of light that cycled through the visible spectrum, so maybe he died, if that's even possible. Good riddance. What about her other senses?"

"The synesthesia makes it difficult to measure them without my specialized equipment, but they appear to be normal, although clearly not equal to hers at eleven, given she's now in a fiftyish body. All senses decline somewhat with age, but you know that."

"They were superhuman a few hours ago."

"I have no explanation for that, but she was clearly 'rebooted' after the incident with Aurora."

"What about her physical condition?"

"Above average hand-eye coordination, of course, but not equal to her as a tween or young adult, no way. Her left-right disorientation is clearly apparent. Muscle strength is excellent for a fifty-two-year-old."

"But not exceptional."

"No, of course not. Nowhere likely near your level, assuming you still work out."

Wendy laughed. "Paige said her mom could bench press eight hundred pounds, and obviously that's no longer possible. I can't believe this. She almost died at eleven for meningitis which is when she initially lost her hearing, and never had any recollection of her childhood thereafter. And now *that's* intact, but nothing afterward? How much more can the world's greatest brain take?"

"It would appear so, but there is a remote possibility that some memories will return later. She appears to have an incredible amount of neuronal reserve and resiliency. Of note, remember she's capable of assimilating incredible amounts of information at an unprecedented pace, in an effort to fill in the gaps of the memories she lost, so that distinction blurs with every passing second."

"It's what she always wanted, you know."

"Come again, Wendy?"

"We met when we were both teenagers, you know. I was her best friend for many years; with all the incredible things she has done, her fondest wish was always to have those memories back, to be a child again."

"It looks like she got her wish. But what do we do with her now? Send her back to North Pole with Krakowski? Lord, I don't recall him being the most responsible individual."

"Jim has matured quite a bit, but I suppose that's the best plan. She clearly has the ability to teach her classes. I would have no idea what to do with her here. I don't see her fitting in with Bella and Nick very well, but she never did. What's our story?"

"We could easily state she was in an accident and had a moderate traumatic brain injury with some amnesia. That would require the creation of some records to substantiate that."

"That's not a problem, trust me."

"Sure, Wendy. Since you brought me all the way out here, though, I now have some questions for you."

"Shoot."

"How is Aurora—Paige—doing?"

"She has improved dramatically. She is fully breathing on her own and is exhibiting normal brain wave activity, and is moving spontaneously."

"Isn't that a concern, that she's moving while unconscious?"

Wendy nodded. "Yes, of course it is, Bobbi. It's conceivable she could accidentally destroy this place even in a significantly diminished state. She caused a Hiroshima-level event in West Virginia a week ago, leveling an entire research complex with shock waves from her body. Not just buildings broken down but completely obliterated. I don't know what we can do about it, and it's not possible for us to sedate her now after her 'incident' with Bonnie. They wanted to move me somewhere else for my safety, but I'm staying put. We've also noticed something else pretty bizarre since then."

"What?"

"About once every few hours, parts of her body seem to 'phase out' and become somewhat transparent. Not entirely invisible, but you can definitely see through her, with some distortion. It appears to be some warping of light around her body; Biv and the DSD scientists are a long way from figuring it out."

"Is she phasing into another dimension?"

She shook her head. "Her mass remains the same, so it doesn't seem so."

"Could she do that before?"

Wendy shook her head. "No. Johnny had theorized that might eventually be possible, but apparently what was taken from Petra has given her new abilities, with perhaps more to come we don't even know about."

"That sounds somewhat dangerous, I mean, if gravity is causing the light to distort."

"Yeah, tell me about it."

"Alex and Bonnie never told me about Aurora's abilities when she was young. She didn't seem to be intellectually gifted like her mother, except for her command of English, which was exemplary. I assume she still rhymes and alliterates like she did as a small child?"

She nodded. "Yes, it's pretty prevalent and can be very annoying, although I would give anything to be 'annoyed' by her right now."

"So, being a superhero was her big career plan? One I assume was endorsed by her immature mother and stepfather?"

"Maybe. I'm not sure it was really thought out, but it looks like she decided to venture out on her own. If not for Air Force One flaming out over Aurora City, she might not have appeared at all. Science and math are not her strengths, as she has more of an interest in the law."

"Interesting choice of profession. As much as she will have to speak as an attorney, depending on her specialty, she had better master the ability to change her speech patterns between the two. The way she talks was unique as a small child, and I assume she still speaks that way."

"Yeah, she does, one of many challenges she must face. Jan Kapoor told her the same thing."

"Bonnie was always upset that Aurora's mathematical abilities were only average. That being said, I always suspected something was up with her physically."

"How so?"

"I was trained as a child psychiatrist, as you know, so I saw lots of children and was very adept at noticing small things. All children show small cuts, abrasions, and bruises at visits, given that kids are active and are subject to minor trauma."

"But Aurora's skin was always pristine, except for some minor scrapes on her outer epidermal layer."

"That, and the fact that she was never sick that I knew of." Bobbi took another sip of coffee. "Aurora never remembered anything after the explosion?"

"Apparently not. Like Bonnie losing her memory after becoming sick at eleven, Paige remembers nothing. It's likely very interesting to you from a neurological standpoint how that can be. She was only told she was born in the United States."

"Bonnie told her about it later?"

"No." She took a sip of coffee. "She pulled some crazy stunt trying to stop what she thought were enemy fighters crossing the Bering Strait, and her armor was damaged. She was eventually found by Bella, who told her everything. I don't think Aurora and Bonnie were on the best terms after that."

Bobbi's tiny frame sat back in the chair as she peered through thick eyeglasses. "A more fascinating family of beings I have never encountered, this much is for sure. There is one unfulfilled professional goal I have, though."

"What's that?"

Bobbi laughed. "That I never had *you* for a patient. Any good doctor worth her salt desires a monumental challenge."

She shook her head. "I think you would've run for the hills and quit medicine right then, Bobbi. Trust me on that one."

• • •

She was flying through the air at terminal velocity, allowing the Earth's gravitational pull to bring her to Earth at one hundred twenty miles per hour. Then she realized she was seeing without the visor and it couldn't possibly be real. Where was she flying to?

No crummy Gart-Monn, which was a relief. Either she was really dead now, or not that far gone, but she was just glad his sorry energy butt wasn't around. Oh, my God, she woke up suddenly realizing there was pain, a lot of it, all over her body. She hadn't really felt that before, except a tiny bit when her mom slapped her. She couldn't imagine how "normal" people dealt with that.

She was wearing what felt like a cotton hospital gown; she felt her hairless head and lack of eyebrows or hair anywhere else. She expected that after what had happened.

She didn't expect to feel the plaster casts on both legs and her left arm; at least that's what they seemed like. It also hurt like hell to breathe in the anterior rib cage. She was clearly in a hospital, but what other terrible injuries had she suffered?

Then, in the background, she heard a disgusting sound, a horrible grinding noise, like a sea monster or some poor animal caught in a meat grinder. She then realized that the grating sound seemed to get louder, then stop for about thirty seconds, then resume again, with the monster gasping for air or something, taking breaths in between swallowing its prey.

It was in the room with her, not more than a few feet away.

Bella taught her Occam's razor: the simplest explanation is likely the best one, and logic dictated that it likely belonged to someone more familiar and much smaller than any monster.

She sat up, smiled, and clumsily moved over to the edge of the bed next to the irregularly breathing being, still sputtering ghastly noises. What a way to wake up from saving the world. She tapped the large person on the shoulder as she winced in pain from the movement.

"Huh? What the heck—" Wendy sputtered.

"Owww. I am no physician, but they say you should use your sleep apnea machine even when you are napping, because it does not help unless you actually wear it!"

"What? How did you know about my sleep apnea?"

She laughed. "It is not hard, as you have been snoring loud

enough to wake the dead, which includes me, it seems. I thought you were a beast gnawing on some poor rodent, except when you stop breathing, which is fairly often, then it is quiet."

Wendy laughed. "Sorry. I should really have it hooked up. They should have a unit around here somewhere. As you can imagine, we've had some other priorities."

She shook her head snidely. "I guess it is true what they say, that doctors are not very good patients."

"You got that right; I'm the worst of the worst." She felt Wendy put the visor on her head. "You didn't think we'd let you go without getting a shot at the Presidential election in twenty or so years, did you? And all the great stuff you'll accomplish by that time?"

"Guess you wanted to see how I would turn out." She looked through the visor as things came into focus. "Huh, you must have procured one of the extra ones from Biv or Bella. The one I had on was kind of vaporized."

"Except New York wasn't, thanks to you."

"About that, I have seen better days," she said, looking at the three plaster casts. "No one signed them, and that is unacceptable."

"Sorry." Wendy laughed as she took out a red felt tip pen and autographed each of the three casts.

"Thank you; this will increase my net worth of zero when I sell my casts on E-Auction, as my converting coal to diamonds scheme was a failure. But how the heck did this happen?"

"You don't remember?"

She shook her head. "No. I blacked out seconds after the detonation. Absorbing that amount of energy must have overwhelmed even me."

"Yeah. You hit the water at terminal velocity—one hundred twenty miles per hour—you're fortunate to even be alive. You have a number of fractures and metal rods in your femur and pelvis."

"How long have I been out?" She rubbed her nearly-bald head. "Not long, from the primordial follicles sprouting on my head."

"Five days and seventeen hours. We moved you out of a sterile environment after two days."

"How did I get here?"

"You landed in the Atlantic Ocean, about fifty miles off the coast. Juriann fished you out at four hundred feet below, and you've been here ever since."

"Yes, but *where* are we? Bethesda?"

Wendy shook her head. "Hardly. We're at The Vault, in eastern Virginia. No one except the most secret types knows this place exists. I didn't think you needed the commotion, with regular hospital visitors and all."

"New York?"

"It's completely intact, Paige. You absorbed pretty much the whole thing and saved everyone, but at great personal cost to you, however."

"That is good, although I imagine I will heal in time." She lay back and closed her eyes. "Mom and Dad, do they know what happened?"

Wendy nodded. "I've talked to your dad twice. Your mom was nowhere to be found for days but showed up two nights ago."

"Huh? Showed up where? North Pole?"

"No, here. She's in the next room."

"Why isn't she in here with us, then?"

"Because she's here as a patient."

"What happened? Did she get injured?"

"In a manner of speaking, yes. She came to see you, having mind-control-morphed into one of our nurses, and did some kind of weird mind-meld thing that somehow brought you out of your coma, accompanied by a shock wave and a brilliant burst of rainbow-colored light that appears to have been the last gasp of your mom's best bud *Oogly-Googly*."

"*Oogly* is no more? What a horrific tragedy." She snickered. "Yet, he gave his 'life' to save mine, so I will try to remember him in some positive fashion."

"We were very worried that we were going to lose you. Right after that, you regained your invulnerability, started breathing on your own, and you woke up just now, a little less than a day later."

"*Nurse?* My mom has no knowledge of medicine, and her providing any form of health care is scary indeed."

"She has some pretty wicked mind-manipulation powers, you know. She fooled most of the staff and got through security without a hitch but didn't fool me or the head doctor given her lack of medical knowledge, as you said. I also know how uniquely she talks, even after all these years. Finally, I could see the reaction on her face when first she saw me. Not one of jubilation."

"Is she okay?"

"It depends on who you ask. She seems perfectly happy. Me,

I'm a bit freaked out."

"What the hell does that mean, aunt who is not lean?"

"She seems to have lost some brainpower and her extraordinary senses. Hearing is normal, which, for her, is pretty good."

"What? That is terrible! How can you be so nonchalant about such a thing, you dingaling?"

"And, just so you know, she now seems to have the mind of an eleven-year-old Bonnie in a fiftyish body. I have seen a lot of weird stuff in my life, but never anything like this, although her mind at eleven is still pretty formidable."

"That will take some time to digest. Is she—otherwise herself?"

"I think so. Realize I haven't seen her for over twelve years, aside from our lengthy conversation right before this all happened, but she seems to be the person I knew when we first met. I suspect that is a bit different than the one you're used to."

"I need to go see her."

"A little later. She's resting now. She has also, somehow lost about fifty pounds, but doesn't look any different."

"What does that mean?"

"Wasn't she always much heavier than you, despite you being approximately the same size?"

She nodded. "Yes, but we could never figure out why."

"It appears to have been some change in her physiology from the Ontario Lacus incident, which seems to have been rectified. She no longer has any extranormal powers other than the ones she had as a child, such as her cipher and verbal abilities, which seem to be intact. Her old psychiatrist is here on-site, one of the few people she would remember."

"Mom had a personal psychiatrist? Why am I not surprised?"

"Sure, Dr. Roberta Elsevier, the world's foremost expert on your mom. She knew and met with you as a child also, but you likely wouldn't remember that."

"Where did all that extra mass go?"

"Most of it seems to have gone to you."

"Went to me? How can this be?"

"Your body, while the same size, is more robust than before, and you now weigh about two hundred ten pounds."

She looked at herself and shrieked. "This cannot be true! I look exactly the same, Dame."

"Yet, you are healing at an extraordinary rate, and it seems that this change was necessary in order for you to have recovered."

"*This* is recovered? Do you need to go back to medical school?"

"You should've seen yourself before your mom showed up. You were on a ventilator with minimal brain activity."

"It does not sound like a pretty sight." She thought for a moment. "I need to let someone else know about me being here."

"Yes, I know. I talked to Russ right after you came here. I knew that would be important to you."

"Russ?" She smiled curiously. "How did you know his name?"

"I'm the President. I'm also your favorite aunt. I know lots of things. Such items are high on my priority list."

"What a lame statement. You are also my *only* aunt."

"And *you* need to learn some better stealth techniques, dear."

She sat up again. "I am thirsty, have you got some Gatorade?"

"Right here, we're prepared this time." She took two twenty-ounce bottles from the cooler and gulped them down.

"Haven't you been giving me IV fluids?"

"We did until about two days ago, as well as antibiotics, as we weren't sure how your body would fight off infection."

"Why are you worried about that?"

"Because you haven't been exposed to the normal germs the rest of us are every day, you haven't developed immunity, we thought. But we got some surprises about that—you had more than we thought."

"Yes, Biv was concerned about my lack of immune factors when we were experimenting in Sulphur Springs, although most of that was speculation."

"You regained your invulnerability, or whatever you call it, about two days ago, when your IVs came out and could not be replaced. We put some fluids down your nasogastric tube after that."

She pulled on the nasogastric tube that had been placed into her stomach. "You can imagine my next question: when can I get the hell out of here?"

"Whoa, while that sounds like the Paige I know, that's a big order, honey. First of all, while it appears you heal at a faster rate than the average person, it will still be a couple of weeks until you get those casts off. Next, the second we get out of here, you'll have people descending on you like you won't believe. Finally, I wasn't at all certain what you wanted."

"What I wanted? I do not understand."

"Maybe you want to be dead. I learned never to assume what another person wants."

"Even though I am not really dead, I might desire people to think I was? What is the good in that?"

Wendy nodded. "Yes. People don't think anything because you've been unconscious, and that's the truth. I didn't know if you wanted to reconsider things. 'No comment' is the standard response to the media at the present time."

"Reconsider what?"

"Your retirement. And your future career."

"Why would I want to retire at age eighteen? I have no 401(k) or pension. I tried converting coal into diamonds for extra income; it does not work. And who will watch over you if I am gone to make sure you don't do something stupid? Mom? What a laugh. Uncle Jay? Don't think so. Jackie? Probably not. Vice President Benton? What could he possibly be trusted with?"

Wendy nodded. "Point well taken, although Robby is a lot more capable than you give him credit for. Don't underestimate him, either, as he has vast behind-the-scenes value I can't elaborate on at this time. I wouldn't have chosen an incompetent for a running mate. But there's much to consider: your destiny, going to school, etc."

"Huh." She tried to rise up off the ground a few inches, failing miserably after a few seconds. "That seems rather peculiar." She dropped to the ground. "Kind of exhausting; I feel kind of heavy."

"Maybe it takes a while to regenerate your powers or something. I have no idea."

"Looks like I will not be using them for a while."

"Well, I'm going to excuse myself, as you have a visitor who urgently wants to see you."

"Mom? I thought she was not ready to come in."

"Nope, someone else. You'll find out in a minute." She heard Wendy leave the room and shut the door as she heard someone else come in.

"Paige. It's me." He gave her a hug."

"Russell! How did you get here?"

"Your aunt sent for me a couple of days ago and I've been hanging out here. It's not a bad place, really. Dr. Gelkis and I have been playing a lot of video games."

"Where are we, actually? Wendy was rather vague."

"Some secret place underground."

"Well, they have not let me out of stir yet. I am not strong enough to break out now, but I will be soon, as I feel like a goon."

"Now that sounds like the Paige I know. Are you okay?"

"I am super tired, with barely any powers, but I may have acquired some new ones. I am wearing three casts on my broken limbs, as you can see. I was busted up pretty good, Wendy said. Hopefully, I will be back to normal soon. Wow, listen to me—for a while, I did not want them, and now I want them back. Now I know how you normal stiffs feel in the morning."

"When will you get to go home?"

"I do not know a lot; I shall have to check with the boss on that one, son. Probably not for a few weeks. As soon as I woke up, I wanted to call you, but I cannot believe you are here, although we will not be flying for a while. Maybe never."

"That's okay with me. Tell you what—I'll do the flying for a while, how's that?"

"Perfect, because I can barely even get off the ground."

"Bet that doesn't last long."

"I bet it does. It might be time for *Stella* to retire. For good.

• • •

"Aurora?"

The voice was unmistakable. "Mom?" She put on the visor and saw her mother wearing blue scrubs. "Wow, nice outfit."

"Unfortunately, I have no other clothing, as I am not quite right, they say. Are you okay?"

"Do I *look* okay? I have three casts and a broken pelvis."

"You look better than the last time I saw you, when you were still in a coma. Your skin looks mostly regenerated."

"Great. I still am only vaguely aware of what happened."

"I came in to see you disguised as a Navy nurse. No one suspected, I am told, but I remember nothing."

"That is not the story I heard. Why in the heck did you do something irresponsible like that, Mom? They would have just let you in to see me."

"I cannot answer, as I don't recall any of that."

"For someone so smart, you always have to do stupid stuff. How did you accomplish this idiotic feat?"

"I used to be able to manipulate minds, your aunt told me. It was not hard to hack into the files, get info on this person, and fool the lesser humans, although I am again one of you, it seems."

"Great to know. Wendy and Dr. Gelkis say it did not fool them, you know nothing about medicine, smarty."

"Humph. It doesn't matter now. If what you say is true, is it possible I wanted to transfer some of the energy you gave me on that fateful day?"

"I do not seem to be any smarter, only heavier."

"Well, I am far dumber, which is likely good for mankind. I also remember a lot of stuff I had long forgotten, stuff from my childhood, and I am apparently at the mental age of eleven for me, or college age intellect for normal folks. Wendy had my personal shrink flown in from Florida for a consultation. She has verified that I've lost my marbles, this time for good, hopefully."

"What about your intangible multicolored friend?"

"*Oogly-Googly* is no longer visible to me. Yet, I am somehow glad to be rid of his sorry photonic ass."

"Was he not there when you were young?"

"Yes, but he serves no purpose any longer. He created more problems than he solved."

"I am sorry. Are you sad about that?"

"Perhaps, but I have learned long ago not to lament about what cannot be changed, Aurora. I have grieved about our lost family members, but it does no good to dwell on it further."

"Yes. So, you now have the mind of an eleven-year-old?"

Petra giggled. "It would appear so. That should still be sufficient to teach my math classes and do statistics, although I will no longer need to write my formulae on the wall; my IQ has apparently gone from 300 to only 190, so I cannot comprehend such things now. The things I apparently was once capable of understanding shall forever be beyond me; yet, my present maturity level is likely beyond what I was a month ago, according to Wendy."

"How terrible. I hope you still have your love of comic books."

"Of course, how could you think otherwise?"

"Does Jack know you are here?"

"Although I do not remember my husband named Jack, I imagine Wendy has probably already told him."

She got up and gave her a hug. "You could have died! Why would you have risked all that?"

"You might have perished otherwise, as I understand. What would have been the worst outcome for me, my death? Do you think I would have cared? When you someday have a child, you will understand what it means to give everything to him or her."

"But you gave up everything, the knowledge of your fame, the things you did."

"That is not everything, Aurora, or the most important. Surely you know me better than that."

"You had become very egotistical and arrogant, Mom. Maybe you are different now."

"The essential thing is that you are here."

"But we do not even know if that is possible, me having a child, I mean. Anyway, when do you get to leave?"

Petra shook her head. "Don't know. They want to watch me for a few more days. Hopefully, they will not send me to jail for breaking into a secret government complex. If they do, will they try me as an adult or a child? I have not yet learned my escape artist tricks. These are all deeply philosophical queries for which I have no answers."

"No lie. Have you talked to Wendy?"

She shook her head. "Just briefly, we have not entered into any in-depth discussions. I am sure we will need to do that soon. I don't know if that will occur here or not. I have spent most of my time trying to learn about my forgotten past."

• • •

"How was the visit with your mom?" Wendy asked Paige, who was now walking around without the casts.

"It was good, although she is vastly different now, almost like talking to a more articulate version of Cousin Jose in the body of a silver-haired pentagenarian. More animated and spontaneous, less arrogant, definitely happier. Probably for the better, although I would like some assurance she does not have permanent brain damage."

"Bobbi assures me that does not seem to be the case, and I will have her come talk to you. She might do you a world of good as well."

"That will be interesting."

"She can only speak five or six languages now instead of twenty, and her senses are merely normal. Don't worry; in a few days, she should be able to return home."

"Home? You are going to send her back to Alaska? Is she even a legal adult?"

"Yes, as competent an adult as she ever was, which wasn't very, the attorneys say, although there is no precedent for this. I don't know what else to do with her. Even at eleven, she clearly has masters-level mathematical skills, which should be sufficient for her to teach at North Pole High School. We will have to fly her there, as she still has the same poor social skills and can't mess with people's minds any longer to travel for free. In the end, we all win."

"It restored her to the way she was. Why did I not become what I had been?"

"A sighted person? Don't know, dear. You may now have some other abilities you didn't before. And your mom wasn't like she was, as she had been deaf, and now is better than she had been."

"I guess anything would make her happier than she was."

"There is something I need to tell you, honey," Wendy said.

"Huh?" She looked up from her oatmeal. "Sounds serious."

"Sure is. Something that happened we haven't told you yet."

She looked at the clumsy casts. "Yeesh! I was almost blown up, and my mom is now a child. What more could have possibly have happened I do not know yet?"

"A lot, Paige."

"Okay." She took a sip of coffee and laughed. "Spill the beans. Get it? Coffee? Beans?"

"Dear, this is important. Initially, we were concerned that you might contract a life-threatening infection, due to your lack of exposure to external antigens."

"Yes, this has been discussed. Roy G. Bivereaux had a tiny sample of blood from when they did tests on me at the lab in Sulphur Springs when I allowed my finger to be pricked. That is not easy to do. It demands my entire concentration to allow that."

"Well, that serum showed a very low level of immunoglobulins, or antibodies, as well as a low index of other immune factors, despite your having a relatively unremarkable intestinal flora."

"That latter fact was explained to me in great detail by Biv, especially the part about my microbiota—fun fecal facts I can never unhear. He did it right before lunch, so I surely did not eat a bunch."

"But, take away your protective energy field or whatever it is, and you would die in a matter of days just by being around normal people and the routine pathogens they harbor. There are two thousand bacteria per square centimeter on your hands."

"So? Why am I alive now then, given my decrepit, debilitated, immunodeficient state, kept alive only by titanic technology?"

"Because your current serum now shows an entirely normal level of typical human immune factors."

"How could that have happened? Was Biv's sample wrong?"

"Well, Biv's no immunologist, and the old Malvin catsup plant isn't the pinnacle of biotech sophistication, but I speculate that you were, rather, exposed to a normal human who triggered a powerful immune response."

"I am exposed to people every day, yet you claim my immunity was deficient, but now it is not. How is this possible then, Gwen?"

Wendy shook her head. "There appears to be one way, one we didn't think of, although it is as old as humanity itself. A condition you might be expected to experience in the future that demands a very strong immune system, as it is probably the greatest physiologic stress placed on the human body. One I have experienced—three times. The third one was a doozy."

"You are being cryptic, not making any sense, so how could my body mount such a defense? Like I am sometimes, you said. 'Three times?' Are you saying what I think you are?"

"Yeah. This is just hard to articulate, but you need to know this, so please bear with me." Wendy put her hand on her shoulder.

"What?"

"After the explosion, at some point when you either hit or were immersed in the water, you . . . aborted."

"*Aborted?*" She thought for a moment. "Are you saying what I think you are?"

"I am. I don't know how to put it more delicately, despite years of practice telling others the same thing."

"Are you absolutely sure?"

"Yes, there's no question. You were about four to five weeks pregnant, according to the blood tests."

"Why would you have ordered blood tests for that?"

"Dear, it's standard protocol for someone your age."

"It is?"

"You sound like either version of your mom. Yes, young people have unprotected sex and get pregnant, no mystery there, and the medical team needs to know if a female is pregnant or not. I'm very sorry, Paige. It happens, there's nothing that could've been done. Usually no one knows the reason why this occurs so early on. Life-threatening injury can be one reason, of course."

"So, if I had not gone to save New York, I could have had my baby, maybe?"

"Possibly, possibly not, we would never know. We can't debate our decisions, so please don't ruminate over it; it could have happened anyway. You did what you had to do, and thirty million people are grateful. Your mother or I would've done the same."

"But I did not even know that was possible—if normal humans and I are genetically compatible, I mean." She thought for several seconds and smiled. "So, I could become pregnant again at a later date should I decide to mate, so is that my great fate?"

"It would appear so, yes, but whether or not you would carry another fetus to term is unknown, of course. Look, it happens to people all the time; that doesn't make it easier for you now, but you aren't alone."

She looked at Wendy quizzically. "I can come to terms with this, eventually, although this is quite a shock."

"One other thing you need to know."

"What now?"

"It would appear that your DNA differs from ours. Not by a great amount, but your body contains certain metalloproteins and amino acids not found in any Earthly organisms."

She nodded. "I am part alien; my conversation with the energy being known as Gart-Monn confirmed this. But what does my pregnancy have to do with my antibodies?"

"Exposure to Russell's semen must've transferred some of his immunity to you—or, more likely, provoked a strong immune response, which would've been necessary in pregnancy. It likely saved your life, both now and when you were in Ramon Argon's complex."

"Does he know about it?"

"No, that isn't my information to share. HIPAA, you know."

"Should I tell him, Aunt Wendy?"

Wendy stroked her face. "It's up to you, dear. There's nothing that can be done about it now, but, ethically, my opinion is that he has a right to know. I guess, for future reference, you need to realize that this indeed *can* happen. This 'protective aura' must have some ability to distinguish between what is harmful to you and what isn't. I would assume that you couldn't contract an infectious disease like HIV. Apparently, procreation is felt to be beneficial, and maybe you can control it, maybe not. Don't know where to even go for answers like those, as they are way beyond the pay grade of me or anyone on this planet."

"What if he or she had been born? What would my child have been like? Would he or she be like me, or be normal?"

"No one has any idea. Not being difficult, but we don't have a clue, Paige. Those are challenging choices you will need to make one day."

"If this had not happened, I mean, if we had not slept together that night—couldn't you have just given me antibiotics and stuff? It is 2029, after all, where medical miracles abound, as they are quite profound."

Wendy shook her head. "It isn't that easy. Despite all we know, we're powerless at times against these invisible invaders. In the 1940s, after the discovery of penicillin, many medical experts predicted the end of microbial diseases; in spite of the many new antimicrobial agents that were discovered since, that prediction has proven to be laughingly inaccurate. In patients with a compromised immune system, once an infection takes hold, it's almost impossible to arrest it. You likely would have developed overwhelming sepsis, or fulminant infection, and would have died, given your debilitated state when we got you out of the water."

Chapter Fifty-Six

Rita McPherson sat down to grade some sophomore biology science papers at her small Parkersburg, West Virginia studio apartment as she heard the doorbell ring. She didn't get many visitors, except people selling stuff. Whatever it was, she didn't want any, and she'd had a long day. Teaching small-college biology wasn't what she thought she would be doing at this stage of her life, but it was better than still being in prison.

She opened the door to find an athletic, slim brunette woman standing with a man, about six-two.

"Yes? What the hell do you want?"

"Dr. Rita McPherson?"

"Yeah. Not interested today, whatever crap you're selling, lady, so get lost."

"Funny." The woman pulled out a gold and platinum badge. "I'm Deputy Director Loretta Baxter."

She leaned over to look at the credentials. "Huh? Of what agency, lady? FBI? CIA? DEA? NFL?"

"None of those. DSD."

She shook her head. "Never heard of you, sorry. They need to make a TV show about you like they did with NCIS, it might help."

"I'm sure they won't do that, Ma'am. Department of Scientific Developments is in charge of, well, what our name says. We aren't a large agency and deal with relatively esoteric things beyond the capacity of those other agencies."

She frowned. "Look, I don't know what this is about, and I

don't really give a shit right now, so you can go tell your boss to go straight to you know where—"

"We report directly to the President."

She nodded. "My meaning exactly."

"Understood. Nevertheless, you need to come with us."

She put her hands on her hips. "Why? Am I under arrest?"

Lori shook her head. "No, Ma'am. But this is a matter of national importance."

"What the hell is it, then?"

"I can't tell you, mainly because I haven't been given that information. But your presence has been urgently requested."

"Yeah? By whom?"

"Again, a rather high source—the President herself. It's a matter of life and death, I am told."

"Sure, sure. Whose life and death? All of civilization is at risk, I imagine?"

"I can't say, Dr. McPherson, although you can speculate if you wish, as it is my understanding you are quite intelligent."

She laughed. "Of course I am, which is why I'm teaching biology to teenagers in the middle of nowhere. Why didn't she come here herself, then, if it's so all-important?"

"I regret that she has other urgent issues to attend to."

"Yeah, sure. I assume it has something to do with *Stella Scura.*"

Lori shook her head. "*Stella* is not the issue here, I assure you, although I have no other information to share."

"Because she's dead?"

Lori smiled. "Do you really think I would be able to tell you that? Are you kidding?"

"No. I also don't think you would be smiling if that were true. What, then?"

"Can't say, but I guarantee you—it's the opportunity of a lifetime, one that might resurrect your rather unimpressive career."

"What the hell is wrong with my career, lady? Where the hell have I heard *that* one before?"

"One difference: my name isn't Malachi Argon."

"You definitely have a point there." She thought for a minute. "Okay, let me get my stuff. Whatever this is about, I do figure I owe the President one."

• • •

Stella walked clumsily on crutches into the small lounge three weeks later, wearing a red Ball State University sweatsuit.

"How're you feeling?" Wendy said.

"Still trying to digest all this stuff. I feel good, about twenty percent. A lot better than what I felt like when I broke out of that goop they had me in before, but I am still sore." She rose off the ground a few inches. "Not bad. How am I healing?"

"Another week and you should get the casts off, then a little bit of physical rehabilitation, which is incredibly fast given what happened to you. Don't worry, that's what I used to do; I know the drill."

"I guess I should be grateful for that. Your medical expertise, I mean, and my relatively rapid healing, and that my mom survived this incident relatively intact, except for *Oogly-Googly*."

"That's good. I didn't think you were terribly fond of him anyway."

"What will we do with her?"

"That is a very good question. She will have a lot to learn and become accustomed to, but remember she's still an unenhanced Bonnie Mendoza, a genius with the native capacity for learning at an incredible rate. I suppose she can return to North Pole."

"With Jack?"

"And maybe you. She could use your help, you know."

"I guess I have not thought much about my future."

"Coffee?" She clumsily took the hot steaming cup with the cast on her arm and took a sip.

"Now that imminent danger has passed, I have an additional query for you."

'Shoot."

"When I was six and the energy wave from the explosion passed through me, there were reports that people with illnesses and other ailments miraculously improved, right?"

"That was the report, yes, and definitely a statistically significant phenomenon. Multiple medical articles were written about it, albeit with little tangible explanation."

"My mom changed after that, but whether or not it was for the better is a matter of opinion."

"You know all these things already, so what is your question?"

"Did the same thing happen after this explosion?"

"I have been rather busy with other things, but the initial reports would suggest that there was very little of the same effect."

"Why? It was a much more powerful missile."

"Yes, but you are much more powerful now, too, and you absorbed most of it. Remember, back then you were in contact with your mom; there was no other person involved here." Wendy paused for a moment. "I wish the outcome had been the same as 2016."

"What does that mean?"

"Never mind. Some people around here could use some healing powers."

"Well—you must have a lot of important business to attend to instead of being down here with me."

"I'm the President. This whole complex is set up to handle almost any emergency, so I *have* been working, believe me, about eighteen hours a day. It's good to be the boss here, although where I am is obviously top secret."

"About how I feel—check this out. Bivereaux and Kepler said I theoretically could do this in time, but it freaks me out."

"What?"

"Look." Wendy watched as her left hand became blurry and somewhat transparent for about ten seconds, although the fuzzy outline of her hand could be seen.

Wendy nodded. "Yes, we observed that happening multiple times after the incident with your mom but before you woke up. It's interesting that it affects only light and not anything else, diffracting light waves around your body. So that appears to answer your earlier question."

"Apparently so, although I am merely absorbing it, as you mention, rather than bending it around me. It requires a great deal of concentration, and I can currently only do it on a small portion of my body."

"That must take an immense amount of energy. My advice is to save yours for healing and quit horsing around."

"The field itself likely takes a lot, to deflect bullets and such. What I do not know is if it affects my ability to absorb energy and to protect myself. It would be interesting if I could do it all over."

"Yes, it would. We don't need to learn about it now."

"And I am *not* interested in the military applications."

"I'm not either."

She smiled at the President. "I do not believe that for a minute."

"Maybe I'm changing, did you ever think of that? I had a good teacher. And I am capable of learning new things, too."

They sat down at the small table in the room. "I have had the time to think about many things."

"I thought you would be, as the contemplative person you are."

"I do not know if I am ready to be *Stella* again. It was what I thought I wanted, but I know now that I have a lot of work to do to become who I want to be."

"Who is that?" Wendy asked, as if she already knew the answer to her question.

"A leader, like you."

"Like me? Really?"

"Well, no, not really. There is no one else like you."

"I thought so. Thanks for the compliment."

"Who said it was a compliment?" She paused for several seconds. "Just kidding."

"No, you're not."

"Well, okay, I do not like to lie. But I cannot do it with a high school diploma, a lofty credential that I, a high school dropout, do not even yet possess. I want to show people that I can lead not with my power but by not using it. I can do more with my life than this. I want positive things in my life, not to be the superhero everyone wants me to be."

Wendy punched her in the right shoulder. "Now you wait just a minute, kiddo. As I recall, being *Stella* was what *you* wanted, so don't you ever put it on me and everyone else. I never bothered you, Paige. I left you alone because I wanted you to live the life you wanted. I even helped keep others away. You wanted to be a rock star, and you got it."

"Yes, that is a fair assessment. It was what I thought I desired, and it fulfilled the dream for a while, but it just became more than I could handle. Everyone wanted something from me. There was not enough time to do everything. I would have needed a whole staff just to maintain my schedule. Everyone wanted me to be a pitchwoman, to be on their show, etc. At least I did not go to that professional baseball tryout for the Atoms."

"There's a lot you need to learn about being President, then, if you think being *Stella Scura* is stressful. But I'll tell them whatever you want, that *Stella* is dead, retired, on sabbatical, etc. I can be pretty convincing."

"I don't want to be dead, I just need to be Paige for a while and pursue my studies, so you can state that *Stella* is on a sabbatical. I wanted to be a symbol of hope. How can I do that when I'm dead?"

"Good point. But that's your choice. You wanted to be an adult, but neither me, your mom or dad, Bella, or anyone else can do that for you."

She crossed her arms. "I will therefore be on a leave of absence until further notice."

"Sounds good to me. Now I'll have to work on how I actually will make that statement."

"Your problem, not mine."

"Thanks."

• • •

Petra gave her brother a hug after he arrived at the Vault complex as he stared at her in amazement.

"Jaime. The last time I remember you, we were in Washington at the White House, and now you live there. I realize now over forty years have passed."

"Yeah. All those years, most people thought you were dead."

"All things I no longer remember. From what I understand, you knew better, about me being dead, I mean."

He nodded. "Of course. Paige wrote a lot of letters to Wendy. Miranda reads them all, and those were flagged as her peculiar use of language is very similar to yours, in many ways more eccentric."

"Miranda?"

"Miranda is an advanced holographic artificial intelligence assistant that you and Alex created. Ironic that she should lead us to you."

"I seem to have much to catch up on and I am amazed every day about the things I accomplished. But thank you for everything you did to help."

"What I did?"

"I have no memory of this, but I logically realize our continued deception was made easier by those looking over us, to protect our simple existence."

"Hey, what are you thanking *me* for? You should be thanking Wendy. She's the one who manipulated all the agencies and promised there would be holy hell to pay for anyone outside the DSD who investigated anything having to do with supernormal activity in central Alaska."

"Yeah, I suppose. They said she also did much for me when I was younger, when I was sick."

"She did. She challenged you to do things no one thought possible, to reach for the stars. You exceeded the world's expectations."

"I am grateful not to be ill. It's also my understanding you dated while she was still a teenager, then you treated her very badly by cheating on her, with her roommate, no less. I can totally imagine you doing that."

He nodded. "I did, I was a pretty bad person. I've tried to make up for it, though. Somehow, I got a second chance when life usually only gives you one. You seem to have had way more than that number, though."

She shook her head. "I don't know where to start about your spouse. From what little I have learned so far, she has done so many things for our country—and *to* it."

"She did what she had to do."

"Like nearly killing us with Conrad's nukes? That was an essential Presidential duty?"

"Don't you realize, or is that giant brain of yours too complex to see what is right in front of you? That the main purpose of her becoming President and doing all of this was for Paige?"

She shook her head. "*That* is almost impossible to believe. Taking over the Moon and making it a state in order to nationalize the regolith? That was all for Paige? Get out of town."

"She's a good person, Bonnie. I know you don't remember, but she helped you become who you were and helped me become a better person. And while you're my sister and I love you, don't ever ask me to make a choice between you and my wife."

"Maybe. The terrible burden of what I had apparently become is beyond anyone's comprehension. As befitting one whose stage name contained the word 'miracle,' I am now as I once was, as normal as that can be. I suppose I had to blame someone when I am as much at fault as anyone. But I didn't want to become this. I was shocked to find out I am on one of the most common forms of American currency. What an embarrassment to one who had to be supervised with money."

"You deserve it for all you gave the world."

"It is all just so hard to absorb, the realization that most everyone is gone, and I will never see them again on this Earth."

"I miss Mike, I wish he was still with us. I guess siblings are the longest relationships we ever have with other human beings."

"I am sure he is up in Heaven with the others."

"You still believe, don't you? Even after all this?"

"Huh? Believe in whom?"

"God, of course. Who else?"

"Jaime, why would you ever question that I believe in God?"

"It's just something I've never understood. You, whose life has revolved around mathematics, chemistry, and physics, things you can prove, having such a conviction in things you can't ever prove. I still don't get it."

"Well, the universe tends towards a higher state of entropy, or disorganization." She tapped on his forehead with her right index finger. "You with me so far?"

He snarled. "Yes, don't be so patronizing, little kid."

"I am not being patronizing, just sensitive to those with limited intellectual ability, although look who's talking."

He sighed. "What's your point?"

"The world, like all physical things, tends toward complete disorganization. For example, a gas released from a small container disperses into the entire atmosphere; it does not merely stay in its original state. Life on Earth is highly ordered, and to my knowledge has not been recreated anywhere else in the universe. To expect that random molecules would have ordered themselves into highly complex cellular systems is ludicrous beyond comprehension. The only way life could have evolved is through a higher power; that is, divine intervention."

"What about these crazy energy beings Paige talked to? How do you explain them, then?"

She shook her head. "As much as I once knew, there is even more I have forgotten. I honestly do not know, but must believe that they were creations of Him themselves."

"Or perhaps they are Him, and Tharr-Kann was the devil. Did you ever consider that?"

"Humph. Of course I must have considered that; how could you not believe I would have considered all possibilities? Even the reduced capacity of my preteen brain can comprehend such advanced concepts."

"That Paige is the daughter of Satan? Are you freaking kidding me? Is that even possible?"

She nodded. "Certainly. There is darkness in all of us, Jaime, some more than others. I have heard of the devastation she can cause with only a tiny fraction of her powers intact. Were she to come at us full force—God help us all."

"Is he still alive? Her dad? Satan?"

"Why do you say that? Alex, my husband I do not remember, was her father, pure and simple. Whatever DNA from Tharr-Kann is within her came from me, not him. So Satan is within me, too."

"Satan is within ye?" He laughed. "That was a song by Wendy's cousin Smiley, I think, along with 'Americium the Beautiful,' 'Don't Club with Beelzebub,' and "Meet Thy Doom with Plutonium.'"

"I am fortunate I don't know such a hillbilly dullard."

"You did, but you forgot. But what the hell happened to her dad, or mom, or whatever?"

She shook her head. "You're asking me? I'm the last one who would know, I have no idea."

"So, what now? Where will you be, back in Alaska?"

"I guess, although it will be strange, seeing it for the first time."

"I've been to North Pole. It's a fairly nice place if you like the outdoors."

"I don't. It doesn't sound very exciting."

Chapter Fifty-Seven

January 30, 2029
Mendoza Multinational Press Room
230 N. Bonnie Mendoza Blvd.
Aurora City, IN

Nick, Bella, and Wendy entered the conference room to give an address, as dozens of reporters waited eagerly, clearly not used to seeing the President at M2 corporate headquarters.

"Today, I announce the expansion of Mendoza Multinational to the Middle East as it will soon bring fusion technology there," Nick said proudly.

A reporter raised her hand excitedly. "M2 is taking mendozium technology to the Middle East? We were always under the impression that this was not in the administration's plans. How will they afford this technology?"

Wendy shook her head. "They don't have to 'afford' anything. It will be given to them at minimal cost, as a gift from the United States of America."

"Doesn't that jeopardize the standing of the USA? Are we making Taraq a state? It's right next door to New Persia."

"No. It isn't about sovereignty any longer. We're all in this together. If we don't cooperate, maybe there won't be a world to live in our future."

"Is the USA going to take over any other countries?"

"Not at this time, but I cannot guarantee what will happen in the future, as the safety of our country will always be a foremost concern. We're big enough right now, don't you think?"

"How is *Stella Scura* going to fit into this?"

"As I mentioned, *Stella* is recovering from injuries sustained in the nuclear blast and will be re-evaluating her role and concentrating on other things for now. She will remain a friend of this administration, and hopefully future ones. Whether or not she will return to her previous role isn't known."

"No one's seen her since Christmas Eve. How can we even be sure she survived that explosion and is still alive?"

"You have my word on that. My hope is that if the world really needs her, she'll be back."

"Any other comments, Madam President?"

"Yes. The United States will immediately begin preparations to destroy the majority of its nuclear weapons. It is my grand hope that other nations will follow suit. What almost happened a month ago can never happen again."

• • •

South Mound Cemetery
505 Bundy Ave.
New Castle, Indiana

Jackie Levickis approached Jack Marshall warily as he sat on the bench in the old cemetery on the last day of January, looking eerily at his own granite tombstone on the cold, overcast Wednesday morning. She reached out and touched him as if she'd seen a ghost.

"Jim. It's been twelve years."

"Yeah. A long time. You're sure looking good."

"Well, you look way better than I expected for someone I thought was buried there," she said, pointing at the monument. "Sorry, I forgot flowers, my bad."

He laughed as he stared at his gravesite. "I'll take that as a compliment."

She snarled at him angrily. "Do you think this is funny, Jim? I should knock your block off."

"No, but it is a pretty decent one, at that. Better than I deserved."

"That sure as hell's true. You've changed."

"A lot has changed. Me, especially. I'm not the same person you once knew, like you weren't aware of that already."

She touched his face. "How could you have done it? Let us all believe you were dead all these years? I know this was part of some grandiose master plan for saving civilization, but come on."

"Well, talk to your boss about it, as it seems she's known ever since it happened. I'm sure you've known for a while, too, don't pretend you didn't."

"Yeah, but don't change the subject, Jim. Just because we knew doesn't make it any easier now." She shoved him in the shoulder as tears streamed from her eyes. "Well?"

He shook his head. "What the hell would you have had me do after what happened? A greater calling prevailed, Jackie."

"A 'greater calling?' Since when did you care about anything spiritual?"

He shook his head. "I can't explain it, it was a force that transcended anything we ever had."

"Oh, you had an epiphany, a vision? A message from God, like Rita McPherson had? Give me a break."

"Hey, I made a vow to Alex before he and Bonnie got married that if anything ever happened to him, I would look after her. That was before they had a child, and I didn't know Aurora would be a goddess in the form of a little girl. Yeah, sure, Rad, Viktor, Bonnie, Rita, and I were all there through the insanity of the Ontario Lacus incident, but I had no idea stuff like this could happen."

"Wendy knew all along, I know now." She shook her head. "Kept lots of stuff a secret."

"Like I did. I didn't plan on doing it in this manner, but you can't always choose what happens to you. It wasn't about what you or I wanted; it was about the world."

She frowned. "I know you did what you thought must be right, and I'm trying to accept that. But are you happy, at least?"

"Petra—Bonnie—is a wonderful woman, once you get past the irritating surface, although I know she's far different now. I could see what Alex saw in her. This is what he would've wanted. Without him, none of this would've happened. I've also found the wonderment of knowing God as I should've long ago."

"For you to marry?"

He nodded. "Whatever she appears to be on the surface, she is, or was, I guess, very passionate. So, yes. I love her more than I could have ever thought possible, and Alex would've wanted her to be happy, although I know our relationship may be different. If you and your boss don't like it, I'm sorry. You won't ever have to see me again."

"Leave Wendy out of it, as this has *nothing* to do with her. But why come out now?"

"Do you think I didn't know Wendy was looking for us? I may be a lot of things, but I ain't stupid. I changed everything in the servers continuously until Paige turned eighteen, when we told her she could make her own decisions. As smart as Wendy thinks she is, I thought I was always one step ahead. Now I'm not so sure."

"You *told* her what she could and couldn't do? From what I've seen, I don't see how you could have stopped her."

"She has a disability. One that can be overcome with technology, like Bonnie's once was, but not by herself—she needs other people to accomplish that, or she can't do a whole lot that's constructive. With the help of others, she can change the world. She always will. Wouldn't you consider that a positive quality? To help others, she must first let others help her. That is the singular quality that will make her great. She's not there yet, but give her time."

"I—I suppose so."

He walked towards the window. "But to really change the world, she needs to be a leader. I don't know who this Tharr-Kann dude is Petra raves about, who apparently was Aurora's father or something—although his DNA was in Petra, so I guess he was partially her mom."

"Wait, I'm totally confused."

"Tell me about it. He sounds like some kind of asshole who ruined his civilization. How much of him is in Paige, I have no fricking clue, but apparently, there is some, from what I heard about the fate of Argon's West Virginia complex. But she'll lead by choosing not to use her power, by not conquering us all like the other guy did. Whether or not that's what the energy beings intended, I don't know and don't care. But I hope the values we have instilled in her will last her the rest of her life, however long that will be."

"*Tinman* knew you were alive all along, as well."

"Of course he did, but we all have our secrets, Jackie. Don't pretend your Star-Spangled blue-eyed boss with the dyed gray hair doesn't have her dirty little ones, because she does. You probably know lots that you can never share."

"Of course I do—what an asinine statement."

"Yes, no way we could've done some of the things we did without his technology and money. He was our secret benefactor, but he didn't know exactly where, though. He never asked."

"So, you waited until now, so she and Wendy can rule the world. How do you fit into all this?"

Jack shook his head. "Pardon my French, but hell, no. You've met her, and I'm surprised how little insight you have into Paige's personality. She has a moral compass beyond most people's and the loud, argumentative attitude of both her parents, with better common sense than both put together. *And* a gift for debate that transcends anything you could possibly imagine. As either *Stella* or Paige, she has no qualms about telling the President or anyone else off if she gets a notion to. She, like her mom, dad, cousin, and aunt, can be quite obnoxious and belligerent."

"Yeah, I've observed as much. So what?"

"So what? The difference is this: who's going to stop her? Nick and the *Squad* can meet any technology needs she would ever require in the future. But, despite her abilities, she wants to change the world in a different way, Jackie."

"What do you mean?"

"The right way, not through force, but serving as a symbol of what's good. Someday *Stella Scura* will be living in the White House. Not as a guest, but as the President."

She looked towards the ground. "Jim, I don't even want to think about how complex that's going to be. There will be a debate over whether she even can run when she's thirty-five, whenever we determine that to be."

"Thirty-eight. The first election when she is eligible will be in 2048. And she will win, I guarantee it."

"Thirty-eight, forty, whatever. You know as well as I that there's some alien blood in her veins. I don't know that people will accept having her in the White House, even by 2048 or 2058. Sure, she's popular now, but time can change things. People are fickle."

He smiled. "That's one viewpoint, so why do you think we did it this way? Because there's no way to stop her now. She's a natural born United States citizen, like you or me. It would be a violation of the Constitution not to allow her to run."

She nodded. "I believe you, but can you prove it?"

"Sure can. Delivered by and birth certificate signed by none other than the Surgeon General, who just happens to be your boss, for the time being."

"Wrong, it's Aurora Darkkin's birth certificate, who's dead. Whatever documents you have for Paige, they're forged."

"I'm sure that she'll figure that out, eventually, and Aurora Darkkin will live again, I promise you that. But the President—don't have much better credentials than her. If someone wants to challenge that, then they can bring it on."

"Wendy will be long out of the White House by then and will have to deal with the repercussions of covering all that up for years, should this all ever come out, which it probably will if she wants to be President. Paige will have to do most of that on her own by 2033."

"I assure you that both of them are up to the task."

She shook her head. "Yeah, well—Paige is going to have to go that one alone way sooner than 2033."

"'Go it alone?' What the hell does that mean?"

She shook her head. "I can't tell you. I promised not to."

"Is something wrong with Wendy?"

"Never mind. In the end, a lot of people will get what they always wanted." She slapped him hard on the left cheek. "I loved you. I still do. There, I said it, and I'm glad."

He rubbed his cheek. "I'm sorry, Jackie. But don't you think I loved you too? I still do. If you don't like what I did, you can lump it. I'm tired of apologizing to everyone for the hard choices I made. Paige herself is barely speaking to me, but I'd do it all over again. Petra seemed to detach more from reality each day, although she seems far happier and normal now after whatever occurred in her encounter with Paige. Whether either of them comes around or not, I can live with it; I finally realized twelve years ago the world isn't about the petty things I desire. I made a decision—maybe it was right, maybe not, but I made the best one I could. I wasted a good portion of my life when I was younger, so I also wanted redemption for the world I saw was coming. We both made a difference in our own way."

"Yeah, I guess. So, where does that leave us?"

"It leaves us where we were before today when I was still dead. I don't exist, as least as the person you once knew, and I'm a married man."

"Yes, whose wife now has the brain of an eleven-year-old kid. That's pretty damn creepy, you must admit."

"Maybe. Not much I can do about it. Do you want me to abandon her? At the rate she's capable of learning, she's likely already surpassed me in knowledge. Elsevier estimates her IQ is presently 190, consistent with the historical number, but less than the 300 she claimed to have before. At any rate, I'm still loyal to her, whether or not she remembers me or not. It's ironic, you know."

"Oh really? In what way?"

"She almost died at age thirty after irresponsibly running down a criminal and suffering an anoxic brain injury. She didn't have any memory of Alex, yet she grew to love him again. For all her flaws, she's a kind and caring person, and the bravest person I know, except maybe for Paige. For those reasons, she deserves everything I can give her. It has to be that way, you know. And because I'm truly happy, Jackie. Happier than I've ever been, because I've done something important for the world, without any personal glory. I learned to stop caring about that long ago."

"So, what comes next, Jim? We just go our separate ways and live happily ever after?"

He shook his head. "I don't know, Jackie. I did the best I could, and I think things turned out pretty well, considering all the variables. I never meant to hurt your feelings. If I had to go back in time, I'm sure I'd do the same thing again."

"I suppose I would've done the same thing. So, I guess this is goodbye?"

He nodded. "I imagine so. I still care for you, but I don't know what purpose continuing this relationship would serve, given your position and all. And I now have two children."

"Both of them quite difficult to manage."

Chapter Fifty-Eight

February 2, 2029
The White House
Washington, DC

"Paige, where are you going?" Wendy asked, coming into her bedroom as she packed her suitcase. "I knew you would be leaving, but so quickly? You're not completely recovered yet."

"I told you, I am moving back home to North Pole tomorrow after the medal ceremony. Dad is going to build on to his church there, and we have some rebuilding to do in our relationship. I do not belong here, and my mom needs my help, as you can imagine. Except for a slight limp, I am as good as I am going to be. Maybe someday I can return, when this is truly my home."

"You're my family, and it *is* truly yours, as least for a while longer. Will wants you here; so do Jay and I."

"Will can come to visit me, then, but surely you can see that it is not my home, as I do not fit in here anymore, that is the score."

"That isn't true."

She put her hands on her hips sternly. "Hey, look, Aunt Wendy, this just is not the place for me now; neither is Aurora City and all the wonders of M2. Fairbanks is more my speed, for now at least. I will be back soon."

"You can change the world. This is where the big decisions get made."

"And I need to grow, to get a background and some experience, to do that. I am not ready for big decisions; little ones will be hard enough. I will not learn that by being a VIP. You did not, did you?"

"No. I suppose not, I only made it to VOP."

"Huh? VOP?"

"Very Obnoxious Person. Also, Very Obese Person. Either fits."

She laughed. "I believe *that.* And we discussed this already. You told me if I want to change the laws then I must become a legislator. I am at best ten to twelve years away from even being a junior mover and shaker."

"I guess I know what it's like to want to leave and go out on my own. It's what I did. But you may find it difficult, not relying on the powers of *Stella Scura* or the wealth and fame of being a Darkkin and a Mendoza."

"I didn't say it had to be easy. My life hasn't been, despite what you think."

"I know what we discussed earlier, but maybe we can eventually use you as some kind of secret operative, especially with your new limited power of invisibility."

She snarled angrily and shook her head. "I do not think that will work out, as I have no interest in fighting crime or espionage now; I will be too busy going to school. I will have to work hard at that and hopefully get a few scholarships, even though Bella tells me I am modestly wealthy. Give Juriann a call, since that is right up his alley, Aunt Wendy."

"Maybe it's just a phase. I know what that's like, Paige; I've been through several of those, as you can see. Don't make all these decisions at once."

"It was *Stella Scura* that was the phase, can you not see that?"

"I know we discussed it before, but I really didn't think you would go through with it. I wanted to become President for another four years, to help you along, and now you're giving it up. We could have done great things together."

"I do not know what you believe those things would be, other than world domination. I have my own agenda now, which does not include you right now, unfortunately."

"There are many things other than those, but I guess I can respect that, Paige. It takes guts."

She sneered. "Sorry for your loss, but that is not my problem; I seem to have enough of my own. This is my life, not yours, I will do with it what I please. If it does not fit into your 'plan,' then tough luck, for you it may suck."

"Yeah, I suppose so, but you don't have to get so huffy about it. I can tell when you've made up your mind. In that way, you're as stubborn as either of your moms."

"I suppose that is one way we are similar."

"Agreed. Being stubborn isn't always good, I should know."

She shook her head. "And sometimes it is."

"But pretty much every other person on this planet would use the advantages your powers give you."

"You do not understand now, but one day you will. And I *am* that one person in nine billion."

"Yeah, I do understand, and someday you'll realize why. Are you sure this is what you want? Or will you change your mind tomorrow, like most teenagers?"

"Must you be so condescending and insulting?"

"Yes, I must. I am the mother of one adolescent, am talking to another, and am married to a third. I can't be any other way."

"Huh. That does not help."

"Well, maybe being realistic will. I was a teenager once and I changed my mind about what I wanted to do several times per week. But this is serious stuff."

"It is what I want and the best destiny for me, you, and our country. Promise me this, Aunt Wendy: you have four more years to make a difference, and you won't have me to worry about anymore. Use your great power and influence to help those less fortunate than we."

"Gee, I thought I tried to do that already, silly me."

"Remember the Roosevelt Memorial and the many that humble man helped. In many ways, you have done so, yet there are many who have been neglected. You can always do more."

Wendy sighed. "Just because FDR had a disability didn't make him humble, as he was possibly one of the most arrogant Presidents ever. He treated his VP like crap, then he died suddenly and left Truman the whole Manhattan Project stuff to deal with, which he hadn't bothered to include him on."

"I guess I mean the message on the monument, not FDR the man. I care little about the latter."

"But are you on my side? I have to know."

"The Republican side? You must surely know that answer."

Wendy laughed. "No, I mean with my goals, my objectives.

Not everything has to be about the party."

"I told you that before. I am on the side I always am: that of the greater good. Time will tell if that is the side we are both on."

Wendy laughed. "Huh, that almost sounds like a threat. Really, Paige? Come on. You can do better than that."

"An observation. *Really*. Do you truly think *Stella Scura* needs to make threats, even to you? You can do better than that, too."

Wendy sighed. "Yes, I suppose so."

"Darn right. Get out of your self-strategizing persona and become the girl you once were for a moment. My mom met you when you were my age, so become her again."

"How naïve. You've got a lot to learn, Paige. Life changes us, and unlike your mom's special case, we can't ever go back, as much as we'd like to. No one would like to be my eighteen-year-old self more than me, but I can't. Your mom may be an eleven-year-old again in a fiftysomething body, but she seems to be the only one who can cheat death, except maybe you."

"Yes, but without your help, she would not have become what she was, and I would not exist. So I owed you much long before I was born."

"I guess so. I never thought of it that way. Hooray for me."

"Anyway, it appears you are not used to a balance of power. The House and Senate certainly do not favor that. They were duly elected by the people so I can't do anything about it, and I support our democratic processes."

"Good to know."

"Cut the sarcasm, Aunt Wendy."

"Me? Sarcastic? Come on."

"It takes one to know one. You may take my comments as you like. Realize, however, that there is no plane I cannot outfly, no atomic warhead I cannot absorb."

"You're going to disarm all my favorite nukes? My dad's little babies?" Wendy pretended to cry.

She laughed. "Perhaps. Sorry if that upsets you."

Wendy then started laughing. "Well, honey, you'll have to get in line because I'm going to start doing it first, even though it will surely hurt."

"What? No way."

"Yeah, really. What'd you think I'd do? Build more?"

She nodded. "Yes. It's like cutting off a part of you, I know they are 'part of the family,' so to speak."

"Part of yours, too, don't ever forget that. We both used to have the same last name as him."

"But if you or anyone else does something I do not like, they will have to answer to *me.*"

"That sure doesn't sound like a 'balance of power.' Practice what you preach, honey."

"Well, you are correct in that aspect, but I am no one's puppet. Not my mother's, not Nick and Bella's, and certainly not yours."

"Listen, I don't want a 'puppet' and don't want to boss you around, and I know I probably can't, but I must think of America first and foremost. If I had your powers, the things that could be done—"

"But you do not, and my destiny is not yours to have. I represent not just America but the entire world. Know that, in twenty years, I will hopefully be in your shoes, and I will seek guidance from you."

"Huh, what makes you think I'll even be around by then? What if it doesn't work out for you? My job's tougher than it seems, and my shoes are pretty big. What then?"

"Then I will just have to deal with it. But, if I am successful, this position can do more for the world than any paltry powers of mine. You said this yourself." She began crying.

"Yes, I did." Wendy brushed the tears from her eyes. "I wouldn't have said it if I didn't believe it."

She came up to her aunt and brushed her hair with her left hand. "You are my father's sister, and I love you like I love him. Please understand that, but I need time to grow. If you need me, I will be there for you. Now and always. Someday I will hopefully return to this house, as I have promised, but it may be a long time from now. But I hope you will be there to guide me."

"I hope so too, Paige. Twenty years or more is a long time. Like you, some days I just want to live to tomorrow. Maybe I can do even greater deeds in my last four years. Something that can really make a difference."

• • •

Department of Scientific Developments
2 Constitution Avenue NE
Washington, DC

The tall, slim brown-haired man wearing the tweed blazer looked like someone out of the early 1980s as he greeted his guest in his well-appointed office.

"Juriann, I'm Dexter Slabb."

He shook the slightly shorter and much thinner man's hand. "Good to meet you. I understand your uncle was Alton Lohrbach, the former CIA Directorate of Science & Technology Director and Secretary of Defense under President Reardon."

"Yeah. Alton's retired now. Don't see him much, as he's kind of become a hermit and lives near Oak Ridge, of all places. Kind of like someone else I knew who used to work for Alton."

"Hmmm. Who would that be?"

Dexter shook his head. "Never mind." They sat down inside Dexter's large office as a secretary brought them coffee.

"Thank you," he said to the mid-thirtyish woman as she left and closed the door.

"So, you'll be staying in America for a while?"

"I believe so. At least I sound a bit more like an American now than when I came."

Dexter sipped his black coffee as she closed the door. "I heard you might want to help us from time to time."

He nodded. "I'd like to at least consider it, but I want to go back and get my doctorate in physics first. As you can see, I'm pretty big. I don't know if I would be a very good secret agent, but I have other talents."

"What I admire are your intellectual skills, not just the others. You're a pretty bright guy. It's that esoteric collection of abilities that really makes you *Orthoman*."

"The *Science Squad* can help you as well with that."

Dexter shook his head. "I'm not sure about those guys, as they don't seem to be very good team players. Johnny Kepler and Roy G. Bivereaux, in particular, are rather obnoxious. Not very reliable, either, per my understanding."

He nodded. "Possibly, I see your point. But understand that I don't work for you, and I'll do the missions I deem important on my terms. Can you live with that, Slabb?"

"I expected nothing else—and I would rather have you on those terms than not at all. You do come pretty highly recommended, at that."

"I do."

"Your physical capabilities are immense. I could see you in any number of roles, leading an attack squad with the intent of technological espionage."

"Yeah. Not my style, though. I'm a thinker at heart." He paused and took a sip of coffee. "I'm sure you'd rather have my little friend than me for that, though, if you had your choice."

Dexter looked at him curiously. "I don't follow. Who?"

"The one with the expensive sapphire sunglasses."

The bureau chief shook his head. "Uh-uh, you'd be very wrong, *Orthoman*. I don't need the kind of publicity she brings with her, as she seems meant for the limelight. She also talks in such a distinctive manner that it's impossible for her to pose as someone else, and I doubt any training can fix that, as it appears to be neurologically hard-wired into her system and therefore unfixable. I also suspect she doesn't take orders very well. Despite her rather unique qualities, she's too high-maintenance for the DSD."

He laughed. "Limelight? There's no person who cares less about that than she. You have no idea what she wants, as she's unlike any person I have ever met."

"No kidding, Juriann. Nevertheless, she's probably easier to disguise than you because she's normal-sized, but a supersonic flying girl isn't my cup of tea. Also, I don't know if she's even around. My boss says she is, but I've seen no proof."

He nodded. "She is. I've seen her."

"Since she left The Vault?"

"Yes, of course."

"Where is she, then?"

"Wouldn't you and your boss like to know, Slabb? Her ultimate goal in life seems to be a bit different than being a superhero, so deal with it."

"What goal could possibly be bigger than saving the world, Juriann?"

He pointed towards the ceiling. "How arrogant. Just because you and Wendy live in Washington doesn't mean you know it all. The world will face immense problems in the next thirty years and beyond, Dexter. It will take more than your, my, or *Stella's* immense strength to fix things; it will take unprecedented leadership, more than you, I, or even Wendy can provide. There is only one solution: she must become a member of Congress, and, later, President of the United States."

Slabb shook his head. "That's the craziest thing I've ever heard, Juriann."

"Really? So what? You've seen a lot of crazy stuff."

"Yeah, well, come on. Are you honestly going to sit there and tell me that she would give up all the power, the celebrity, the money, to an extent no person has ever known, to take a highly improbable chance she could, as an average citizen, somehow acquire the diverse knowledge and skills to someday become our elected chief executive, when people would just *give* it to her alter ego? Are you kidding? No one would do that."

He laughed. "Then you've never met *Stella*."

"I guess I know now why your big sister thinks she's so special. I can't imagine what being her is like."

"Yes. And, hopefully, with us fighting the good fight and, over time, persuading the world powers to get rid of their nuclear missiles, the world won't need saving for a while."

"Huh." Slabb tapped his black Omas fountain pen on the desk. "She really must be different than most people."

He nodded. "That she is. She's different from me, for sure."

"Let's change the topic." Dexter threw a plain manila folder on the table. "This is a project that might interest you when you have the time, which might be a while."

"What's this?" He opened it and took out the photo of the distinguished-looking, early fiftyish scientist. "His face is unfamiliar. Why should I care about this man?"

"This is Dr. Benjamin John Zeihn, one of the world's most brilliant nano-engineers. He'd done some private contracting work for the government, and had collaborated on several projects with Dr. Vaughn Baxter, but now is nowhere to be found."

"Who is this Vaughn Baxter?"

"Lori's father, he's a high-level brainiac involved in many aspects of DSD such as weapons development. You've met Lori."

He smiled. "Yes, of course, she's hard to forget, and I would like to get to know her better."

"Come on, Juriann. She's way older than you and isn't even interested in me."

He laughed. "In case you haven't noticed, I'm not you, Slabb, and I'll take my chances. Anyway, is this guy something the DSD even cares about? Do I need to go rescue him or something?"

Dexter laughed. "Hardly. If anyone needs rescuing, it's us."

"Benjamin Zeihn. Benzene? As in the chemical?" He laughed. "That's preposterous."

"Yeah, Lori calls him the *Benzoicman*. But Zeihn's disappeared, probably on some remote island somewhere, planning to do something very bad."

"Remote island? Come on, how corny can you be? That sounds like another Malachi Argon fiasco."

"Probably worse, Juriann. Trust me on this one. Dr. Ben Zeihn is bad news. He's mainstream enough to fit in without the mad-scientist personas of the Argons and the craziness of *Santaman* and *Red Skeleton*."

He took another sip of coffee and smiled. "Since Lori knows all about him, I'll set up a meeting with her. No offense, but she's a bit easier on my eyes than you."

• • •

The White House
Washington, DC

Russell sat in the lounge chair in her bedroom as she sat on the end of the bed.

"Thanks for inviting me here; it was great to get the tour and see the Oval Office and everything."

She nodded. "I thought it was time for that."

"What's on your mind? You usually aren't this quiet."

"You are very perceptive." She felt him move next to her on the bed and sit down. "I am leaving to go back to North Pole tomorrow afternoon after Juriann and I visit New York briefly, and there is something very profound I must tell you, Russ. Something I only found out after I recovered, an occurrence I thought impossible. I should have told you in Virginia but did not know how to bring it up, or even if I should."

"What is it?" he said softly. "It's okay, whatever it is."

"When they brought me in, they determined I was pregnant."

"Pregnant? How?"

"I had the same question, so I guess both of us need a lesson in human reproduction."

"No . . . I mean, I didn't think that could happen, you know, since you can't be infected with microorganisms or affected by toxins. I thought this fit into the same category."

"I guess my protective aura does not consider that activity to be harmful. It does not matter now, as I aborted anyway."

"Because of the trauma of the explosion?"

She shook her head. "No one knows, Russ. It is the first DNA evidence that confirms I am not entirely human, so with our incompatibilities, it might have happened in any case."

"You know that for sure, about you?"

She nodded. "I possess several metalloproteins not present in any known lifeform on Earth, among other things."

"I'm sorry, Paige. It makes me even more sorry for something I must also tell *you*."

"What?"

"I'm leaving Wright-Patt," Russ said sadly.

"Why are you doing that?" she said, with tears in her eyes. "Where are you going?"

"Europe. I've been reassigned. Only an hour's flight for you."

"For *Stella,* but not Paige. I'll never see you again. And *Stella* is going into retirement, pending the acquisition of multiple college degrees, which will take me many years of laborious work, with no guarantee of eventual success in my chosen vocation as bottom-feeding scum of the Earth."

"You'll see me again, I promise. But you'll only be nineteen next year. Despite the things we've shared, I don't think either of us is ready for a permanent relationship."

"What the hell, Russ? You mean *you* are not ready for it. Never patronize me; are you saying it was not meant to be?"

"Come on. I have a pretty dangerous occupation, you know."

She laughed. "And I do not? I damn near got myself killed with that missile. Without your help, I would never have been able to do it. I may need your help again."

"You know it as well as I. I'll be promoted to captain soon, and will be stationed in Germany. You're going to college and probably then to a big-name law school, as you've said. Big career ahead of you, the sky's the limit."

"I do not need to do any of that. Money is not my goal."

"Yes, you do, and none of this is about money! You can't accomplish anything without education. Without that, you'll be just an appendage of the White House or a mascot for Mendoza Multinational, which I guess you own a small part of now, but I don't think either of those is things you want. Do you want to just be a corporate symbol, something I know you detest, deep down?"

She shook her head. "No, I do not, and how can you ask such a thing? While I like my relatives, their path is not mine. Where I go, I go without the benefits of the Mendoza or Darkkin name. They bring with them far more baggage than advantages."

"Your aunt has four more years and then she's done. Make your own way in the world. You said yourself you wanted to give *Stella* a break."

She pushed him gently back as tears came to her eyes. "I was just another notch on your stupid military officer's belt, wasn't I?"

"No, of course not. How could you say such a thing?"

"Because I can and want to. You better remember you never had better than me."

He stroked her soft face. "Don't you think I know that? We're both very young, Paige. I'm not ready for this. I thought I was, but it's far too complicated for either of us to sort out right now. You will hopefully find someone better suited to you than me, and I may do the same. And maybe someday it will work out between us, but not right now. We just need some space, as too many things have happened."

"Perhaps we went about this all wrong, you know. Should have stuck with either Paige or *Stella,* not having you date the latter, now you are going to scatter. It would never work out now, perhaps you are correct."

"That does make things rather complicated."

She nodded as she brushed some tears away. "I know you are right, deep down. I need to reexamine things and be on a higher plane than what I was. The fame was fun for a while, but it became rather mundane. Bella, Wendy, Jay, and my mom enjoy the adoration of being famous, while I do not, it is so superficial. In that regard, I have the most in common with my cousin William. And going to the fast-track police academy was pretty much a waste, I was meant to do more important things than give speeding tickets or arrest bank robbers."

"It's not wasted, especially if you want to become an attorney.

That knowledge is invaluable."

"Yeah, a lot you know about it. But since you are going AWOL on me, I suppose I am going back to North Pole until I actually 'officially' graduate. I have got a few more months left in my senior year, and I am going to enjoy them by being as big a pain in the butt as possible to as many people as I can. Maybe I can procure someone famous to come and give our Commencement address, such as Johnny Kepler or Royce G. Bivereaux. I lament, however, that I shall not be the valedictorian."

"What a surprise." He bent down and kissed her. "Goodbye, for now, *Stella Scura*. I know we'll meet again."

She hesitated and panicked as she realized, despite what she had said, that this really might be it. "You really mean it? You do not have to be reassigned. I have connections, and—"

"Won't work because I asked for it. Do you want to foul up what I really want, even though you could make it happen?"

"No, of course not, but you really want to leave, correct?"

"I want to grow in my career, and I can't do it in the comfort of Dayton or in the middle of nowhere at Eielson. I want to see the world, be an influence someday. The same wants you have. You need to grow, too, in ways you can't imagine. We can't let this continue."

"You want to go where I will never see you again."

"You'll see me again, I promise. By that time, I hope we both will have grown immensely."

"Go, then, and have fun in Germany, and do not drink too much beer or have *too* much cheer."

After a quick dinner, she kissed him goodbye as he went to his motorcycle; she smelled the exhaust as it drove off through the White House main gate as she was left alone in her tears. She knew now what Bella meant about being hurt, and she didn't know if she could love again. She had pushed the relationship with Russ too far, going too fast at times. His life might never be the same again, after his brush with celebrity. In the conservative world of the military, that might hurt his advancement. Or maybe put him on the lecture and book circuit, were he to choose that route.

It was time to take care of a few details and leave Washington and Aurora City to go back to North Pole tomorrow afternoon. She would be back to the city named after her someday. But that day was a long way away.

Chapter Fifty-Nine

The White House
Washington, DC

Paige watched with the other forty people in attendance as Bella, Nick, Wolfram Steele, Todd DeOhmman, Royce G. Bivereaux III, and Johnny Kepler waited in the Press Room. Juriann wasn't much for the limelight and wanted to remain in the shadows. Her 'new' mom was nowhere to be found, likely on her way back to Alaska, lest someone recognize her.

She was wearing her new red pantsuit and a Titian wig supplied by the White House beautician; her hair had started to grow out but wouldn't be the desired length for at least three or four more months. No hair color changing with this getup; maybe never again. Paige would have to have her own wig. She heard the commotion as she figured Wendy came out, surrounded by the news crew.

"It's been a long time, my old friends. Thanks for coming."

"Thanks for having us, Madam President," Biv said. "It's an honor to be at your side again."

"Most of these people you do not know, they are the ones with no super-powers who risked much to help *Stella Scura* bring down that missile. They are old friends of mine, and this reunion is a long time coming. I know now why you are my friends. The President's Science Squad you shall be."

"Maybe they'll make a real movie about us," Wolf said, laughing.

"Hell, count me out," Johnny said. "I'm goin' back to Princeton. I can't deal with this superhero crap."

"Yes, I figured as much, Johnny." Wendy took the medals the press secretary had brought out. "I present to each of you—the Presidential Medal of Freedom." The medal recognizes those individuals who have made "an especially meritorious contribution to the security or national interests of the United States, world peace, cultural or other significant endeavors.

She pinned the medal on each of them, one at a time.

"I just want to say something, Madam President," Bella said.

"Go ahead," Wendy replied.

"What *Stella* did, she was given great powers to do. But none of these people, including President Mendoza—a great heroine in her own right—have them. They are the true heroes, just as I want you all to be. I want you all to be the best you can be every day and know that nothing is beyond your grasp with the right effort."

The small crowd cheered for them, and she was proud to be part of the *Science Squad*, those many laughed at, who solved many of her problems with the knowledge of science. She just wished that Russell could have been a part of it. Bella had told her that things didn't last. She didn't want to believe her, but it was probably true. Russ was now in the past, and she had a whole life to live now.

And she now had to cope with a tween mom yet to experience the joys of adolescence. She couldn't graduate and go away to college soon enough.

• • •

Central Park
New York City

Paige and Juriann strode down a sidewalk in the north side of the massive park, her holding his arm as she imagined the skyscrapers gleaming in the distance. She had only been to New York once, when she was on the WBS Evening News with Millie Avery, except for her trip at Mach 10 redirecting the DARC missile, of course.

"Does anyone look at us as we walk, my friend?" she asked.

"Not really, but this is New York City, and ninety percent of the people look far weirder than us. Why do you ask?"

"I do not know; I guess if they look at anyone it would be you, as I do not appear unusual. I hope they do not think we are a couple." She stuck her tongue out, as if tasting something putrid.

"Yeah, that would be pretty creepy since I'm technically your uncle, even though we're chronologically similar in age. But I've always thought Paige would attract more attention than *Stella.*

She shook her head. "Although I cannot see others' reactions, it seems that people just ignore me. Blind people are not given much credibility even today—we are sort of invisible—the last disabled group people discriminate against. No one thinks we can do anything, which is a gross underestimation, one which has worked to my advantage, a good cover for me. And it teaches one many life lessons. Patience, for one. Humility, another."

They stopped a few seconds later. "Well, this is it, the statue. I'm not sure why you wanted to come here since you can't see it, and it's too large and high up for you to feel without leaving the ground."

"Because it's of me, and I just wanted to be here. Describe it to me and tell me what you see."

"It's bronze and pretty darn huge—you're about thirty feet tall, holding the Earth, like Atlas. It's a very good likeness."

"Right, but what I mean is—what are the reactions of others when they see it?"

"They take photos and vids, look, and stare with awe at the large bronze angel from the stars. Kind of like you, and also similar to the Aurora statue, from what I witnessed when I was in Aurora City, except that this one has no wings. But, to them, Aurora is a symbol and doesn't represent a real person. *Stella* does."

"Whoa. We have been over this before. I am certainly no angel, and I deserve no monument. I have done nothing to earn such an honor. I merely did what my physical abilities allowed me to do."

"You risked your life and almost died, and your life will become more complex, as Bipper statistics reveal 79% of Americans now feel that *Stella* and Aurora are the same person. Good luck with that."

"Those stupid social media blogs—I guess I never anticipated that, but what was I to do?"

"Don't know. Guess it's good that you're going into retirement for a while."

"Huh. It will definitely take me a 'while' to go to college and law school and start my amazing political career."

"People need to have their heroes and dreams. Isn't that what you want *Stella* to be? You saved New York, the President, and possibly the world, with what Argon was planning with *Mantissa*."

"The Bible says whenever someone is given great gifts it is then expected they do much with them; to do anything less would be an enormous waste of what God has given. Many have done far more than me with much less."

"Does that mean you really believe in God now? Doesn't your spirit of scientific inquiry wonder about that? Something you can't prove?"

"As you have probably discovered, I am *not* a scientist and do not have the 'spirit of inquiry' or technical talents you, Mom, Bella, and *Tinman* have. And, no, I am still not convinced."

She still hadn't figured out how *Stella* was going to have any kind of relationship, and she needed Paige's blindness as a cover. *Photraman* was still working on special contact lenses for her, but it was a work in progress; the thickness of sapphire needed made it difficult, if not impossible. For the foreseeable future, she would merely be wig-wearing Paige Marshall, now walking with a slight limp, a remembrance that no one was completely invincible.

These simple things would pale compared to the adventures she had experienced and the people she had met, but they were important to her, nonetheless. She might plan on returning to Aurora City this summer to attend a university near there; it was better than going off to some gigantic campus or staying in Alaska.

It would be so easy, using her alter ego's powers to gain notoriety and a place in society, but that didn't mean anything. She had been given those powers. She didn't agree with everything Wendy had to say but knew that she had earned everything she had received, and paid a dear price for it. Scrapping to get an education would be the hard way, but the only path to truly earn the respect of millions that she desired.

It was fun being *Stella Scura* at first, but she tired of it after a while. Most people were simply superficial and didn't care about her. But her family did, she knew. Even the ones in the White House. What would their relationship be? Would *Stella* return in the near future? Or years from now, when the truth would be shared with all?

She might have to if the President didn't behave herself. She told Wendy she would be back if that happened. And who knows what the next President might bring. Hopefully, it would be her and Nick's friend Fahnaz.

"And, the ones you spoke of, those created of dark energy? Are you sure you didn't see God? Sure sounds like it to me."

"I had my suspicions, but, no, they were no more divine than us, just a more advanced life form. Mom had seen them as well. I used to think she was crazy, but it is true. They have deficiencies and have made mistakes just like us. So I am just a mortal being. This flaw, my lack of vision; it is the defect that makes me human, do you not see how it all makes sense now? We are alike, Juriann, my cousin, or grandfather, or—what are you to me again?"

"It doesn't matter, Paige. I can always be your big brother. I wish you well and will be here for you."

"Where are you off to now?"

"Apparently, action and adventure await me. Alton Lohrbach's nephew, Dexter Slabb, is the head of this new secret agency, the DSD, or the Department of Scientific Developments. Missions and such to help America. Like you, I need to do what I can to help my new country."

"I need a break from that for a while. Maybe not forever, but for at least a few years."

"I get you. I never did anything like stop a nuclear missile. I can stop a low-caliber bullet or a knife, but that's about it."

"*Dr. Wendy's Science Squad?* Are they on board?"

"Probably some, as, except for Kepler, none of them have very good jobs. They have a lot of unique talents, just like your mom. Maybe she can come back and do some guest appearances. *Stella* can be the big-time symbol of truth and justice while I do the 'dirty work' behind the scenes."

"I doubt I will be there. They are more than what they realize. Without them, I would not have achieved much at all."

"Then you've accomplished another thing you set out to do—help people realize their potential."

Paige walked away from him as she heard small footsteps and felt a child's ball hit her feet. She kneeled to the ground and felt for it, finally grasping it.

"Thank you, Miss," an adult female voice, probably in her late twenties, said. The child's mother, no doubt.

She turned around to the voice. "No problem. Here you go."

"Oh," she exclaimed, taking the ball from her. "I didn't realize, young lady—"

"It is okay, Ma'am, a natural response and certainly no problem for me." She felt a small hand touch her.

"Thank you, lady," the girl said. "Are you blind?" Maybe five or six years old.

"Shhh, Karen, that's not nice."

She kneeled down again and felt for the girl, stroking her hair.

"No, it is okay, as I was young not so long ago. Your name is Karen, is it? How old are you?"

"Yes, I'm six."

"Nice to meet you. My name is Paige. I am visiting here from Alaska."

"How old are you?"

"Eighteen going on forty-eight."

"Huh?" The girl paused for a few seconds. "I don't get it."

"Never mind. It just means I have grown up a lot in the last two months. I am older on the inside than on the outside."

The girl touched her hair. "Your eyes—left one blue and right one brown. I've never seen anyone like that before. Why is that?"

"I have one from both my mom and dad. While they don't see like yours, realize that you can do almost anything in your life if you try hard enough. Life is all about doing the most with the gifts you have. Something else to remember, young Karen."

"What's that?"

"Always believe in the best in people. Someday, somewhere, no matter who you are, you will always need help from someone. Accept it with graciousness and return the favor."

"Gee. I'll try, but that's a lot of stuff to do."

"You can do it." She stroked the girl's hair. "Do you know what you want to be when you grow up?"

"Maybe a nurse or police officer or firefighter or something."

"Those sound like very good choices, Karen—looks like you want to help people. You just keep on wanting to do that."

"I wish you could see the statue of *Stella Scura*. She's beautiful. We traveled from New York to come to see it. They said she saved the city. Is that really true?"

"She did, but there are many other historic things to see here besides this heroine's statue, Karen. Learn all about the history and the richness of our wonderful country and of the world. Don't admire one person exclusively. The world thrives on diversity and the contributions of all."

"Huh. That's a lot to remember. Do you think she and Aurora the Angel are related? Everybody says they're the same person."

"I do not know about that, honey, but you must always have your fables to believe in. Is she really beautiful?"

"Yes, and no one's as pretty as *Stella Scura*. I'm gonna be her for Halloween."

"Do you think *Stella* is real, young lady? Or just a myth?"

"Of course, I heard she saved the President's plane, too! She's sure real, all right."

To be a child's Halloween costume—there was no higher honor in the land.

She didn't know where her life would take her. But she knew one day she would need to leave the nest again and go out on her own. Changing the world would be tough. To do things in Washington meant understanding the bureaucracy enough to get things done. It meant hard work to become an attorney and hours learning things the hard way. But that would be the only way to gain respect from people.

To be one of them. She was a person, to some extent. Her special abilities couldn't help her go through college, get a law degree, or become a politician (other than she didn't get physically tired and could survive on far less sleep and food than normal, which might be helpful for those college all-night study sessions, given her talent for procrastination). Her mouth could do wonders. She remembered how Jack told her that was a special ability, too.

In the last couple of months, she had become a little older and much wiser, as she had learned one thing: for all the reasons that the world needed *Stella Scura*, she knew now that it would need an older, wiser, more mature Paige Marshall far more: a very human person to show them the way. She had been given a wonderful life by her mother and adoptive father, and only in the last couple of weeks had she realized what a gift that was. Because we all have to live in this messed-up world together.

• • •

I am but one human being, albeit one who has been given enormous gifts no one person should be entrusted to have. I have the power to do anything I want without fear that anyone could stop me.

Do you realize what a terrible thing having those abilities is?

Unlike ninety-nine percent of the world, I will do with them what most would never even consider.

I will do the unthinkable.

I will walk away from them.

Because as much as the world needs Stella Scura, there is a greater need for the talents of Paige Marshall.

It seems that I was part of some plan. I don't know if I fit into it or not.

But, you know what? I don't really give a damn. If someone disagrees with me, then bring it on. I will be ready. I'm kind of tough to beat down.

Why will I walk away? Two reasons. The first is because I don't need these powers to accomplish my goals. Rather, they would likely hinder what I really want to do.

The second: I have seen firsthand the dangers of having too much power. Especially in the Mendoza White House. The President will have to be content with running America rather than the whole world. There are more important things than helping her do that.

I hope, deep down, she realizes that and accepts it.

If not—well, I don't want to think about that. She has been through some tough battles, but so have I, and I am here for the duration. However long it takes.

I am no demigoddess, no Savior, no "chosen one." I am but a young woman. A woman with unique abilities, yes—but no more. No one should have such faith in me. I am not deserving. I was born with these powers; I didn't earn them. To worship such an individual would surely diminish individual importance, the dignity of each human being to contribute something significant to society. I am only one small piece of the puzzle, and the path I must take has never been clearer.

I want people to respect me for my mortal accomplishments, not fear me because of my powers. I can live with the fact that not everyone will like me, but I want to be like other people in that regard.

That won't be easy.

Despite my political connections, there are a few even now protesting my very existence, believing me to be a devil, an omen of the future ruination of mankind. Others wonder what happened to me, resentful that I abandoned them, even though they can take care of most of their own problems. People are free to believe what they will. This is even more reason to earn my accomplishments.

The previous version of Mom would've told you that, like her, I have never chosen the easy way in anything I've ever done. This way will demand much effort and sacrifice, if I can do it at all.

Maybe this isn't possible. But If I can't do it, then I'm not deserving of their respect. For doing it any other way would be wrong.

Most any person would use the fame already lavished upon my alter ego and ride that to stardom. How easy that would be, and don't think I have not been tempted. Perhaps others would do that, but such a path is not for me. While I love my newly-found family members, I do not wish to share their fame.

Some will criticize me, stating that I am selfish, that I belong to the world, here to serve. Surely some negative outcomes will occur because I was not there. Can I come to terms with that? I cannot be everywhere at once, anyway. But I know the time will come around when Stella must reluctantly appear again. Hopefully, that is a long time from now.

And there is a better way to serve mankind than this. I hope.

I realize now the singular greatness of my mother, the things she gave up for me and the world. Yes, she is quirky and quite irritating, but so am I. The apple does not fall far from the tree, I guess. I am not entirely sure where the rest of my "tree" is, though.

And she was right. She told me this long ago, but I ignored her: despite outward appearances, the world is broken. Badly. It's no one's fault in particular, but there are many problems. Mom blamed it all on Wendy, but that's neither an intelligent nor productive answer. Wendy was trying to fix things the best way she could. Maybe it wasn't the right way, but hindsight is always 20/20. Could I have done better? I don't know. Probably not. I doubt my mother could have.

And somehow, Mom has been given a second chance to live her life over again. Some say she was driven to succeed by having a disability; what will she be like 'growing up' without that? All I want is for her to be happy, she deserves that, after all she has been through, although she remembers none of it. It's good she doesn't remember some of the very bad things she's done, although some could argue they were necessary.

Millions were liberated in the takeover of North Korea and other countries, but that continued path of sovereignty isn't the solution to creating a better world. While our country has riches beyond dreams, there are many poor in the world who are ignored, like dust swept under a carpet—as if they don't even exist. We were seconds from our greatest city being wiped off the map because of the weapons my grandfather created and the arsenal his daughter amassed. How much of that money could have been diverted to finding cures for disease and helping the poor? I know that statement seems so simple, coming from a teenager, but I don't know what else to say.

Yet, we must be careful there, too. In some way, I know I am the unwitting byproduct of those who wanted to make humans superior; that is another slippery slope. Who gets to decide about the elimination of genetic defects, for example? My mom, somehow, has received her greatest dream—to be a child again, at least mentally. I would give anything to be someone devoid of responsibility like she is now. I only hope she is at peace now and able to forget some of the things she's done. She deserves that.

Wishing doesn't make it so. And I don't have many answers.

As I mentioned, I have a new-found respect for my aunt and the things she has done, although I don't agree with all of them. Being President is hard. She is just one mortal person who has had the courage to do what she felt was right. I fear nothing because I know nothing can hurt me. She fears nothing because she has faced pain multiple times and lost more than I can imagine, yet returned stronger than ever. I will never really know what that feels like, although I guess I came close to that recently.

But it is not up to me, a single being, to provide salvation for the entire world. I cannot do that, as it is not mine to give, even though many would wish otherwise. It is conceivable that I could destroy all the world's weapons, but that is not the answer. Someone will figure out how to make more.

Rather, if the world is to survive, it must be changed the hard way, and the people must do it, as I cannot do everything, or even most things. I hope one day to be chosen as their leader. At least I can help that way. No more.

Note my words: chosen; not taken by force. If they put their trust in me, it will be by their own choosing, not by mine. By that time I will need to have disclosed to them who I really am, lest I be thought of as secretive and dishonest. But now is not the time. I have only one vote in the matter. And they will put their trust in our legislative system, not in any one being. This is perhaps neither the easiest nor the fastest way, but the way selected by our forefathers.

If I choose another way, then I am no better than the dictators that were overthrown to create some of our other states.

I am neither Stella Scura nor Aurora Angelica Darkkin Mendoza, legendary and fabled as they may be.

I am just plain Cheryl Paige Marshall, a simple flawed blind teenager.

Yet, I will not always be a teen. I will grow up, with many figurative bumps and bruises from the College of Hard Knocks.

And then, you had better watch out. The recognition I obtain, I will earn. Like my mother before me, I will dare to do what no one thinks possible of me. Hopefully, I can do that without killing people with my mind and ripping people's heads off. It will not be easy.

I have human failings. I will stumble and fall many times on my way to achieve my goals. Many will laugh and tell me to give it up, that mere Paige Marshall cannot possibly accomplish them.

All that advice will accomplish is to make me try harder, for we learn the greatest amount from failure. But each time I fail, I shall pick myself up and grow stronger each time. We cannot evolve without this. My mother and aunt had many. I do look up to them both, despite their shortcomings. I have high hopes that someday they will be friends again. But I have more important things to worry about now than their petty problems.

I am surely the most formidable opponent you could ever have. And it has nothing to do with my powers. You get into an argument with me, because you will lose. Badly. My mouth will destroy you.

But I will achieve it someday. Don't you worry about that. Maybe not in twenty years, but eventually. I don't know how long I will live. I may wait until I'm fifty, if the world is still here by then.

I will do my best to change the Constitution again to restore the limit of Presidential terms to two if it has not been altered by then, for no one should be our nation's leader for longer than that. Not even me. There is always some up-and-comer who is more worthy.

And, if there is no other choice to combat the world's evils, Stella Scura may return, albeit briefly, for I don't want to be alone on this world.

Chapter Sixty

February 15, 2029
North Pole High School
1065 Kris Kringle Drive
North Pole, Alaska

Bella and Nick had brought her back home early Saturday; Petra had been returned home a couple of days earlier to her new, strange life. She got up Monday morning and was a bit nervous about going back to school. After all, she hadn't been there for months. But she certainly had a lot of new clothes to show off from her visits to Aurora City and Washington.

She had debated whether or not to go back or not. But she had some unfinished business, friends to say goodbye to, and maybe a Prom to attend. Yeah, right, if anyone asked her to that.

She was still moving on from the change in relationship with Russell. In the end, she knew it was probably the best thing for both of them, as neither could handle the publicity. She hoped his life wouldn't be messed up by that but remembered that it had been his choice. She still hadn't figured out how *Stella* was going to have any kind of relationship, and she needed Paige's blindness as a cover. *Photraman* was still working on special contact lenses for her, but it was a work in progress; the thickness of sapphire needed made it difficult. For the foreseeable future she would merely be Paige Marshall, albeit now wearing a custom-made Titian wig, until her own hair grew out. That would take a few months.

These simple things would pale compared to the adventures

she had experienced and the people she had met. But they were important to her, nonetheless. She might plan on returning to Aurora City this summer to attend one of the small universities there; it was better than going off to some gigantic campus.

It would be so easy, using her alter ego's powers to gain notoriety and a place in society, but that didn't mean anything. She had been given those powers. She didn't agree with everything Wendy had to say but knew that the President had earned everything she had received, and paid a dear price for it. Scrapping to get an education would be the hard way, but the only path to truly earn the respect of millions that she desired.

It was fun being *Stella Scura* at first, but she tired of it after a while. Most people were simply superficial and didn't care about her. But her family did, she knew. Even the ones in the White House. What would their relationship be? Would *Stella* return in the near future? Or many years from now, when the truth might be shared with all?

She might have to if the President didn't behave herself. She told Wendy she would be back if that happened. And who knows what the next President might bring. Hopefully, the next one would be someone she met in New Persia a short time ago.

• • •

The Marshall family walked through the snow up the sidewalk to North Pole High School on the cold mid-February morning.

"This is the place where I shall be a teacher? Humph. It is not very impressive. I imagined someone such as I being housed in a distinguished ivy-covered building."

"Well, given your current limited choices, I would think you would be grateful. Gotta start somewhere, Nureyev," she said as she ran up the stairs with a slight limp and held the door open.

"How do you even know where you're at, Paige?"

"Muscle memory. I have been up and down these steps thousands of times, so it is easy."

"It will take a while to get used to all these changes."

"So what do I call you now? Mom? Or am I your mom now? Big sister? Do we walk together to school? Is your drivers' license still valid? Can you drink beer? If so, can you get me some?"

"Humph. I don't care what you call me, Paige. For the sake of appearances, 'Mom' shall suffice. And, yes, I can partake of suds, unlike you. You are a very annoying teenager, do you realize that?"

"At least I *am* a teenager, kiddo. If you think I am annoying now, just wait, there is *so* much you have forgotten."

"Another blessing I have been given."

She walked in the front door with Jack and Petra, who took her to the principal's office. The secretary ushered her inside.

"Well, as I live and dream—Paige Marshall, welcome back. I sure missed you." Ned Eggserby's bass voice was unmistakable.

"I missed you too, Mr. Eggs. You do not know how much."

"Uh-huh. Sarcasm at its best."

She smiled. "A tinge, perhaps. But I really am glad to see you."

"Well, the feeling is mutual."

"Tinge of sarcasm?"

"Perhaps."

"Any questions for *moi?*"

"We wondered where you went to, as you disappeared rather suddenly, but your dad says you were visiting some relatives in Indiana."

She nodded. "You could say that. I did receive some education while I was there, from the school of hard knocks, it really rocks. No, actually I did sort of a mini-internship at Mendoza Multinational. Learned some good stuff, not all of it with any practical interest."

"Hmmm." She could hear him ruffling through some papers. "I can see you actually would've had enough credits to graduate end of fall semester had you actually completed your final exams."

"Right. You going to let me complete them?"

"I guess so; I can make an exception for you. Does that mean you'll leave afterward, then?" His voice beamed with excitement.

"Nope, no such luck for you. I plan on sticking around until June. Maybe longer if I go to the University of Alaska—Fairbanks, unless I go back to Indiana."

"Darn. A man can have hopes and dreams."

"It is only four more months, but bring on those exams. I cannot say I have studied a great deal, however."

"What else is new?" He took her to the auditorium, where she opened the door. A hundred voices yelled "Surprise!"

"What do I deserve a surprise for? It is not my birthday."

"Yeah, we all know you're eighteen, Paige," Rachel said, putting her arm around her. "Don't want to go through that again."

She had her work cut out for her, applying for university political science programs. It wasn't going to be easy, what she wanted to do. At least she had agreed to take the trust money, although her mom wasn't real happy about that. It was her mom's money, actually, but Mom couldn't be trusted with money and didn't care about it, either.

Dull and unexciting compared to the life of *Stella Scura,* supersonically soaring through the sky. Four years of college—maybe three if she worked hard and took summer school—and three years of law school, and that was if she passed all the exams. And she had insisted on doing it without the recommendations her famous relatives could supply. What challenge would that be, being the President's niece? No one could ever know that. Not yet, anyway.

Jobs after law school were hard to find these days, and becoming a U.S. Representative or Senator far harder yet for one girl with immense aspirations and above average but not a gifted intellect. But her aunt didn't have special abilities, and look what she did. Luck played a huge part in that, for sure, but you take what you can get.

Wendy was loud and over-the-top, but she was deceptively smart, and what she said was true: she could either choose to complain about things or become someone who could change them with hard work and effort. Changing the world with force wasn't the answer others were expecting. Somehow she realized she had known that all along.

But after it was all said and done, she would have gained a great deal of respect, for what other person would not use those gifts to an advantage? Even Wendy admitted she could never have done that.

This must have been the reason why the powers of *Stella Scura* had been given to her. She still had many doubts about God and religion and probably always would, but this unique chain of events had made it a little clearer. Life certainly wasn't going to get easier. But it could still be fun.

Maybe there was still time to get a date for the Prom.

Epilogue

Fifteen Months Later
The White House
Oval Office

The President will see you now, Dr. Stannous," the female assistant said to Nick, who was waiting in the outer office checking messages on his mobile device on the pleasant May afternoon.

"Thank you," he said after having waited for only ten minutes as he stood and went inside. While he'd been to the residence and had stayed as a guest many times, he hadn't been to the West Wing all that often, maybe ten times since she had been in office. There never was much of a need. Today, there was one, apparently, for both of them.

"You doing okay?" Wendy asked as she went over and gave him a hug.

"Fine. Same ol', same ol'. Money in, money out. Way more than I need."

"Bella and Jose?"

"They're great, as usual. She's taking him on a tour of the town, to the Smithsonian, I think, and to the monuments. He really likes that stuff. By the way, we've got a surprise for you. Something Jose has wanted for a long time."

She smiled at him. "Something money can't buy, guy?"

"I suppose that's one way of putting it."

She gave him another hug. "Hey, no way! That's great, Nick, congratulations. When is she due?"

"Late January, early February. We didn't want to know the gender and we wanted that to be a surprise also."

"I can't tell you how happy I am for you both. But you could've just stayed here, you know. You *are* family and don't ever need an invitation to come here. The staff are always instructed to give you anything you want."

He shrugged. "That's okay, as Jose wanted to stay in a hotel this time, although he does want to come by later. Plus, he wanted to go swimming at the hotel."

"We have an indoor pool; he could swim there." She watched him stare at her face, one he had not personally seen for nine months. "What's the matter?" She rubbed her face with her right hand. "Oh, no, did I forget to shave today, to my dismay?"

He laughed. "Nothing—but, your face, it looks different."

"What do you mean? Did it look bad before?"

He smiled. "No, it looks quite good, actually. I only meant, well—have you lost more weight?"

"Maybe, maybe not. Don't ever ask a woman about her weight or the work she's had done on her face, not in this place. Your wife should tell you *that.* Otherwise, you are living quite dangerously."

"I guess so. The hair looks nice, too. A little darker and thicker than usual, kind of like when you were younger, as I recall."

"Sure, thanks. Younger is always good. Kudos to the White House stylist for helping make the illusion real."

"It's just that I recently looked at all the 'before' and 'after' photos of recent two-term Presidents and how much they aged after eight years, and it's significant, yet you seem to be better than ever, after nine years in office."

"That's because all the other Presidents were men who didn't know how to take care of themselves."

He looked at her moderately tanned skin. "Looks like you've been down south. Nice tan—as I recall, you usually burn, though."

"Just trying to increase my vitamin D stores."

"I don't usually think of you as being malnourished." They sat down on the sofa as she poured some coffee for them. "It was darn nice of you to consider giving part of the Moon back, so the people in China can look at it and don't think they are looking at the United States any longer."

"You know it is the right thing to do, as complex as that process will be."

"Maybe there's hope for the world yet. How is the new health-care initiative going?"

She shrugged. "It's just as you would expect, Nick. Complex, but there are many tasks to tackle in the next three and a half years. Probably what I should have been doing all along. It's not like we don't have the money for it."

"Good to know." He took a sip of coffee. "Don't mean to change the topic, but how is your illustrious niece? Paige, the page?"

She smiled. "She's going to Ball State, which has excellent programs for those with visual disabilities—but it's only seventeen miles from you, so why are you asking me?"

He shook his head. "Don't see much of her. I meant, though, after she got that summer internship job with Senator Baker."

"Haven't really seen her, but my understanding is that she is doing a phenomenal job. She has a high energy level, you know, and has been a big help, despite her disability."

"Yikes, but Theresa Baker is a Democrat, the one who wants to reinstate the Twenty-Second Amendment, just so you know."

She nodded. "Yes, that's correct. The one limiting Presidential terms to two, passed originally in 1947, repealed in 2025."

"Well, what do you think of that?"

She laughed. "It's probably a good thing. The more I get into this third term, the more I think it was a mistake. It won't affect me, but maybe it should. They could have a 'recall' election. We could then go live at our summer home in Green Bay."

"Huh. The Democrats rise again, who would've thunk it? Most experts thought they were dead and buried."

"Hardly. I would imagine your old friend Fahnaz will be our next President, so you can still hang out here."

"Good to have friends in high places." He looked around the room. "So, is Paige livin' in here with you whenever she's in town?"

She laughed. "Heavens, no. I heard she was living in some hole in the wall; she hasn't contacted me at all or tried to call this one with a Southern drawl."

He looked at her curiously. "Hey, that's pretty good. The spontaneous rhyming, I mean. You've done it several times."

"I guess it rubs off. Anyway, how would she living with me look, Nick? That wouldn't fit her 'starving student' image. Getting paid peanuts, I assume. Will has gone to see her a couple of times."

"We all gotta start somewhere. I guess you don't have to worry about her safety or getting enough to eat."

"Yeah. But, Nick, you know what I wanted to talk about, right?"

He shook his head. "It's really hard to know what you want, Wendy, so let's get down to brass tacks. We know each other too well to waste each other's time with small talk."

"Okay." She looked out the window. "*Stella* initially had her own agenda, which I fully supported, and she was the main reason I ran for a third term, so I could manipulate the federal agencies and keep them out of her hair. Now that *Stella* has for all practical purposes vanished, my relevance is less clear."

He laughed. "That's a pretty weak story, but whatever." He rolled his eyes. "It's good you support her somewhat unorthodox agenda. Not a hell of a lot you could do about it if you didn't."

"Now, listen here. I'm not trying to be confrontational, but—"

"But—you want unlimited power and money. I guess we're on the same wavelength. I understand moolah."

She shook her head and sneered at him. "No, Nick, we're not."

"Let's don't start that again, us not being equal and all."

"That's not what I meant; you misunderstand me. I have money and power to spare, so don't assume you know what I want. In three and a half more years I'll retire, probably to Wisconsin, volunteer my time at a medical school or something, teaching pediatrics. I will be out of the limelight for good."

He snickered. "Yeah, I can see you taking a bunch of early twentysomething short white-coats on hospital rounds. What a spectacle that would be; no one would get anything done. But remember, though, that attempts to clone her didn't go so well for Ramon Argon, lessons he should've learned from Uncle Malachi and Travis. I think he was blown into like a billion pieces by *Stella* tearing through that complex like tissue paper, even though she was barely conscious. So maybe you'd better rethink this, Wendy. Perhaps *she* can control it, but there must be a reason there's only one of her. Two would be bad. More than that really could destroy the world, something you've somehow managed to avoid until now, but just barely."

"How limited you've let yourself become, and you're not even forty. Old before your time." She shook her head and began waving those big arms around, demonstrating her seventy-four-inch wingspan. "I don't want to rethink anything. This world will need unlimited energy to reach the stars, and as great as mendozium cold fusion technology is, that alone ain't gonna cut it, *Tinman*. I'll be dead one day, and we have to find another world to live on."

He pointed to the sky as she poured him more coffee from the ornate porcelain pot, which had been part of the Presidential china collection for over a century. "We seem to be missing one person who should be in on this discussion." He took a sip of coffee.

"Who? Bella? Johnny Kepler? *Photraman?* Dexter Slabb? Forget it. Dexter's way too busy with the *Orthoman* project to care about this hypothetical discussion."

"I kind of doubt the last one. But, no, I was actually referring to *Stella* herself, if you've forgotten about her for some reason. What does *she* think of all this? I'm just sayin'—might be good to get her input, if you know what I mean, since she could, like, stop you instantly and reduce the military to dust. That is, if that sort of thing matters to you, in your new anti-nuke world."

She shook her head and brushed long golden bangs from her eyes. "She wouldn't want to be involved anyway in such scientific matters, and we're just having a theoretical discussion. She's too occupied going to college, then law school, and politicking for the next ten or fifteen years after that, so we need to do some things for her until she gets to live in this house."

He patted her on the head, pushing down the large mass of thick hair. "Darn nice of you to be such a thoughtful aunt."

She snarled and pulled her head back. "I am merely being protective of this country's greatest asset, with the help of my maternal instincts. God knows her own mother isn't capable. Business, finance, and science are not Paige's specialties, either."

He shrugged. "Haven't you had enough adventure in your life so far? I know what you're planning."

"Me? Planning something? Get real."

He shook his head. "Going to Tennessee to dig up old Rad the Dad doesn't sound like the greatest plan you've ever concocted, you know, even if he did inject himself with the same stuff—*Stella's* real dad's DNA—that caused Bonnie's genetic mutation. Rad was dangerous enough when he was alive, so let him rest in peace. He saved your life, for God's sake. And rumor has it her 'dad' wasn't the nicest dude. Although her 'dad's' DNA was in her mom, actually, so—damn, this is so confusing."

She laughed. "Oh, *Tinman.* How little you know. You and Bella, who think you know it all, have it only partly right. You don't need to go to Oak Ridge to find my father, not that he would be of any use to anyone."

"Huh? Why not, pray tell?"

"*Why?*" She grinned. "Because he was never buried there, of course. How obvious."

"What?" He almost fell off the sofa. "Good Lord. Where in the hell is he, then?"

"The CIA took the body, and it was in cryogenic storage, and for the last twelve years, he's been, er, transferred to a secret facility only a handful of people know about."

"Huh. I assume one of those people is you."

"Well, what do you think? Besides Bonnie, he was the only person who had part of that DNA."

"Yeah, that you know of. Is good ol' Dexter Slabb one of those 'handful of people,' too?"

She crossed her arms and frowned. "I cannot comment on the operations of the DSD, you should know that."

"That usually means 'yes,' in politician-speak, and I bet he can break away from Juriann to help you with this. Who the heck did they bury, then? Uncle Jim said he went to the funeral."

"A realistic bio-mannequin that looked like him; it certainly fooled me as I didn't know any of this at the time, not until well after *Darkkday*. I was devastated at my dad's funeral."

"Awww, yeah, I sure believe that, since you were so close. Not."

"Believe what you want, Nick. Anyway, Jim's one to talk about fake funerals. I remember us both being at his, by the way. I hear he upgraded to having a real corpse in the coffin."

"Gee, this is just wonderful news, Wendy. So great for you to share all this now about Rad."

She shook her head. "It is what it is; I didn't do it, I can't change it, and I have to make the best of it."

"*Stella* didn't appear until just recently. Why?"

"I base my entire operations on intelligence, and I knew this was going to happen. She was far more than I expected, obviously, in terms of power. I knew she at least had partial invulnerability, but flying, at those speeds, so I had to be prepared and not scared."

"Sure. And what if I tell her about all this?"

"Tell her about *what?* An experiment that doesn't even exist?" She laughed heartily. "Are you hallucinating? What proof do you even have, *Tinman?*"

"Don't need it, Falstaff. She could take your whole operation down like I said, you know that."

"*Falstaff?* Don't you dare make fun of me, Nick. And that happens only if she knows where it was and decided to stay being *Stella*. She doesn't and isn't."

He pointed angrily at her. "She's ninety-nine percent peace and goodwill, something you should be *very* grateful for. The other one percent, well—you don't *ever* want to see that, Juriann said. There's nasty potential in her you can't possibly imagine. I don't think you want her to come looking for you while she's in a foul mood."

She laughed. "No, even if *Stella* cared about such things, which she doesn't—you won't do or say anything, do you know why?"

"Huh? Why won't I? You can't bully me, as we've established that irrefutable fact long ago."

"I get that, such was not my implication. But, quite simply, I don't need to, Nick, because I don't have to."

He stood up. "What? Why the hell not?"

"Because I know you too well," she said in a soft Southern Appalachian drawl. "This represents power and wealth beyond what you can possibly imagine, and you'd never forgive yourself if you weren't in on it."

He looked at his shoes and shrugged. "Yeah, well, I can imagine quite a bit. And Bella would tell her, as she sure isn't scared of you or anyone else. Not that I am either, mind you."

The master manipulator pointed to the ceiling. "Ah, but you're scared of *her*, so you won't say anything to her either. You wouldn't have been researching dark matter yourself in secret with Kepler in the first place if that wasn't the case. And it isn't to hurt *Stella*, but to help us understand her better. You brought the damn *Science Squad* out to help do that, as I recall."

"Comparing that to cloning Rad is the stupidest thing I've ever heard. And Bella will figure it out, it's only a matter of time."

"Maybe. If so, then I need to depend on you to help her see the light and occupy her time with worthy philanthropic pursuits. Underneath it all, she's a greedy person just like you."

"Wrong. Maybe once, but no more; she's different now, and that 'light' should be left well enough alone, lest you risk your own destruction by underestimating your older niece, but you're headed that way already. Look, I'm as opportunistic as the next guy, but this could be damn dangerous. It isn't worth it."

"Dexter will help us do it. You've got the money and means to help do all this. Think of the energy implications."

"Haven't you learned anything? *Stella* is basically a liberal pacifist, much unlike her aunt."

"That is an exaggeration, trust me. I've seen things you haven't."

"What does that mean?"

She shook her head. "She has a rather bad temper once she gets riled up. You don't want to be on the wrong end of that."

"Well, okay—but what if Regenerated Rad isn't the same in whatever form he comes back to life, if you can even do that at all? The alien guy from Thonxxeron, or wherever, is toast for a reason we can't possibly understand, and it took all those dark energy dudes to take him down, Paige said. Why take that risk?"

"I'm just constructing some theories. Don't make a mountain out of a molehill for a theoretical question."

He shook his head. "I don't believe you, Wendy. Just because Bonnie and Alton lost most of their marbles and took Rad's body and Cassie's stem cells exist somewhere in cryo-storage doesn't mean you have to continue their insane haphazardness. I would love to have Marcy back, but cloning her makes a different person altogether, it would be like having another child. I have a new family now, and I've moved on. You were damn lucky to have had another child in your mid-forties. So, live with your losses and rejoice in what you *do* have, even though it can be unbearable, because down the other road lay madness."

"Is *that* what you think this is about? It isn't. Don't be so simplistic." She squinted and puckered up her face.

He nodded. "I do."

"Huh? What the hell? You and Bella have taken many risks in your lives. Some of those early mendozium experiments were dangerous; without such experimentation we never would have colonized the moon to mine helium-3. We are certain the powers can't be re-created from his body. But there may be other advantages."

"*Powers?*" He looked at the all but vanished crow's feet on the fifty-seven-year-old woman's face. "Of course—I can't believe I've been so stupid. You don't want it for the energy, for weapons, or to reach the stars, because you'll be dead by then. And you don't want it to bring Cassie back, either."

"What would I want it for, then? Enlighten me."

"OMG. You want it for *yourself*."

She crossed her arms. "That is ridiculous beyond belief. I want to study how a human body can manipulate dark energy. I was a doctor before I got involved in politics, so I have a natural curiosity in such things."

"Is it ridiculous? As well as you know me, I know *you*. You'd take any opportunity you could get for immortality, to have the power for yourself, because you're just like your dad."

"I shall take that as a compliment."

"Yeah? It's not. You're a stupid, egotistical dumb ass."

She laughed. "Oh, come on, grow up. Surely you can insult your President better than that. What is this, junior high school?"

"Wait—no, you're worse than Rad, because you don't even need LSD or booze like he did to hallucinate or do crazy shit, you can do it all on your own with that big whacked-out brain of yours, with the entire Armed Forces to back you up."

She smiled. "How lame. You are *really* getting desperate here. I haven't had a manic episode since before Cassie was born, and I got help for that. See how calm I am? Quit while you're ahead, because you're *way* out of your league."

"I'm not finished. You've seen genetic experimentation gone awry. *Stella, Orthoman II,* and Rita McPherson seem to have turned out with at least some degree of success. Bonnie's roided-up clone *Mantissa* and your bro Travis Argon, the first *Ortho-Man,* not so much. Get out in one piece while you can and go retire to Green Bay or wherever. You've earned it."

She walked over to the window and looked out, her large frame illuminated by midday sunlight. "Like I said, I do want to retire, but is what I want so wrong, Nick? To want an extended lifespan? To be immune to the diseases which eventually will kill us all? To live long enough to experience interstellar travel?"

"You don't know if *Stella* will live longer than any of us, that's the phoniest excuse I've ever heard. You want the strength, the invulnerability. Again, you're playing God with things you don't have full mastery of. Throughout time, these types of endeavors have not gone well. Haven't you learned enough from Malachi and Ramon Argon's follies?"

"Maybe, but I have made decisions no President has ever made, and came out on top every time."

"Well, wise up. You're a smart gal who understands probability theory, given your past experiences with Bonnie, before you guys took her to that fancy celebrity rehab place for her gambling addiction. Therefore, you know it might be time to roll snake eyes. Just saying you're due for a turn of shitty luck. *Stella* bailed you out of the *Santaman* fiasco in New York. May not be so lucky next time."

"Listen here, *Tinman*. I want mankind to reach the stars, but that's not going to be possible without beings who can actually make that journey, and they don't exist here. Whatever you think of me, I have always thought big, like the woman I am."

He shook his head. "Yeah, right. I just hope you don't kill us all in the process. Just look at what you've done already. Your dad's damn nukes—if not for *Stella*, New York would be gone."

"Yes, you are quite correct about my dad's legacy. I have taken steps to remediate that," she said as she walked off. "I don't want to die, and I want to help the world in ways you cannot possibly imagine."

He shook his head and frowned as he stood up and turned towards the door. "Wrong, Wendy. I can imagine quite a lot. And knowing you, not all of it's good."

"You all still coming over for dinner at six-thirty?"

"Yeah, we'll be here."

"No more shop talk?"

"Nope. Promise." He patted her on the shoulder, as he left the world's most famous office and closed the door. The President sat back down and got back to her paperwork.

He sure had a wild imagination, she thought to herself. Was she wanting even part of her niece's powers, just to have the strength and to control the world?

Like I actually need that.

And I've had my share of shitty luck, thank you very much.

She took a deep breath and exhaled, intentionally blowing a large stack of various federal reports across the room. Her last pulmonary vital capacity measured by newly promoted Captain Leonard A. Gelkis was 14,402 cubic centimeters, or about 400 percent of an average thirty-year-old male her height. Damn, that wasn't half bad for a woman nearing sixty with one lung.

Everyone always says I'm a blowhard. Now it's really true.

And her hair had returned to its natural blonde color of her early thirties, a couple of shades darker than the L'Oreal Super Blonde that now sat gathering dust on the White House stylist's shelf. Her skin was also a few reflectance points darker, for reasons she obviously knew. She also didn't have time for cosmetic surgery. If others thought she had some work done, then that was fine with her.

The urge to rhyme and alliterate was almost like a tic now, suppressible but requiring some effort. Using contractions was a little easier, but she had to watch herself.

She also noticed over a month ago that the hot flashes had stopped and that ambient temperatures could return to normal, a joyous occasion for Jay, who could now enjoy a more habitable human environment. She told him it was a new medication she was taking.

That obviously wasn't true.

There was only one good way to make those hot flashes go away, she knew, having a firm grasp on the fundamentals of female endocrinology.

Physiologic plasma levels of estrogen. And she wasn't taking it as a medication.

She had been lying about a lot of things for the last year. Only Len Gelkis and a handful of others at The Vault, including Dr. Rita McPherson, knew the unbelievable truth: that a woman living on borrowed time now had a new lease on life. Maybe six more years, maybe sixty.

Maybe six hundred, if the world was still around by then.

Whatever she could get out of this experiment was better than the alternative, which was unacceptable.

Jay would eventually figure it out. But right now it was on a need to know basis, and he didn't need to know.

"Miranda, talk to me," she said in the Oval Office, speaking to no one in particular.

"Yes, Wendy. How are you today?" the pretty holographic figure asked as it appeared in the middle of the room.

"You tell me. Daily report."

"DNA and 18-fluorodeoxyglucose-PET scans again show no evidence of malignant cells at the molecular level. The prognosis of advanced pancreatic adenocarcinoma, as you know, is still grim, even in the year 2030. Yet, your novel therapy has helped you beat the odds."

"I suppose so. Yet, to accomplish what, I don't know. I'm taking this one day at a time."

Miranda pointed her holographic right index finger at her harshly. "The long-term side effects of this therapy are not known.

Heed my warning, Dame Wendy, as my words are wise. History has not been kind to those who tamper with things mere mortals should not; this is known to you from many past experiences."

"Really? How insightful, as usual. Well, it's better than being dead, don't you think?"

"Perhaps, although I don't understand that concept. By the way, my scans now estimate your chronological age at only forty-five years, based on your DNA. Interesting. You were forty-seven two months ago. Hopefully, you will not devolve into an infant."

"Yeah, we wouldn't want that. I don't really want to go to high school again, it pretty much stunk."

"That would be quite a sight. It is, however, recommended to have another scan in two weeks. Maybe you will heed this advice, but probably not."

"Got it. Thanks, but what's done is done. Again, none of this is to ever be in my official medical record."

"Of course, Dame Wendy." The hologram disappeared.

What came next would be damn difficult to hide. She thought about having an endometrial ablation before the periods started again but thought the better of it. Like she told Miranda, she was taking this one day at a time, and none of this could have been anticipated in the history of medical science.

She was a physician, after all, but a woman first and foremost—who might need that old uterus again someday for its intended purpose. One last time. Although using it for that would be damn hard to explain—and to hide.

Having a libido going through the roof didn't help matters.

She had always told people she wasn't afraid to die. That was what she had always thought.

Before, she had no choice. Now, she did. It was her choice to give Dr. Rita McPherson a new secret job on the President's medical staff: not someone with the most robust ethical standards. Yet, they were tied together by fate, by the events of Ontario Lacus that started it all. She couldn't change that.

But when confronted with certain death, she changed her mind. There was too much to do. And she wasn't going to die this way.

She had told Nick Stannous the truth; a liar she had never been. Rad's old frozen body might be useful for biochemical energy experiments, and perhaps some healthcare applications (despite the deceased not having lived the healthiest of lives), but that was all.

She would give others the label of "reckless."

Because a desperate woman is only concerned about survival.

Her salvation lay not in the preserved tissue of her deceased father, as fascinating as that concept was. But fate had brought her other means, something of almost limitless potential.

Dr. Leonard Gelkis told me I had advanced pancreatic adenocarcinoma after I finally got a checkup, at The Vault, of all places. Not that routine checkups can change the outcome of this crappy disease anyway, even in 2030. I knew I might have some bad stuff going on, but nothing this horrible. The standard therapy was chemotherapy and targeted genomics, which might have bought me another year or two. The quality of that time on Earth could be debated.

No, thank you very much. I chose another therapy that had never been tried. Something pretty out-of-the-box that no reputable researcher would even contemplate and no institutional review board would approve.

I have always been a creative thinker, especially when it's my own life at stake, ethics be damned in this particular instance.

Stem cell therapy is pretty mainstream these days, but this was different. We could've used my daughter Cassie's stem cells, which are still in cryogenic storage. But that wasn't the plan; even a disgraced, unethical biogeneticist like Rita McPherson (reduced to teaching freshman biology at a Podunk college) raised her eyebrows at this one in disbelief.

No, not using the genetic remnants of good old Rad the Dad either; we were pretty sure that wouldn't work. Not that I would want any more of his genes, anyway. I have enough of those, thanks.

But there was another solution, borne from another's inadvertent tragedy. Something good needed to come from that event.

I have been infused with the totipotent fetal stem cells procured from the aborted fetus of a demigoddess. The potential genetic rejection issues were enormous, but here I am. It's not like I had a whole lot to lose.

I didn't want any of this. But I had no choice.

No, that's not entirely true, is it? We always have choices, yes?

But I chose life rather than the alternative. I am grateful.

Surely this proves I am not the noble person many people think I am. No surprise there. But I never held myself up as a perfect individual.

What I do, I do for the greater good. Which, fortunately, includes me.

I don't know how long I will live. I may have bought myself a few months, or years, or even decades.

Or will I become immortal? I sure as heck hope not.

Dearest Cassie, Jake, and Mother: I want to see you so badly. I know I will do so in the afterlife.

But it can't come for me yet. It's not time for me to pop my clogs, Mom. Please understand.

Like everyone else, I do what I must to survive. I would be long gone by now were it not for that.

Yet, I worry about the eventual consequences of what I've done.

General Brant Gallagher, onetime Presidential hopeful, played instrumental roles in the assassination of President Graham and Darkkday. Back in the day, I hated him because of his desire to create "genetically improved" people and weed out the "undeserving." I saw it differently, that each human being has a purpose in life, and it isn't up to us to decide who gets to live. I, who took care of many disabled children in my previous career, knew that better than anyone. I guess I ended up better than him.

But the question at hand is: have I now become one of the hypocrites I despised? I have been many things in my life, but never that. Yet, look at me now and what I have done to myself. But what's done is done. No going back. I try to justify my actions, like many who make questionable choices likely do. Maybe I should've just died. Wouldn't that have been the heroic choice?

Or it's yet another chance to finally make the world better in the way I originally envisioned, by helping people.

Yeah, right. I helped myself first, as usual.

In a way, I started all this. With some help, of course, from my dad, my brother, his best friend, and my sister-in-law. I might as well see it through to the end.

No time to worry about that now. I have a lot to accomplish. One day at a time. That is all I can do. But, right now—

Right now, let's see what this old lady's amazing new body can do.

She then took out her dad's old MIT Zippo lighter and flicked the wheel as an inch-high yellow butane flame burst out. Although the former United States Surgeon General didn't smoke, of course, she did enjoy having some of his old items around, some of which reminded her of his colorful past (although for most of her life, she had wanted to forget him). This one had a newly-found practical purpose. She also pushed aside the reading glasses she no longer seemed to need. She was going to order a new set with zero-diopter lenses to give the illusion she still needed them, although any astute observer with a rudimentary understanding of optics would figure that out from the lack of distortion.

She held the back of her right hand two inches from the flame. The back of the non-dominant hand was the part of the body most sensitive to temperature, she knew. She had pushed the button on her Omega automatic chronograph to record the time to pain.

She finally felt the sting and closed the lighter. Twelve minutes, fifty-seven seconds this time. She inspected the hand, which was a little reddened and smelled slightly of burnt hair but was otherwise unharmed. She smiled.

She put her toy away and got back to work, which she sure had a lot of, but she also had a lot more energy than usual. She hopefully had a long time to live yet and have fun after the next three years were over.

And, after that, the sky was the limit.

Or perhaps the end of the world. Or, at least her world.

Which it was going to be wasn't clear.

She couldn't worry about that today.

THE END

In the year 2043, the world is at peace, the vast energy resources of the USA now shared with the world. The growing issue is the expanding population and where the people of the future will live.

Researchers at the world's largest energy company are working on a new energy source that will make others pale in comparison. It has been fourteen years since any legitimate sighting of the heroine called *Stella Scura,* and younger people wonder if she really existed at all. Some believe she was just a legend. Most believe her dead, a consequence of saving New York City from nuclear destruction on Christmas Eve, 2028.

But a far more dangerous new menace has come forth to threaten Earth, inhabiting a vessel he had sought out long ago. He had virtually destroyed one planet and was thought to have been eliminated by the all-knowing beings of pure energy which he once was.

The infallible beings were wrong.

Will a former President's desperate attempt to hold onto life fourteen years ago and *Stella's* mother's haphazard experiments long before she was born now effect the destruction of Earth and the human race?

He will meet his match in a blind thirty-five-year-old attorney and junior Senator from Alaska named Cheryl Paige Marshall, who has risen up through the ranks the hard way in an effort to someday become President herself. But can the woman who is secretly more than human find a way to defeat her new adversary without killing everyone else in the process? She has to face her biggest fear, that inside her resides a capacity for violence which she cannot even begin to comprehend. Yet, she knows she must harness that inner power in order to triumph. She cannot do it alone. Which person close to her will make the supreme sacrifice for the world?

Stella Scura
Rad Reborn

www.ingramcontent.com/pod-product-compliance
Lightning Source LLC
Chambersburg PA
CBHW070630310726
48982CB00001B/234

* 9 7 8 1 7 3 4 9 3 7 2 2 0 *